KILLING WIDOWS

KILLING

WIDOWS

CLIVE BIRCH

Matador
9 Priory Business Park,
Wistow Road, Kibworth Beauchamp,
Leicestershire. LE8 0RX
Tel: 0116 279 2299
Email: books@troubador.co.uk
Web: www.troubador.co.uk/matador
Twitter: @matadorbooks

ISBN 978 1789014 631

British Library Cataloguing in Publication Data.
A catalogue record for this book is available from the British Library.

Printed and bound in Great Britain by 4edge Limited
Typeset in 10.5 Aldine by Troubador Publishing Ltd, Leicester, UK

Matador is an imprint of Troubador Publishing Ltd

Original artwork by the author

For my grandchildren; may they never witness such horrors.

1

THE SNIPER

Spring 1937

His friend slipped away already a ghost and Miguel hid his eyes conceding that all he held dear was lost. It was taken in the bitterness of the last few days and worse, that sweet girl who loved him never would be found amongst the tumbled stones of her burning village. Now the implacable Rodrigo without a word and with barely a backward glance slipped away mute in the chaos of surging emotions. But the unspoken exchange rearmed the other powerfully; they had work to do.

He dropped to his knees, lowered himself cautiously onto the uncompromising stony surface and by pressing his elbows into the dew-dampened ground formed a stable base from which to support the heavy rifle. He lifted his upper chest and shoulders to look forwards towards the distant road. In the process of settling himself, in preparation for the action to come, he scuffed the toes of his old army boots making indentations in the hard earth to further secure his firing position. It was then that he picked up the almost imperceptible sound of the still distant advancing enemy as it drifted in on the light wind. He smiled a bittersweet smile. Incongruous as it seemed, considering the circumstances, he looked in wonder at the pure beauty of his surroundings; there was a strange unreality to this place of pastoral innocence as the sun filtered through the morning mist. Soft green undulating meadows gave way to deciduous forest as it climbed the steepening hillsides. It was rich in a variety of the finest trees, integrated and interdependent displaying differences by shape, colour, light and shade with enviable harmony. Yet, as did Eris who lurked in the Olympian shadows waiting to spoil the day, the Peña de Francia hunched malevolently within the obscured distance.

His mind drifted back to just a few moments ago as they parted; a touching separation of ways underlined by an undeniable sense of finality. It was awkward and more emotional than on other occasions both knowing chances of survival were slim. He watched with sad stillness as Rodrigo scuttled down the exposed hillside moving from rock to rock with a skill they had developed over the months they had been brothers in arms.

He could still hear the children wailing, a haunting and depressing sound for which he could do nothing to help. He willed Rodrigo to send them on their way with undeniable need for urgency and God's guidance to a place of safety before the battle started. Miguel laughed bitterly; some battle this will be! Me against the hundreds carried in stolen lorries, the variety of which a witness to livelihoods destroyed and many an owner lying cold and yet undiscovered in some distant ditch. Anger iced his blood and cleared his mind of everything except the need to kill.

The Moroccan mercenaries aided cruelly by Spanish Legionnaires had cut through the ranks of the Republicans with contemptuous ease and carried with them a justifiable air of invincibility. Onward they continued unconcerned that the midge might bite again. It would be nothing more than an inconvenient, irritating pause; an incident to be swatted away as they made their way north to steal from the impoverished, spill the blood of the brave and claim rape as their reward. He watched with growing agitation as the convoy trundled slowly along still some distance away, travelling as it did at an incautious, idling pace.

Miguel was thankful for the extra time awarded to Rodrigo as he would need every minute, comforting and advising the distressed refugees on the best action to keep them and their children safe, yet the soldier in him was annoyed with the apparently dawdling convoy. There should be greater caution especially as they escorted senior officers into the next theatre of war. *Where are the outriders?* he asked himself. *Even men on the small Patria motorbikes would do, emulating their supporting Fascist mentors as they do on BMWs according to the manual of best practice, "Motorised Patrols subsection, defensive action".* Miguel chuckled to himself over his ridiculous thoughts; a parody of Nazi German behaviour. But here, at this very moment, there should be at the very least well-armed Spanish Nationalist soldiers in light-armoured vehicles. However, their mistake was to his advantage; maybe God was on his side after all. Miguel cast that vain hope aside as the Nationalists had already declared they were fighting for a Christian Spain. *Odd how they get their centuries-old enemies, Moroccan Muslims, to do the work of our Christian God.*

The women were now quiet, sent by Rodrigo on their way he assumed. His mind switched back to the job in hand as the lead car approached the first marker. Not far ahead of the advancing convoy was the second marker, with the distance from the firing position calculated earlier by Miguel. This was a good marker easily picked out under pressure, a combination of a distinctly rounded boulder and a solitary olive tree known now to be 200 metres from the ambush position and the sights on the rifle had been set to match the distance.

He kissed the stock of his Remington M1871, an old long-barrelled, bolt-actioned, single-shot rifle; ancient it might be, but it had a great reputation for accuracy. He had used his sergeant's rank when in the army to lay claim to it, much to the objection of the then present owner and it had never left Miguel's side to this day. It was not the reputation as a sniper's rifle that attracted Sergeant Miguel but the beautiful replacement walnut stock skilfully crafted by some caring technician. It was so different from the crudely formed stocks of many of the repaired rifles thrust upon the mainland Republican soldiers of lowly rank. Miguel's acquisition had received special treatment with the butt being formed from some Walnut burr rich in swirling patterns of chestnut brown against the paler, more closely grained wood. It was the pattern of expensive bedroom furniture found only in the houses of the bourgeoisie and Miguel cherished it as would the lady in silk. He caressed it once again as if it was that lady and chuckled to himself.

He pulled the butt comfortably into his shoulder and with his cheek against the stock he nestled into his old friend checking the alignment of the sights onto the rounded boulder.

He watched them close in on the prearranged position and timed his breathing perfectly. In, now out slowly, in again and hold. Everything was rock solid as he squeezed the trigger. His concentration was so intense he did not register the sharp sound of the shot; he was far too busy reloading and, in his imagination, tracing the fall of the bullet. He knew he had struck his target as the windscreen distorted. The big car turned sharply left, leaped the drainage ditch and with no perceptible loss of speed ploughed up the adjacent bank towards the trees violently throwing the occupants about, leaving the driver broken against the steering wheel. Aware that the troop-carrying lorries were taking evasive action he did not allow his concentration to waver; he would not be distracted from the task in hand. Smoke billowed up from beneath the bonnet and Miguel caught the first flickerings of flames as the right-hand front door opened cautiously. A lanky young officer emerged keeping as much of the door as possible as cover against the sniper's art. He leant across to open the rear door then bravely used his body to give cover to the senior officer now being forced from his place of safety by the denser billowing smoke. Miguel shot the young man between the shoulder blades; the impact threw him against the opening door and with arms outstretched as if expecting an embrace, he twisted away and fell, exposing the older man who turned and foolishly tried to re-enter the burning car. He was driven back by the scorching heat and forced to turn again to hobble away as Moroccan mercenaries rapidly fired towards the sniper's position. Miguel felt, more than heard, the bullets hiss and buzz about him too close for comfort but he would not move until the job was done. The old man hunched within his greatcoat and holding firmly onto his braided hat shuffled away to find shelter. Miguel fired, and the round struck the officer high on the shoulder turning him so that he peered in grotesque surprise up the hill towards his assassin; the final shot slapped him in the throat and with blood-swamped hands hopelessly holding what little remained, the old man folded towards the ground.

Miguel knew he had been hit by at least one if not two rounds; glancing blows he vainly hoped, knowing the crushing hammer blows told a different tale leaving parts of his body thankfully numb. Now he must defend himself with as much vigour as possible to keep the beasts at bay. Rodrigo would still need time and certainly the women and children did as they strove to find a place to hide. Miguel hoped that his friend would stay where he was and not try to return to the hill. This was no place for an unarmed man.

Putting all personal discomfort out of mind he watched with soldiers' eyes the mercenaries approaching on two fronts; unsurprised, he gave credit to the advancing rebels. *Very sensible*, he thought. It made it difficult for him, constantly having to change his direction of fire, which would become more demanding as he felt the effects of his wounds. The dulling numbness gave way to mind-searing pain; his wounds were worse than he had at first hoped.

The advancing soldiers knew they had no effective opposition; the enemy was outnumbered so they were not going to take unnecessary risks despite their bellyaching officers shouting at them from the rear. They still wanted their squad to be the first to over-run the enemy because you never knew what little treasures there would be for the taking.

Unknown to Miguel a third group was advancing from the rear and although faced with a difficult climb, they may well have had the best chance of reaching him first. Their eager colleagues to the front knew this so they made haste with caution.

Miguel fired as quickly as possible switching from the section on his right to those on the left as they sprinted forwards a few more metres under the covering fire of their colleagues. They were eating up the ground and as he swung his rifle to the left once more, a bullet struck the treasured Walnut stock splintering it and driving the fragments into Miguel's cheekbone; he saw stars, was stunned and seemed to lose his presence of mind as he pushed himself up from his prone position. In that microsecond, he felt his only hope lay in escape by launching himself over the sheer rocky drop to his rear. Within that same second a bullet struck his knee collapsing him awkwardly to the ground. *Oh God*, he thought, *I'm done for.* The Moroccans advanced rapidly with knives drawn only to pull up in surprise. The helpless, heavily wounded enemy was a solitary being, a brave man no doubt and such courage gives greater value to trophies to be taken. They smiled dark smiles. Know you how treasured are the bits cut from the fiercest bull in the ring?

Miguel did not register his head being pulled forwards as sharp knives removed his ears, but the bayonet pressed through his nose with such callousness was all too much.

He was lifted awkwardly. Shards of pain like spear thrusts coursed through the limped flesh as dark hands moved to discharge his mortality into the space beyond the rock. Airborne his soul slipped its Earthly ties and with fleeting care was carried by the breeze; spirited away like spiralling dust on a still warm day but with certainty his soul would seek the girl with laughing eyes. The power of this final thought was undeniable. Estrella would be waiting in the enveloping mist that was the final dream. *God help us, why did this begin?*

2

THE BEACH

August 2009

The day started much as any other day when on holiday in the Landes, the sun already creeping towards its zenith and Natascha late for breakfast. She had been coming here ever since she was born and over twenty years later here she was again. It was almost a ritual but more probably the result of an assumption that this is where the extended family would join up and share with each other the events of their year. It was a place where they would eat, drink, make merry, play games, compete, and generally annoy each other. As usual there was the scramble for accommodation, some claiming rooms in the house, others having to make do with the caravan or tents they brought for themselves. Natascha quite enjoyed camping on the grass under the great pine trees relishing most of all the peace found when tucked away in her own compartment reading or just listening to music. The shortcomings were few but being disturbed by the noise generated by her brothers in the adjacent compartment was one, and secondly being called by Mama to carry out tedious tasks. These were regular, aggravating occurrences but she still loved it and most of all going down to the beach at Cap de L'Homy. The beach was magnificent, stretching as far as the eye could see in both directions; even at the height of the summer you could always find a place to picnic, lie out in the sun and doze. Throughout her young life she found the sea irresistible. It was the best part of the day by far. Enormous waves generated hundreds of miles out into the Atlantic Ocean travelled unchallenged across the Bay of Biscay to expend unequalled energy on the beaches of western France. Black-suited surfers bobbed distantly upon the surging seas as they waited with undue patience for the right wave, whereas Natascha and family threw themselves into the boiling surf with a skill that easily outstripped their recklessness.

Today was to be different. Everybody agreed that nostalgia was to be the order of the day and instead of the easily reached Cap de L'Homy they would venture off course to seek out the remote beach of Yons. In the early days infants were hauled upon shoulders as the family crocodile navigated the disintegrating cycle track that led to the steep, soft dunes that divided land from sea. Now, in the later years, the steepness and the shifting of sand under foot made the climb most difficult for the once invincible few and carrying the lightest bag was enough to make the final obstacle a task close to impossible. These were the same people who only three decades ago could jog up the impossible hill carrying beer bottles and a barbeque stove, let alone a bonny daughter shoulder-riding and gripping Father's hair to secure her seat. To repeat the venture was to refresh the memory, recalling visions of stepping through the comforting shade of deeply scented pines and into the surprising heat of the midday sun and then to squint through darkened lenses seeking out the coolest track through sun-baked sands. The climb was always hard but soon forgotten when the comforting breeze lifted by the upward-sloping dune cooled tortured lungs.

The leggy, impossibly energetic child had changed. Now it was a tall, elegant and introspective young woman who took to the forest track. The brightness of her personality still sparkled, but those who knew her well perceived shadows of concern. Natascha had changed and it was nothing to do with the brilliant recovery that rescued her academic career. There was something else, an incident perhaps, maybe an unpleasant one; whatever it was it happened between the third and final year at university. On several occasions Natascha had talked to her mother about her social life and the absence of a decent boyfriend. When asked about her time spent in Spain she spoke with enthusiasm expressing her love of Salamanca and day trips into the surrounding countryside but when the discussion turned to the time spent in Béjar her comments were short on detail. If she was to be believed, it was all rather dull.

The path beneath the pines was clearly marked. Feet had reserved areas from the encroaching heather and bracken and the remnants of the "piste cyclable" were easier to walk upon than the shifting sand. Without awareness Natascha had gained some distance from the family group who chattered and laughed at often heard tales of the discomfort of others. She would have been the centre of such happy nonsense not so long ago, but since Spain other tales less amusing had wormed their way into her chest of reminiscences. Beyond the laughter, corrupting images dissolved the source of joy, projecting the mood from light-hearted silliness to irrational sadness in less than a moment. It was happening again. It came like a thief; nothing seen, and nothing felt until the damage was done.

She walked ahead happy to be left with just the rasping sounds of cicadas as they called out to lost lovers from lone trees subjected to the relentless sun. Pine cones snapped open in the heat folding back their woody petals to reveal precious seeds. How she loved these sounds enveloping her as she moved towards the base of the dune. The trees thinned, and the shade disappeared as she climbed the dune following a wrecked boardwalk in between great bushes of broom. Picking her way upwards using the remnants of once secured boards she breathlessly reached the top. The sound and sight of the surf breaking on the broad expanse of beach momentarily carried her back to her carefree childhood. She turned about from her elevated position and scanned the tops of the cushion-formed forest of stone pines. The deep viridian green of softly rounded foliage belied the penetrating sharpness of the needles. None could deny the beauty, the calmness created by the constancy of form and colour, a blessed sight of rich green shadows and sun-drenched highlights like polished aluminium. She stood leaning on the extended pole of the sun umbrella letting her mind absorb the certainty, eternity and contentment exuded by the sky, the sea and the forest. It pushed back into the recesses of her mind, just for that moment, the intruders. Lost in the beauty of all that surrounded her she was unaware of the family as they struggled up the last few metres to the crest of the dune. She was standing back from the path as the family filed past, the youngest whooping with joy as the sea came into view. 'Come on, Natascha. Thought you'd be down there by now; look at the waves.' They sprinted along the top of the dune then launched themselves down the steep slope to the beach. She stayed screwing the umbrella post into the sand making sure it stayed in place even though there was presently little wind. Opening up the canvas parasol, she hid from the unremitting sunlight, settling into the welcoming shade. She did not understand why she was not thrashing about in the waves with everyone else, but she felt at peace and that was all she sought at times like this. Time passed easily; she was seduced by solitude.

Her father sat upright on the beach with his long legs folded so he could grasp his knees. Peering out to an empty sea, there was nothing but waves turning in on themselves on hidden sandbanks then reforming to run swiftly across the shallowing water and breaking yet again upon the perfect beach. Comfort surreptitiously eased into an angular mind as the sweet monotony of constant sound subtly subdued the anxiety of life; large waves plunged, accelerating the onward rush with a crescendo of shingle upon fragmented shells whilst sunlight faceted to flash diamond-like and harmonise with wet pebbles masquerading as polished gems. He turned his head to the left and watched the boys plunging in and out of the advancing waters. The waves grew to be more demanding on their second breaking as the tide deepened the water on the distant sandbanks. The cleanliness of the forward wall of the advancing wave glowed amber and agile bodies shimmered as they plunged through to the other side.

Time for him to swim, he thought; but where was the sleekest fish of all? Where was Natascha; she who lived for the waters; a mermaid, long-legged, tanned golden by the sun who flipped with unequalled skill as she moved through the uncompromising tumult with the grace of a dancer? But it was his turn now. He loved the challenges of the sea, to ride the mighty seventh and think not of risks. They gave an edge to the excitement, the triumph, the shared laughter, the bruises gained as trophies on a painful landing. But where was Natascha? He turned about and looked towards the dune. The blue and white stripes of the parasol were still in place and there was an unhappy loneliness of such a simple sight. This girl, this beautiful but awkward young woman should be here, he thought. This is her domain; this is the place that draws from her infectious laughter, the joy of life, the irresistible charm that uniquely transports her back to childhood.

He loped across the sand towards the foot of the seaward facing dune and climbed, struggling against the backward shifting sands until the firmness of the crest. There she sat at just a short distance holding her knees to anchor her posture. The shade cast by the parasol gave some comfort, but the sun-heated sand reflected light and dried the air. It was not an easy place to stay. Her chin was on her chest as she slumped forwards, and the hat lay unattended just out of reach. He was breathing heavily and could not call out her name. She didn't move; there was something about her very stillness that generated a surge of concern. Standing still for a moment he came to terms with something outside his experience. He was puzzled; this extrovert young lady would normally deliver some cutting remark when disturbed. He stepped forwards cautiously and called her name. 'Natascha.' Again he spoke, 'Natascha, are you not well?' He lowered himself to sit beside his daughter careful not to touch her, for the tension was palpable. Her chin remained resting on her chest and he watched as a small tear ran across her upper *lip to fall unnoticed towards the hot sand. Persistent cicadas rasped their presence barely heard over the thunderous plunging of Atlantic waves as they crashed upon the shifting beach. 'What's wrong, darling? Tell me.' He put his right arm about her shoulders and she turned her head slowly to face him. He tried not to let his expression register his concern as he recognised fearful confusion within the eyes. Had he ever looked so closely? In the past, contact had been on the hoof, in passing and too brief within their busy collective lives. All had accepted with a sigh of unjustifiable tolerance, the vagaries of growing up. Irrationality, selfishness, deception, mischief and infectious charm, a combination of which miraculously produced this graceful young woman. This was new. 'Has something awful happened,' he paused for a moment before adding, 'to you?'*

'Look, Dada, I feel as if I have been pushed into a world full of nastiness that no one can put right.' He waited for her to carry on not really understanding what her concern was. He knew already that the world was a dog-eat-dog environment with all those in power pretending to be men of the people whilst feathering their own nests. She continued. 'I eventually started to take my studies seriously.'

'Yes, and not before time I might add,' he interjected.

'Stop, Dad, and listen to me; I know what you thought of me and you have a point, but what I am about to tell you has only a little to do with me. Now just listen,' she warned him. 'Please say nothing.'

'Before you start do you want to walk down to the beach and have some lunch?' Her look already told him this was a silly idea.

She stood up abruptly as if she had been re-energised, brushed at her clothes vigorously then turned to him and said, 'No, come let's go sit under that tree, it's got to be cooler there.'

Having settled down into the cooling shade provided by the foliage of dense bushes of broom and with their backs pressed against the trunk of a huge fallen tree, Natascha started to speak intermittently holding up her hand whenever her father tried to interrupt.

'Dad, I've only just worked out what has happened to me and before I tell you this upsetting story, I want you to know how I've struggled with the consequences of what I have learned and what I experienced.' She spoke softly but with an intensity that demanded his attention.

She explained how she did not know whether it was something, a mood with no rational basis or something else that has logic but is elusive, hidden in her mind. Her father lifted his head and looked closely at her conveying his cynicism; she dismissed his unspoken words with a look, halting his attempt to speak with a single raised finger. 'I am no madder than you nor am I less sane; let me continue.' And she did, pausing for but a second. 'These unwelcome mood swings are poisonous and creep in uninvited and unnoticed at the most inappropriate times and however legitimate the joy of that moment is I feel compelled to leave the comfort of my friends.'

She smiled in unspoken relief and it dawned upon him that she had been moved from there to here, transformed; no longer a morose, unhappy child but one in control in her world. The power of the confessional, he thought; devils cast out in the stream of incomprehensible words. Natascha chose to ignore the uncertainty that flickered within the doubting eyes. 'And now I can tell you the story. It's not pleasant; in fact, it is tragic and there will be events that will make you angry. But it's over and you can't do anything about it.'

Her father continued to listen but remained hesitant to accept her analysis of the perceived problem.

'This all started with what Mamie told me before going off to university.'

'That doesn't surprise me,' he said expressing his intolerance with outside interference.

'Don't be silly, Dad. What Mamie told me was very interesting although I didn't take much notice of what she said at first. But during one of the lectures that history professor, I've spoken of him before, said something that linked up with what Mamie had told me. I got interested; I really wanted to know more. It was what I learned in Béjar that upset me and I'm sure even a grumpy, cynical old man like you would have felt the same. It's not gone away, you know; I'm still affected by what I found out; I will never shake it off and I don't think I want to.'

'What are you going to do now? You may have controlled your demons, or let's be fair, you're starting to control them, but I sense you want to do more; am I correct?'

She nodded vigorously affirming what he asked but said nothing. She stared unfocussed into the middle distance as her father waited with growing agitation not knowing what to do with the suspended conversation. Turning back to him she asked in an accusatory way, 'Don't I owe it to Mamie and others to tell people what I know?'

Taken aback by the way she spoke to him, he replied, 'I'm not responsible for what happened; and I'm not sure what happened, anyway. If you think something ought to be done, you do it.'

'I'm not blaming you, Dad, but it just shows, if you, who has an opinion on everything, know nothing then something must be done. In this age of apologising for this historic brutality, and that suppression of an undeserving people, and taking responsibility for the slave trade and many other foul events then what about the horrific injustices of that time in Spanish history? It wasn't such a long time ago, you know, and some of the brutes whose crimes were covered up by the Franco regime may yet be still alive.' Natascha paused then spoke softly with her voice edged with concern. 'I hate to say this, Dad, because I love the Spanish people for many good reasons but lying beneath the surface of their society germinate the seeds of the same fascism.'

'But all western democracies allow freedom of thought and speech. We in France, and in Britain for that matter, have political groups that have fascist tendencies too; nothing so special about that.'

'Mmm, OK' she conceded. 'But I want to do something about bringing justice to the hundreds of thousands of victims in *this covered-up atrocity and the only way I can do that is through journalism.'*

'Good news, but do you have the qualifications?'

'All sorted, Dad; now, would you like to listen?' She paused for a moment then took hold of his arm. 'Before I start I want you to know this is about what happened to Mamie's godmother, Joan. The cruel events she suffered later in her life were dormant on the day she married her Spanish husband, Rodrigo.'

3

THE WEDDING IN BURGOS

May 1932

Once they had passed through the grand arched exit from the station they looked out over the city. The rooftops of the nearby buildings obscured much of the scene but could not hide the towering spires of the cathedral. The sun caught the tracery of the pierced stonework on the higher reaches of the spires. 'It is magical,' said Mary. 'It has a sense of improbability about it; how can such delicate lace-like lines be produced in stone?' They were viewing only a small part of one of the most impressive Gothic architectural works of art in Europe. 'Joan told me that Burgos has many wonderful places to see and if they're half as good as what we're looking at now we have a treat in store.' Harry nodded in agreement and continued to stand with his mouth half open.

Joan, at the foot of the steps and close to the taxi ranks, spotted them as soon as they emerged from the shadows of the station. Though impeded by the tightness of her ankle-length skirt, she tripped elegantly up the street avoiding motor taxis and the horse-drawn carriages as they jostled for space to claim passengers at the foot of the steps. 'Mary,' she called again and again to no avail. Both were so engrossed with the view that they were unaware of what was going on at pavement level. Joan had reached the base of the broad stone steps that led down to the taxi ranks. Cupping her hands around her mouth she shrieked in the most unladylike manner, 'Mary, I'm down here!' Only then did Mary pull herself away from the view of the cathedral to wonder who on earth could be calling her name. Joan was determined not to have to climb the steps towards them so stood waving manically trying to attract their attention.

Mary grabbed Harry's arm and pointed down the steps. 'Look, there's Joan; she's come to meet us. How wonderful. She's on her own so no Rodrigo at the moment, I fear.' Pulling her dress up to knee level she ran gracefully down the stone stairway and threw herself into Joan's arms. Harry followed in a statelier fashion struggling with the luggage. Hugs and kisses were exchanged, and the young women entwined in each other's arms danced a short jig of delight. Harry stood and waited slightly embarrassed with a grin upon his face until they had done with their silliness.

Joan shepherded them towards a taxi she had reserved for their arrival as they struggled to resettle hats and push loose hair back into place. 'How did you know when we were going to arrive?' asked Harry. 'I'm so glad you did. God knows how we would have found the hotel.'

'We do have such things as telephones in this country,' she said laughingly. 'I rang the station office and they told me there had been a few delays; one at Vitoria over troubles with the Basques; I hope you weren't worried?' Mary pulled a wry face; the memory was disturbing.

The taxi had moved off turning right into La Merced drawing gasps of appreciation from both as they looked across the river towards the towering cathedral once again. They crossed Puente Santa Maria catching sight of the magnificent Arco de Santa Maria before following the road beside the river. 'I'm really glad to see so many great monuments dedicated to me,' said Mary with false pomposity. 'Maria is the Spanish equivalent of Mary, is that not so?'

'But that is not all; the most beautiful of all monuments is also dedicated to you, "Saint" Maria.'

Harry rolled his eyes as Mary said with an undisguised sense of superiority, 'Not the cathedral as well, Joan? How appropriate, don't you think so, Harry?'

Harry shook his head gently, murmuring to himself but loud enough for all to hear. 'I'm in for a difficult time with you and your mischief, no doubt.' They all laughed.

The Hotel La Puebla was once a nineteenth-century *hostal* which maintained a sense of history and comforting charm created by rich wood panelling and chestnut internal doors; beyond the elaborately carved portico stood magnificent age-blackened doors studded with oversized antique nails. Harry ran his fingers appreciatively over the studded door and shook his head in wonderment. 'Wow, these must weigh a ton; they're truly magnificent.'

The smell of coffee was enticing but Joan chased them upstairs to their room warning them not to come down until they had rested. 'Because tonight you are going to meet up with my lovely Rodrigo and family. I will bring you up a cup of coffee in five minutes so don't go to sleep quite yet.'

True to her word the coffee arrived, and Joan explained that she was staying at this hotel too, but Rodrigo was housed somewhere across the other side of the city. She explained Rodrigo's family were going to eat locally and had asked that they might meet them for pre-dinner drinks.

'So, wash and sleep; it could be a long night,' she said as she left.

Much as Mary was looking forward to meeting with Rodrigo and his family she peered longingly at the bed realising how much she needed to sleep.

'Don't you dare lie down,' warned Harry. 'Tired as we are, we mustn't let our heads hit the pillow. We'll never wake up if we do.'

They had planned for it not to be a long night and Joan, not wishing to tempt providence on this night before her wedding, decided not to join Rodrigo's family. She delivered Harry and Mary to the restaurant's door and told them they couldn't possibly miss Rodrigo, as he was the most handsome man in Burgos. Mary had to agree, for as soon as they had entered the room a dark-eyed young man stood up and walked towards them. '*Señor, señora,* I am Rodrigo, the most privileged man in the world because tomorrow I will marry your beautiful friend Juana.'

'How do you know who we are?' said Harry with a smile that matched Rodrigo's. 'We could be anybody.'

'I would not know you, *señor,* but Mary has been described to me in great detail by Juana, and she has been accurate in every respect,' Rodrigo continued appraisingly.

Harry chuckled to himself. *Compliments flow like water here, but no wonder*, he thought as he looked around at his surroundings.

They were both taken by the charm and gravitas of Joan's groom and although there was only one other English speaker amongst the group they enjoyed the warmth and generosity shown by the entire family. Rodrigo explained to his parents and friends that Mary and Juana had nursed together in London and that Mary would be Juana's special guest at the wedding. 'Also, my friends, my beautiful bride of tomorrow is godmother to their lovely child, also called

Mary; sadly, she is not here but in safe hands in England.'
He finished with a flourish kissing Mary on both cheeks.

When Harry and Mary left it was late, but they left
reluctantly. 'Who's "whanna"?' said Harry mimicking
Rodrigo with a grin on his face as they walked slowly back
to the hotel.

'Joan, you dope,' said Mary. 'Juana is what they call her
here; it's rather nice I think.'

'God, I'm tired, Mary; can you believe it? We've been
travelling for days. It was all the hanging about in Paris that
got me, and then not knowing what was going on in Irun.
Thank God we met up with Doctor Martinez and his pals.'

'You can thank me for eliciting the attention of the
lovely doctor, Harry,' she said pompously. 'Whilst you were
practising your schoolboy Spanish to no avail, I was using
my female intuition to good effect,' she said teasingly. 'Did
I not save the day?'

'Yes, you did, and it was the middle of the night by the
way,' responded Harry grumpily. 'Also, I saw the look you
gave the handsome doctor; and that wasn't about getting
information about the trains, Mary.'

'Yes it was, and anyway, it was he who showed interest
in me, not me in him.' She squeezed his arm even more
tightly. 'That's enough of this silly conversation.'

'You've gone a lovely shade of pink, Mary; it must be
that glass or two of Rioja you had earlier in the evening.'

'I would prefer to think it is the presence of the best
man in England or possibly Europe; and it is he who is
taking me to his bed.'

'Outrageous hussy,' said Harry, 'but I like the idea.'

It had been a long and demanding journey through
northern France towards Paris and beyond to Spain, with
the sleep of yesterday being intermittent and ineffectual.
Tonight it would be different. How welcome the comfort

offered by this beautiful bed and true to its promise it carried them softly into dreamless sleep unaware of what the Burgos of tomorrow would bring.

Harry and Mary had decided to walk to the church taking a route that would keep them close to the river. There was much to see and so little time to see it. Being such a clear, still day with the sun high in the heavens they decided to enjoy as much sunlight as possible. How they had missed clear sunlight over the last few months in England. They declined the taxi and explained to the receptionist what they wanted to do. She dismissed their concerns by saying he had plenty of other people to pick up and he would not be out of pocket by their absence.

Harry was wearing for the first time a pale grey suit that Mary had borrowed from her brother but was concerned with the image he created, and Mary chuckled to herself as she noticed the slightly uncomfortable look on his face. The suit fitted him well but normally he was much more comfortable with the invisibility a dark suit provided. 'I'm much happier merging into the background of the multitude wearing dark suits than parading about like a gigolo.' She responded, with mild annoyance, accusing him of calling her brother a gigolo. He looked towards her apologetically and she smiled brilliantly in response.

'You wouldn't think I'd had a baby not so long ago would you, Mister Gigolo? You may be pretty but quite properly I am receiving all the attention.' *No wonder*, he thought. She looked amazing in an ankle-length dress, heeled shoes and a fabulous broad-brimmed hat all subtly coloured by the predominance of a dusky turquoise trimmed with understated pink.

'Not quite the costume for a long walk in the sun,' Harry remarked with some satisfaction. 'I bet you're sweating under all your finery.'

'We glow, Harry, we don't sweat; that is for you and your unsavoury male friends.' She smiled seductively in his direction and took hold of his arm.

'I can't deny it, you look beautiful; you are always beautiful but today you are exceptional.'

As they walked up towards the bridge they took the short linking path towards the main thoroughfare to be immediately faced by the Arco de Santa Maria. It was a truly magnificent monument with a façade turreted and elaborately decorated celebrating the lives of past dignitaries. They walked on passing through the coolness of the arch but making sure to leave plenty of room for the fast and noisy traffic as it bounced over the uneven cobbles.

As they moved on into the adjoining square the western front of the cathedral loomed over them. They were overwhelmed as eyes rested on tall, lacy spires with others perpetuating the same fragility as they clung delicately to the main edifice. 'How can that be stone? It's more like the delicate patterns we scissor-cut from paper.'

'Couldn't put it better myself, Mary, but I wonder what it is going to be like inside if this is the detail we are treated to on the outside?' Harry then took her arm. 'Come on, darling, I can't wait to see it. What a place to have a wedding.'

'Hold on, Harry, the wedding's not here. This is the cathedral; the wedding is in San Nicolás Church, behind the cathedral.'

'What a shame,' he said with feeling. 'This place to be substituted for a dull old chapel; I was hoping to have something glorious to occupy my mind during the ceremony, which is bound to be heavy with Spanish and Latin.'

'Come on, you old grump, Harry, all the churches in this city are historical gems. Let's just wait and see.'

Looking across to their left towards the wall enclosing the northern boundary of the square they watched a number of people climbing the broadly-spaced steps. All were dressed in their finery; gentlemen in neat suits and ladies extravagantly adorned in the bright colours of a celebrating Spain. 'It looks as if they're off to a wedding as well,' said Harry. 'And thank God some of the guys are wearing pale suits.'

'Cast your eyes beyond the lovely ladies, Harry, towards the building at the top of the steps. Can you see the church? If my instincts are correct that is our destination, San Nicolas.'

They crossed the square and climbed the steps and then followed the sloping pathway towards the beautiful Gothic arched doorway set in the simplistic durability of a cut stone wall. The famous carved chestnut doors became visible. The church was built into the terrace of houses so an independent west end did not exist; hence the main entrance was in the southern wall.

The fear that Harry would be left to endure a dull little building evaporated. The enormous doors caught his attention but there was not much time to stand and stare as the following guests pressed them to move on. They shuffled into the semi-darkness of the incense-scented interior. Heavy wooden pews lined the aisle and Harry and Mary were escorted to a place close to the front. Mary knew this was at Joan's request, as she had wanted her to have some active role during the ceremony. It remained a mystery, but she knew it would not be too challenging. Rodrigo sat apprehensively across the aisle from them in the front pew. Great candles were being lit on the simple white marble altar by assistants as the priest adorned in the gold and green of his regalia over a pristine white laced surplus drifted towards the congregation.

The organist struck the first chords of the processional hymn prompting everyone to stand then turn in anticipation. Joan walked alone as small girls trailed behind in delicate dresses of pure white cotton carrying simple posies of brightly coloured flowers. Since the death of her father Joan had told Mary that she needed to be strong and do all that was necessary on her own; no one could replace her dad and that was that. It was a powerful image, which drew people's thoughts to her absent father; Mary believed that was exactly what Joan was trying to do. She looked amazing creating an image of fragility and strength at the same time. The veil fell lightly about her shoulders making her appear even more slender and the dress fell away to the floor using layer upon layer of the finest translucent material giving the impression she was suspended, floating lightly towards her awaiting groom. As Joan came level with Mary she stopped and turned towards her passing over her bouquet of sweetly-scented freesias. Mary was taken by surprise; she had not been expecting this. She looked through the folds of the veil into Joan's enormous eyes as they smiled in happiness. Mary relaxed and mouthed thank you. Such a simple action carried with it the importance of their friendship and Mary, overcome by the gesture, hid her eyes within the shadow of her hat. Harry knew how this would have affected her and put a comforting arm about her shoulders; even a stranger from the pew to their rear leant forwards and touched her arm. It was a simple acknowledgement of acceptance from a warm-hearted people.

Harry, believing that all wedding ceremonies followed roughly the same pattern, was staggered by the time taken by every little event. He had been correct; Latin and Spanish in great volumes linked a process of incomprehensible events; turning, kneeling, praying, kissing inanimate objects, folding ribbons and wrapping hands of the couple together whilst holy water and incense were splashed and waved about liberally until the crowning glory, Communion.

Despite the element of cynicism, he was drawn by the integrity of the ceremony, however relief came through the wordy passages from feasting eyes on the gilded stone wall behind the altar. That was not all; every corner he looked into was yet another amazing, colourful declaration of faith. *And this is just a small church* he thought to himself; *where on Earth did they get the money?* A nudge by Mary brought him back to the wedding, which had now reached a conclusion with the congregation applauding as the newlyweds made their way down the aisle towards the outside world and reality.

This was a community event confirmed by the number of witnesses housed within the church to be doubled by those who had waited outside. The Spanish, a noisy, exuberant people, loving contact with friends and neighbours on occasions such as this demonstrated their zest for life. Family was everything to these joyous people. The crowd swept the bride and groom with guests following closely along the street towards the feasting place passing between those shopping but now standing and smiling. Others were throwing flower petals and calling out their best wishes and compliments. Harry and Mary knew not a word said but understood everything. The movement of the celebrants swept through the streets and hooting car horns added to the cacophony. 'I hope we're not causing a hold-up; in England a disagreeable row would be brewing by now.'

'I'm sure no one minds being delayed by a wedding, even in England, you old misery, Harry. You can see how much everybody is enjoying themselves except that miserable pair over there under the arch.'

Harry looked across the road to men in military uniforms. 'You're right, they don't seem to be enjoying themselves.' As Harry walked by, he kept his eyes on the two men. They seemed to be concentrating all their attention on him and Mary. He was unnerved by the way they stared and unwisely took it as a personal affront. Typical of Harry he chose not to ignore it. Stepping towards the men he spoke in English. 'Have I done something wrong, gentlemen? You seem to have made me the subject of your attention.' One of them flipped his hand as if telling Harry to move away. Harry felt his annoyance turning into something worse but before he could react he was grasped firmly by the elbow and forcibly turned away by one of the guests.

'Take no notice, *señor*; those are *Guardia Civil* and those two are particularly unpleasant men. I know to my cost. They have great power here and will arrest anyone for the simplest of things; there is not much that can be done about it.' Harry recognised his rescuer from the first evening they had arrived. He was a close friend of Rodrigo.

'Thank you, José Ramón, I'm sorry if I've caused you any embarrassment. Come, let us go on and enjoy the party.'

José held firmly on to his arm restraining him for a little longer. 'I'm so pleased you are enjoying my beautiful city, Harry, but Burgos is a place dominated by privileged people who despite the poverty suffered in much of the country will do anything to preserve their way of life. And those two and others like them have the means to do it.'

Harry understood exactly what José was saying and acknowledged his appreciation of the information received by a knowing nod of the head.

Mary, disturbed by the whispering that went on between the two men was grateful that nothing unpleasant happened and gave José a kiss of gratitude. He laughed and spoke to Harry. 'I hope we have another event from which I can rescue you if I am rewarded each time with a kiss from a beautiful lady.'

As they entered the restaurant Harry looked back at the two guardsmen and unsmilingly they continued to look.

4

THE SCHOOLMASTER

June 1934

Juana loved Burgos; every corner she turned in this beautiful city revealed architectural treasures and evidence of a regal history. Her marriage to Rodrigo, the kindness of his family and above all the birth of Alicia in this friendliest of places made her wish that all her days could be lived here in continuing happiness. The hospital had been pleased to employ her working with sickly children now that she had mastered the language. Her work lifted her spirits further as she nursed her precious charges back to health and she gained much joy from returning them to the arms of their loving mothers. Rodrigo's wishes to return to the province of his birth could not be denied; he spoke constantly of his childhood and how much he needed to recapture it for the sake of Alicia; the joy of the forest and the snow-capped peaks beyond and everything else but he knew Juana loved Burgos and all the historic drama associated with it. She was an historian at heart and her passion was to unravel the mystery surrounding "El Cid". Where did lie the truth amongst the wealth of myth?

Family contacts had informed Rodrigo that the church wished to employ a schoolmaster in a village not far from the town in which he had grown up. 'This is fate,' he declared passionately to Juana. 'This is meant to be. You will love it, I know you will love it and Alicia can go to my school and grow into a beautiful woman just like her mother.'

'You haven't got the job yet, Rodrigo,' she replied phlegmatically. 'And before you get too excited why don't you go to see the priest? He might be the most awful man you would find impossible to work for.'

Rodrigo returned from meeting the priest and a senior cleric from one of the ancient churches in the centre of Béjar. He immediately made a connection with the older man whom he remembered from when he was a child, much to the chagrin of the village priest who was distant and superior complaining it was not an old comrades' reunion but a job interview. Rodrigo was a little disturbed by the spark of anger in the younger man's eyes but chose to ignore it and not mention that to Juana. Undeterred Rodrigo continued with enthusiasm to convince Juana of the importance of the job to him. 'However, I managed to persuade even the superior priest that my ideas and methods would benefit local children.' He paused and looked thoughtful. 'He did say, however, more than once, very annoyingly, that he expected me to work closely with him as the teachings of the church are paramount. I'm not convinced the Gospels are paramount to this particular priest, he thinks it's him; so full of himself.'

'Well, you haven't said if you got the job or not.'

'Of course I got the job. Who could possibly turn down my exceptional talents?'

Juana flung her arms about his neck and kissed him, for the joy he exuded in gaining the job but not for the thought of leaving her beautiful Burgos.

Everything happened very quickly and there was need to say farewell to their friends and colleagues. There was great sadness at their leaving, but many hopeful promises to visit and keep in touch eased the sense that something precious would be lost.

It was an awkward journey having first to stay at Ciudad Rodrigo overnight then pick up whatever could be found as transport from there towards Béjar. 'Look at a map, Rodrigo; we're almost doubling the journey.'

'I have a family member who delivers goods between Ciudad and Burgos and he can carry all our belongings between the two towns. He will also give us a bed for the night and supper before our journey to Béjar the next day.'

'I suppose you are right; I believe you know what will be best for us.' She gently touched him on the cheek. 'But I don't want Alicia suffering any more than she has to, over the journey.'

'This is the best way; we will be with family, so we can stop whenever we wish and believe me, Alicia's welfare is as important to my cousins as it is to us.'

It was a long and lumpy ride to Ciudad Rodrigo, but the welcome was warm and generous with Juana being temporarily relieved of her child by gentle hands whilst she was invited to wash away the grime of the journey in a large tin tub of hot, scented water. They slept a dreamless sleep and rose with the dawn. More sad farewells and vain promises as they climbed into the lorry cab with Alicia held firmly in her father's arms. The road twisted along the lower edge of the Sierra de Francia and continued to snake its way close to La Alberca before the easier run into Béjar.

'I'll take you straight up to Santo Domingo from here,' said the driver, indicating a road to the right. 'It's not quite as steep as the road from the town centre which I'll use on the way down from the mountain.' *This long, dusty journey has undone all the good of last night's bath*, thought Juana, *but I'm glad I don't have to travel on any more switchback roads.* Of this she was wrong and within a short time she was clinging firmly to Rodrigo's arm. The road wound up through the most beautiful forest rich in birch, ash, oak and beech with the sunlight breaking through the leaves and patterning the forest floor with pools of shimmering light. The fear diminished as her mind imagined creatures tripping through the deep covering of fallen leaves. The place was magical; no wonder Rodrigo loved it here. The road followed the ridge above a mountain stream in the latter part of the journey taking some bends that almost came back upon themselves. The driver skilfully used his gears to control the noisy vehicle, as they approached a great pile of boulders. Juana had lost sight of the road as it disappeared behind bush and boulder; she held her breath as he used the complete width of the crumbling road to negotiate hidden left-hand turns. It was ridged and steep but in the lowest gear the lorry negotiated with relative ease the short drive up into the village.

'What a difficult turn and such a spooky place; I'm sure that jumble of rocks and twisted blackened trees could tell a few blood-curdling tales and maybe in the future tell some more.' Despite the heat she shivered.

'Yes, those big rocks make it difficult to turn into the Santo Domingo road. It's only spooky because that spot gets all the run-off rainwater during the frequent heavy storms and they wash away much of the vegetation. But the ditch on the far side of the road has been recently dug; that should help to deal with winter downpours,' explained the driver. 'Anyway, this is the end of the journey for you. Looks like you've got a welcoming party,' he said pointing towards a group of people standing under a tree to the left.

Rodrigo passed over an envelope to the driver as he stood by the back of the lorry unloading their worldly goods. 'Thanks so much for going out of your way to deliver us here. Have a safe journey back home and pass on our love to my cousins.'

The welcoming party gathered them up as a mother would her children, telling them that the only duty they had tonight was to eat and sleep. Miranda, the wife of Rodrigo's old friend Jorge, had all of that under control. Immediately Juana felt at home. 'Can we meet everybody tomorrow?'

Miranda nodded her agreement and sent everyone on their way calling out to them, for Rodrigo and Juana's benefit, that tomorrow would be special. 'Yes, we've even organised tomorrow's party for you so you'd better sleep well tonight.'

As the gathering dusk slipped away into the deeper shades of the lamp-lit darkening night Rodrigo took Juana in his arms and whispered, 'Thank you, kind lady, love of my life, for letting me return to this perfect place. This dream of mine is built on sweet memories and let us hope such good things will be repeated. What is certain, my English rose, is that it will be all the better for me because I can share it with you and our delightful daughter.' Juana nestled her cheek into his chest as he enveloped them both in protective warmth. 'In Santo Domingo we are protected from the meanness of a greater world; we will be forever safe here.' He took her by the hand holding Alicia in his other arm and led her to the soft, clean, alluring bed. 'Now we must sleep in the safe thought that nought can hurt us here.'

5

THE LECTURE

June 2006

This was the fourth of six lectures she was obliged to attend; no one said you had to, but her mother was emphatic about her going to all lectures and not to waste any opportunity that would enhance her chances of success. Anyway, her mum would find out soon enough if she appeared to be slacking; she seemed to have a spy on the campus. Getting into Albi University to study English and Spanish was unexpected; it was probably her competence in English that got her there, but her Spanish wasn't bad. Her father almost gave up on her as she never seemed to work and was good at keeping the truth at bay. As she listened to the lecturer droning on, it puzzled her why Spanish history should be important if you were just studying the language, but something in the back of her mind niggled and seemed to give it credence. She was convinced it was something to do with what her Grandmother Mary told her a short time ago. It was about a relative; no, in truth, not a relative but her grandmother's godmother, called Joan. Anyway, she thought, whatever it was, the memory brought tears to her grandmother's eyes convincing Natascha that powerful events of the past could affect you for the rest of your life.

This lecture was all about an invasion and a war; it held her attention because she remembered her grandmother, known in

34

France as "mamie", talking about soldiers from Africa taking over the country. *Now this has some relevance,* she thought. How she wished she had listened more carefully to the preceding lectures; there must have been reasons for the foreign invasion. With that she made herself a promise to look up the notes and other scribblings she made almost absentmindedly at earlier lectures to see if she could get a better understanding of what had been going on.

The lecturer continued and by paying closer attention she started to feel for the people who were involved. But all these facts being presented were very dry; they were as words on a page; no life in them, just ink on paper. Maybe the lecturer had lost all feelings for the real people who were affected by the war as a result of the number of times he must have given the lecture in the past. It was very different for Natascha who had been drawn back to the time of her grandmother's tears. She was disappointed that the dry facts lacked feelings. These were events that destroyed people's lives and Natascha felt that the lecture needed a bit of theatre to generate emotions, so the students could relate more closely to those awful times.

It was a war amongst themselves, brother against brother, and it was vile. It was hard to work out who was right and who was wrong. And who was on whose side anyway? It was complicated. What was patently clear was that many who had done no wrong were swept up in the troubles, driven from their homes to be left destitute or brutally murdered. As Natascha's grasp of the sequence of events became more secure she made a pledge she would concentrate on this tragic period in Spain's history if only to understand and respect her grandmother's account of that time and place.

The fifteenth century saw Spain's rise in fortune and influence, but this slipped away in the following centuries. Despite their diminishing power, the powerful and wealthy seemed to ride out the storm. The poor suffered worsening conditions and starving peasant communities out of necessity found a voice. Muscled agents of the rich and the Guardia Civil, regarded as the private army of *the wealthy, set about punishing the "troublemakers" by destroying homes, breaking heads and even murder. The church called upon the poor to remember their place and obey their masters.*

Locked up in her room in voluntary isolation Natascha did her best to catch up on what she should have listened to more carefully in previous lectures and was surprised by how much she enjoyed it. Her notes were better presented than her expectations and she gave herself a congratulatory chuckle of self-satisfaction as she settled down to absorb the facts.

During this period of greed, moral absence, and to a certain extent, national feebleness in the 1920s King Alfonso XIII sought to reclaim some admiration from his people by covertly organising a war with the Moroccans. A war that should have been easily won was easily lost to the shame of the nation.

Natascha felt her brain was working in overdrive and needed time out to cool down. She pushed aside her papers but made sure the books lay open at the right pages. Getting up to stretch her legs, which were suffering from the onset of cramp she was tempted to pour herself a glass of wine but with a great deal of self-satisfaction settled for water. 'I'm changing for the better, no doubt. In the past I would have tried to wipe out all irritation in a glass of Madiran or two.' Her mind returned to her work feeling compelled to know more and with that she sat down and peered studiously into the books.

General Primo de Rivera, an honourable man, took control of the country, appalled by the corruption that existed throughout Spain, with a justice system which seemed to work only in the favour of the privileged and against the poor. He was a decent man who tragically failed to bring about a fairer society; the opposition was too strong.

A picture of the past was slowly forming in Natascha's mind but there were still quite a few years to catch up on before those which were relevant to her grandmother's life and that of her lost godmother came into focus. There were very few who were willing to make a difference to the miserable lives of the many as the power lay with the wealthy. The church used its influence to maintain the "status quo". Primo de Rivera turned to the emerging workers' groups and organisations inviting them to become involved in government, but many regarded his efforts with cynicism.

In January 1930, he resigned, and left the country to live in Paris. Within a few weeks he had died, bitterly disappointed, overwhelmed by his failure to bring peace and order to his beloved Spain.

The more she learned, the more Natascha felt herself become emotionally connected to the plight of the anonymous and neglected poor. 'For goodness' sake,' she thought. 'What a waste of time. Nobody with any power seems to care for the great majority; they're only interested in themselves.' The King turned to Admiral Juan Bautista Aznar in the hope it would allay the fears of the prospective Republicans and bring peace to the striking workforces. Aznar instructed elections should take place in April 1931 in the hope they could re-establish an order to their liking. Early in the morning of 14th April 1931 the country awoke to the news that the first Republic was born. The Liberals and Socialists had been voted into power. King Alfonso XIII abdicated, collected his belongings together with his family and slipped away unseen, unloved and soon to be forgotten.

Natascha felt more confident having gained so much more knowledge from her last-minute intense study sessions in the library when others were urging her to party. She was becoming a better student. Today as she listened intently to the lecturer she wanted to be more than a dedicated note-taker and passive listener; she needed to know more about what he was talking about. This was the subject area that had most relevance to her, but how was she to extract more information from this dull and seemingly disinterested man? She suddenly felt empowered when another student interrupted his delivery of dates and facts.

'Sir, these are just a set of facts to me; a list of faceless people who dominate our interest today and disregard the mass of people *who had no say. Their lives were made worse by an arrogant, self-important, privileged few.'*

'This is a narrow-minded observation, not a question,' he replied then paused with a superior smile upon his face. 'Who are you, anyway? I don't know who you are; maybe I can call you Mr Trotsky. Yes, why not? A commissar who makes observations also from a position of self-importance.'

The student tried to respond to the unjustified comments, but the lecturer waved at him to sit down. Natascha was incensed by the dismissive way in which the lecturer had treated her fellow student and she felt empowered by the courage shown by the young man.

'His name is Pierre, sir.' She started with her mouth dry and her knees trembling. 'It wasn't just an observation, it was a comment which seeks further information that would add life to your dull words.'

'Well, well, well, what have we here? An amorous union lending strength to each other?'

'No, sir, I'm sure there are more than just two students who would like to know more about the effects such a war would have upon people just like ourselves.' Natascha looked about the hall for support.

The professor turned away from her quite pointedly, almost dismissively, and directed his responses to the first questioner. 'Well, Monsieur Pierre, I'm sure you can fight your own battles without a girl's help. Let us put this discourse back on an even footing: you ask a question, I will supply an answer.'

'Sir, my apologies, but we haven't been studying this for very long and have not yet become aware of the details.'

'Question M Pierre, if you please.'

'I'm getting there, sir.'

'Well, hurry, if you don't mind. I'm sure all of us want to be elsewhere.'

Natascha stepped in before Pierre had got his question together. She was still smarting from the lecturer's dismissive comments and the fact that Pierre had said nothing to acknowledge her support of him. Was it just men ganging up on her? 'We are language students, Professor, Spanish speakers. Very soon we will be speaking Spanish in Spain, with ordinary people, living ordinary lives. We're not likely to meet the elite,' she smiled, 'certainly none of your generals or politicians you've mentioned I'm sure. I want to know how the ordinary people in the thirties and the forties were affected. What happened to them?'

'A little blood, a little gore, you want to know the bloody details?' he barked at her seemingly cross.

'Yes,' she said equally strongly, 'if it gives me an insight into the culture, the traditions, and the "hang ups" of these poorly treated people.'

'Can you all wait a little longer?' he said with a small smile on his face, and then turned to the general audience. 'Do you mind if we extend this lecture by about a further ten minutes?'

There was a subdued mumbling of disapproval, but most were enjoying the sparring going on between Natascha and the professor.

'First of all, Natascha; it is Natascha, isn't it?'

'Yes, sir, it is; I just want to know more, and I hope I didn't come across too strongly?'

'No, Natascha, you've got me wrong; I admire your tenacity; this is what university is all about. You have challenged me and by doing so you have favoured everyone in this room by your intervention.' He turned towards Pierre. 'You too, Pierre, thank you, both.'

With that he turned to the hall full of upturned faces and spoke in sombre tones. 'To this day, just about all the Spaniards I have met do their best to avoid talking about the past. Mind you, it is no wonder when you get to know what I now know. It's a taboo subject and this is the reason that this set of lectures seems so dry and dull; we can't deliver the colour. I have no wish to trample over people's sensitivities. I am not the victim, the people we talk about are the victims whatever side they happened to have been on and we must respect them. Note both sides of the conflict have much for which to be ashamed, but some were worse than others.'

The hall was hushed; they felt the tension of this impromptu discourse. This was truly an extra-time drama and no one wished to miss a word. Feet shuffled as students made themselves comfortable, a soft cough or clearing of the throat was heard but not a word was spoken.

'I can do no more than give you a list of quotes and verified actions, that is, those that are documented, which apparently give them credence. Hopefully these will become a reliable base on which you can allow your imagination to work. But I beg you do not over colour the images. Reality is crudely coloured already.'

The professor settled himself against the lectern; he closed the file containing his lecture notes and dropped it heavily on the floor beside his feet. He sighed and seemed to be lost for a few moments. Lifting his head, he spoke. 'I have avoided doing this all the years I have been a lecturer. The reason is that there is no absolute truth; yes, we have mounds of paper, much of which is statistical evidence of numbers involved in this or that offensive, lists of those killed in the various actions but these are primarily about Nationalist combatants; the dead on the Republican side were not treated with the same amount of concern.'

A student closer to the front of the hall than Natascha raised a hand. 'Sir, do you have numbers of those that were killed?'

'Be patient please, it's not just about numbers. Anyway, it is sometimes difficult to determine the number killed in battle from those who were just murdered. This is particularly difficult with the numbers of victims on the Republican side and these were in the hundreds of thousands.'

He closed his eyes and lifted his head speaking clearly into the space above their heads. His articulation projected the determination to tell the truth regardless of how painful it might be. It was a confession seeking absolution. It was compelling.

'The strategy employed by the Nationalists destroyed whole communities; they were destroyed by them regardless of whether they

were a threat to the rebels or not.' He brought his hand sharply down on the face of the lectern to emphasise his next comment. 'Mola gave instructions to his invading army of foreigners to give no quarter.'

He paused and looked around the hall. 'You don't know who Mola was, do you?' A general murmuring affirmed this. 'Well, he was the architect of the rebellion and at this critical time was situated in the Basque country and Navarra, while Franco was just across the water in Morocco; no, forgive me, he was actually in the Canaries at that time but soon to travel to North Africa as part of the greater plan. Mola was associated with the Carlist Requetés who were Royalists but were against Alfonso's royal family and they also deplored the Basque and Catalan separatist movements; they were very pro-church, great soldiers and brilliantly disciplined. General Mola led them towards Madrid at the beginning of the war and this is all I want to say about him at the moment. I hope that's OK with you?' But he continued explaining Mola's influence on how the war was to be conducted. 'I struggle to recall his exact words, but he said something about smashing the cruel rabble with a hammer blow that would paralyse the left.' He carried on explaining that there is not much wrong with encouraging your troops with colourful imagery. 'But what message does this give to your troops when you use extreme violence to shock the left into paralysis?'

He gave time for the words to be absorbed. 'What do you make of these comments? Is violence against the left legitimate because they were declared racially inferior? What is extreme violence, anyway?'

The professor paced up and down on the podium. He was not reading from any notes but trying to inject a little life into the proceedings. 'I don't hear any rumblings of discontent from you, the representatives of a liberated society. Where are your cries of outrage? Maybe I have been a little too cautious with my comments.' He stopped talking, stood and looked out at his audience. There was no sound from them. 'Help me, is this any good?' he called out throwing his arms apart.

'Well, not really, sir, I'm sure we've got this message already from what you have said in the past.'

'Point taken, and as we don't have much time to get the message over all I can do is give a few examples. Be warned, they are in my own words, but hopefully they will give you a better understanding of what it was like to be there at that time.' He paused to collect his thoughts and decided to use neutral language so as not to show prejudice but it would be difficult; he knew it. 'First let me quote from an account written by one María Lejárraga, a Socialist observer, who in 1933 made a study of the way country folk lived. You asked how the poor lived at this time, well, these are a few words from this lady's report.

"In the front row sat a number of wretched women, each with one or more children on her lap, their misshapen heads connected to their skeletal bodies... their bellies swollen, their little legs twisted into incredible shapes." Apparently, this was quite normal during these times before the war.' He paused on hearing a sharp intake of breath from those closer to him then continued. 'Talking about evidence of starvation I am reminded of an account I read somewhere given by an eyewitness. It was said that a group of starving workers found acorns in a pig trough, stole them and started to eat; they were discovered by the Guardia Civil who set about them with riot batons beating them unconscious.' (Lejárraga, 1933, cited in Preston, 2012, pages 30–31)

Someone called out, 'But why? Why pick on the starving? How could they do any harm?'

'Wait, please wait.' He continued. 'Nobody was safe during this dreadful time, both sides did appalling things to their opponents. The Left was accused of extensive abuse of the clerics of the church. Priests burned inside their churches and nuns were raped and slaughtered. These figures were greatly exaggerated by the Nationalists for propaganda purposes but nevertheless such things did happen. I must add that one of many investigations into reported atrocities created wholesale disapproval from around the world. It was reputed that

Republicans raped nuns, but the investigating body found no evidence to support the claim and only one case contained a semblance of truth but there was little to verify even that. It is interesting to note this enquiry took place in 1946 when Franco was in power.' He paused to draw breath and give himself some time to get under control the strong feelings he had over this appalling period in Spain's history. He must continue, he wanted to purge himself of these bad images, but he knew it would be dangerous delivering the details to such a vulnerable audience. Clearing his throat, he continued.

'The war was very one-sided. The Nationalists had the most experienced soldiers and the most dynamic senior officers. Their strategy gave no quarter; the slightest possibility of opposition was ruthlessly crushed.'

He stopped pacing up and down on the platform, bent down and picked up the file he had thrown down earlier. Lifting it onto the rostrum he opened it and started to search for something at the beginning of the file. 'I know this is taking longer than any of us expected but bear with me, I have just remembered I have something here that you might find interesting.' Dropping his head once more to concentrate on the written page he flipped over several sheets of handwritten notes. 'Ah, yes, here we are,' he exclaimed. 'Did you know Franco was involved in the suppression of striking workers in Asturias in 1934?' He looked around the hall seeking some response. There was none.

'No, you don't, we've overlooked that event, I can see. He, Franco, referred to this action as a frontier war. He said that Socialism and Communism were frontiers that would replace civilisation with barbarism; this is mild stuff and effectively covers up horrors of that event. The miners and other workers were declared as genetically inferior to the ruling classes and were not truly Spanish; they were the same as Arabs, Jews, Freemasons, etc., etc. It was declared that their annihilation could only do Spain good.'

The professor puffed out his cheeks and sighed heavily as he sought out in his mind the next direction he should take. 'General Queipo *de Llano, one-time supporter of the Republicans, was employed by Franco to arouse bloodlust in the attacking forces and terrify their opponents. Many of his broadcasts through Radio Seville dispersed the foulest propaganda and included instructions to use rape as a weapon, leave no one alive who may oppose them, destroy all assets and loot to their hearts content. Never fear, whatever they acquired in their glorious liberation of Spain would be sent back to their families in Morocco.' The lecturer paused in his delivery then returned to his notes. Thumbing through the pages he stopped at what he must have been looking for. 'Yes, here we are; I have been taking up much more of this extra time than I expected and I'm sure many of you must be as hungry as I am so I intend to conclude as quickly as I can but I need to leave you with images that will more than adequately illustrate the brutality of these people. It seems that this conflict gave succour to sadism.'*

He turned back to the selected page of notes. Anyone with sight of this page would recognise it as a photocopy of a newspaper article pasted into the centre of a piece of paper with many hand-scribbled notes surrounding it. He sighed loudly, paused, then wiped his brow with the palm of his right hand several times pressing hard into the skin as if trying to eradicate something painful from his mind. 'I quote the American journalist John Whitaker:

"Four old peasant women dead and left to decompose in a ditch... Republican guards tied back to back with wire... and burned alive..." (Whitaker, 1943, cited in Preston, 2012, page 332[1])

'How about this by Antonio Bahamonde:

"In working-class districts Regulares went up and down streets throwing grenades through windows, blowing up women and their children in their homes and raping and looting at will."'

He looked about the hall, his impassioned eyes scrutinising the upturned faces. '"This was done with the approval of their senior officers".' (Bahamonde, 1936, cited in Beevor, 2007, page 85[2])

---

1   Preston, P. (2012). *The Spanish Holocaust.* London: Harper Press
2   Beevor, A. (2007). *The Battle for Spain.* London: Phoenix

He paused yet again allowing his latest comments to penetrate. 'Let me finish on this and not say another word. I quote Whitaker once again:

"I stood... with the Moorish major when two Spanish girls, not out of their teens, were brought before him... after questioning them he had them taken into a small schoolhouse where some forty Moorish soldiers were resting. As they reached the doorway a ululating cry rose from the Moors within. I stood horrified in helpless anger. He smirked when I remonstrated with him. 'Oh, they'll not live more than four hours,' he said."' (Whitaker, 1943, cited in Preston, 2012, page 334)

He closed his file and then taking the large red handkerchief from his breast pocket softly dabbed his eyes and lightly blew his nose. When done, he tucked it back into the same pocket then lifting his head surveyed his audience. Not another word was spoken, but much was communicated by the eyes still visible within the shadow of his face. He turned and without a sideways glance walked away. The students sat in reflective silence until the door swung closed behind him. He was gone.

They shoved books back into bags, stood and looking towards neighbours silently posed more questions seeking answers with a glance. Others reached across aisles to touch and comfort friends disturbed by old, appalling news but by looking to the East may that yet be happening today? They filed from the hall subdued as gentle whispering gave way to voices laced in protest, enough now to submerge the sounds of boisterous youth. Everything had changed.

6

SALAMANCA

Spring 2008

She cursed softly beneath her breath. She was not ready; there was still much to do and her idle roommate, Belle, was still asleep. Hardly a belle, Natascha thought viciously; 'Why did I stay out so late?' she grumbled out loud to herself, loud enough for the sleeping Belle to turn restlessly beneath her duvet. 'Oh God, I don't need you waking up and giving me a hard time; I've got enough people on my back as it is.' She kept on grumbling as she moved around in the dim light of dawn stuffing underwear into the last recesses of the rucksack. 'God, how much underwear have I got? Did I pack any last night? I can't remember.' She tried pushing her hands down inside the rucksack to see if she could come across anything. 'How I hate these stupid sacks, everything is lost forever once it's pushed inside.'

'Will you stop talking to yourself? It's like living in a mad house.' The now fully awake Belle lifted herself from her pillow and pulled on the light switch. 'What are you doing at this time of the morning? I heard you come in late last night or was it early morning?' She looked around the room as Natascha continued with the packing. 'My God, what a mess, I hope you're going to leave the room tidy before you go.'

Natascha emitted a strangled scream of frustration. 'Shut up, Belle, I'm trying to count.' She stood still in the middle of the room counting off the items she felt she had packed last night. 'Tops, shorts, socks, woolly jumpers, shorts.'

'You've said shorts already,' said Belle laughing at her.

'I haven't, have I?' She suddenly looked startled. 'Oh my God, what about shoes? Have I packed any shoes?' She bent down and started feeling the bottom of the rucksack. 'I can feel something; I think they must be shoes. Oh God, I hope they are. Wait, I can feel my books and other things; yes, I remember I put the shoes in when I packed the books.' She looked at the clock that stood on the communal dresser and with a cry of despair noticed she was already late. The coach would be waiting; she couldn't afford to miss it. It was the only one that linked up with the Spanish network in Irun.

Loud whispers came from behind the bedroom door followed by a frantic rapping. 'Natascha, Natascha, come on, we're going to be late. For goodness' sake, are you dressed? Come on, we're not waiting for you.'

'I'm coming,' she shrieked loud enough to force Belle to put her hands over her ears and to evoke complaints from adjoining bedrooms. Her eyes swept the room for anything she might have forgotten. 'My God, look at that, it's my entire make-up.' She stomped across the room and with her arm swept everything in sight into a conveniently available plastic bag.

'Hey! I hope you haven't taken anything of mine,' called out Belle, in angry concern, as she started to disentangle herself from the bedclothes.

Natascha vigorously pushed her back onto the bed. 'Stay where you are, madam,' she said with emphasis on the word madam. 'Stay out of my way.' She searched the room with her eyes, knew something was missing but couldn't place it. 'There isn't enough room for both of us to move about in here; anyway, what makes you think I would take any of your poisonous make-up? What a horrible idea; I might end up looking like you.'

'My God, Natascha, you can be such a bitch. You're foul, worse than any other bitch I've known,' spat back Belle with venom.

'Not bothered,' said Natascha, her eyes then alighting on her passport lying on the floor under the bed. 'My God, look, my passport; Christ, where's my ticket?'

Someone banged hard on the bedroom door again. 'Natascha, for goodness' sake, get a move on, the driver won't wait more than another minute; we've held the bus long enough. Come on, come on, now!'

'Coming,' she shrieked, then burst through the door and ran down the corridor doing her best to catch up with her friend. The door of the room lay open. Belle ignored it, snorted and buried her head under the duvet. Natascha ran as best she could; out of the building, through the gates with her rucksack thumping away on her back and wheeled suitcase knocking the paintwork off the door frames and flying over the uneven surfaces of the pavements.

'I'm here, I'm here,' she called out breathlessly. 'Oh God, come on, help me, you lot.'

The driver, clearly annoyed, peered darkly from beneath his cap as he looked up from his crouched down position by the luggage compartment. 'Give me your case and your rucksack.'

'Why?'

'They've got to go in the storage compartment, it's the rules.'

'My things, snacks, water; I need them on the journey.'

'Too bad, you've kept me waiting long enough already; give me your ticket and get in. You're lucky I'm still here.'

Panic seized Natascha; where was her ticket? Her passport was still in her hand and she opened it not knowing what else to do. There it was, right where her mother had put it. 'God bless you, Mama,' she said loudly and with exquisite relief.

She climbed the steps and noticed all the best seats had gone; she had no choice but to sit beside someone she didn't know; a man, older by many years than herself. She gave him a withering look, he was unconcerned and just turned away not at all bothered *that he took up most of the seat or that the remnants of his early breakfast decorated Natascha's place. It was then she noticed she had a headache. 'Why did I stay out so late last night and what on earth did I drink? It wasn't much, I'm sure,' she moaned, settling back into her seat as comfortably as possible, resting her aching head against the removable linen headrest cover. She sat up quickly. 'What on earth is that smell?' she called out and looked around. She could see her friends laughing to themselves, and then turning to look at her neighbour she discovered the culprit.*

There was nothing she could do but put up with what had been delivered. It was her own fault and she needed to count her blessings; she was on the bus, she had found her passport and, thank God for an amazing mum, she had her ticket. She was exhausted and, coming to terms with the unpleasant aromas, it was not long before she was asleep. Sunrise came and the morning went by unnoticed. It was only when the driver spoke to his passengers over the loudspeaker system that she woke like a startled rabbit. He informed them that they had turned off the motorway and were aiming for the Spanish border and it could be as long as one hour to reach the customs post, all depended on the amount of traffic about at this time of the day. Natascha wondered to herself with agitation why he needed to wake her to tell her that; they hadn't got there yet. She realised she was leaning into her smelly partner and pushed herself away promptly. He didn't seem to smell so much now; maybe she had just got used to the odorous tramp.

After straightening up her belongings and trying to disentangle her messed up hair she looked around at her friends and fellow students. One or two seemed to be asleep, others staring out of the windows with blank looks upon their faces much devoid of thought. There was no conversation to be had from that dull lot, she thought, so she gave herself over to her own thoughts. The first things to pop into her mind were the words from her grandmother.

It was such a convoluted tale and it had happened such a long time ago that Natascha was only half listening. Did it matter

*anymore? She couldn't shake off the feeling that Mamie had put
her faith in her and expected her to find out what she could. She
had wanted to say to her that Spain was an enormous country and
to find anything out was almost impossible. She would try but as
Spanish boys were reputedly good-looking hopefully they would
take up much of her spare time. She laughed to herself at her silliness
inwardly assuring Mamie she would do what she could.*

The Spanish border came and went with the least of fuss
particularly as they didn't have to change coach. It was going to
be the same coach and unfortunately, noted Natascha, the same
driver to take them all the way to Salamanca. He collected together
everyone's passports and submitted them for inspection. The border
guard climbed aboard and stood at the top of the steps counting the
number of passengers. He flipped through the bundle of passports
trying to count them, but several fell from his hand; in frustration
he passed what was left to the driver and told him to move on. The
driver then pushed the passports into Natascha's unwilling hands
and pointed to the ones lying on the floor saying, 'Earn your keep,
girl, and give those back to whomever they belong.'

Natascha stood up open-mouthed and was about to say
something unpleasant but as he had started the bus and was in the
process of pulling out into the traffic she changed her mind.

The Irun to Bilbao motorway was like a racetrack with huge
lorries belching diesel fumes jostling for the outside lane. The coach
driver seemed to enjoy the competition slipping into a lower gear to
retake the juggernauts on the hills only to surrender the position,
once more, as they overtook perilously on the downward slope.
Bilbao passed by and on towards Burgos where they travelled
with greater calm, the lunacy left behind. Burgos was the place
her grandmother had mentioned. Yes, this was the town in which
Mamie's godmother had married. Natascha remembered how
Mamie had pointed an ancient finger at a sepia coloured photograph
of two ladies, one holding a baby standing beside a man. She had to
admit she paid more attention to the man; he seemed to be very nice

and good-looking in an old-fashioned way. She was certain he was called something like Rodney. The motorway skirted the beautiful city of Burgos, but the thirteenth-century Gothic cathedral could be seen clearly. Many of the travellers were sad that no time had been set aside to visit the amazing city of "El Cid".

The road took them through vast agricultural areas of softly undulating hills for what seemed to be hours on end. There was not much to capture the imaginations of the young people as the only action available was from distant tractors disturbing the soil and trailing great sun-masking dust clouds in their wake. Mountains appeared as remote shadows to the north but too far to insinuate any secrets. Passing close to Palencia and skirting closely to the panoramic view of Valladolid stirred some interest as guidebooks were thumbed through to find out a little more. By the time the page was found the place was gone. Tordesillas was reached and passed by and no one, but the driver, noticed the road had changed. It was slower and narrower but he warned them that they were approaching their journey's end.

'We're not going to be able to take you up to the university as the old bridge, it's Roman, I think, is unsafe and coaches have to deliver their passengers to the bridge south of the river.'

A groan went up from the weary travellers assuming the worst; they were going to have to traipse miles through the town with heavy loads or spend some of their precious money on taxis.

'Don't worry, someone is going to meet you at the bridge and guide you through the town.' He chuckled unkindly to himself and continued, 'It's not far for youngsters like you; it's all up hill and the first there, gets the best rooms.' He laughed loudly feeling very happy with himself.

The slip road led them down towards the river and the coach pulled up into a parking place just after the bridge. 'Stay in your places, please. Wait until I've opened the luggage compartment, and then leave the bus from the front.'

Natascha was determined she would be one of the first at the university; she wanted a decent room for a change. She was glad to *be away from Belle, who wasn't such a bad girl but their room in Albi was so small.*

Natascha was so weary. Travelling always took it out of her making her very grumpy but she couldn't comprehend how the driver had kept going. 'I'm exhausted just from sitting, how on earth did you manage to drive so far?'

'Had little choice; at Irun the relief driver was sick but I did have a break at the service station close to the turn off to Pau. You didn't notice because you were fast asleep. Anyway, I'm good at catnaps.' He smiled for the first time at Natascha and seemed after all to be a nice man. 'Don't worry, I'm going to get my head down as soon as I get rid of you lot.'

With all luggage collected most sat on their cases disconsolately, others wandered around but a few pored over the maps inside their guidebooks to work out the quickest way to Plaza del Concilio de Trento. There was much finger pointing across the river to where they ought to be going and, ludicrously, some pointing in completely the wrong direction.

Hola', called out an attractive dark-haired lady, waving vigorously as she tripped across the ancient bridge towards them. 'Did you have a good journey?' she called across to them in Spanish. 'So sorry, I hope I'm not late; have you got a leader?'

No one responded but they all walked towards her then moved in closely to surround her. She felt intimidated and looked startled. A few of the boys asked the others to move back and give the lady space. Natascha, always unafraid to speak her mind, used Spanish to convey her true feelings. 'Señora, we have had a long journey and are quite weary and when we arrive here the driver abandons us and you are late.' The lady looked a bit taken aback; she hadn't been expecting any criticism.

'Well, mademoiselle, you are early and I am here on time,' she said checking her watch. 'Now you have a long walk over difficult terrain; I hope you can keep up with me?'

Natascha was the victim of a few hard looks from her friends.

'*Nice going, Natascha, just the comments we need to make a good impression.*'

'*Well done, Natascha, just the way to make new friends.*'

The university receptionist set off at a brisk pace despite the elegant shoes she wore. The heavy luggage bounced upon backs and the capricious behaviour of the wheeled cases slowed everyone down as all quietly cursed Natascha and wished her an evil time. The curses worked for as she dropped her wheelie case off the first high curb the right-hand side wheel collapsed into useless bits of broken plastic. She was left firmly at the back of the group dragging her case, wheel-less along the cobbles. No one responded to her cries for help with most enjoying her discomfort.

The students filed into the small office towards the back of the fabulous university. Every building they had passed was dressed in warm sandstone and the elaborate facades and intricate carvings constantly drew admiring comments. Natascha was a good distance behind the main body exhausted by the difficulty of her walk up the hill with her case bouncing manically along the broken road. She knew she was doing it irreparable damage but didn't care. All she needed to do was to get there in time to get a decent room. Arriving late she had to stand by the door. The receptionist worked at her desk quietly ignoring the group until one of the young men spoke up. 'Señora, I am sorry you think us rude, it is a shame for most of us appreciate the efforts you make on our behalf. Can you forgive Natascha for her inappropriate comment? It is not the way we felt.'

'Ah, Natascha,' she said out loud. 'Now, where have I seen that name? Yes, here it is.' She lifted her head and searched the room for Natascha's face. She noticed her standing in the doorway. 'Just got here, Mademoiselle Natascha? Bit of trouble with your case, I hear? Shame. You're very tired, you said so, I'm sure you will be able to sleep anywhere, I've got just the place for you.' She turned her attention to the sheet of paper in her hand, scanned it briefly then looking up and pointedly catching Natascha's eye smiled briefly and turned her attention to making alterations on the list.

Natascha knew exactly what the lady had done and resigned herself to being accommodated in the least desirable room. 'C'est la vie, as the English would say,' she said, in English, loud enough for all to hear. A few giggled about her and the receptionist demanded a translation from those closest to her.

A dear friend of Natascha mischievously translated the words as, 'She's pleased you are giving her special attention.'

The lady snorted. 'We'll see about that.' Getting up and moving from behind the desk she pushed her way through the crowd calling all to follow her. The students obliged with Natascha bringing up the rear yet again; she had no expectations of being given her room any time soon.

There was a difference in the standards of accommodation but Natascha felt content with hers. Although she might be a little remote from the others, she didn't have to share and the bathroom wasn't too far away. She settled in quickly having to leave most of the small items of clothing in her damaged suitcase, which she tucked under the bed. She had room to hang her best clothes behind a curtained cupboard and a small desk and chair at which to work. The others had a comfortable chair in which they could sit and read but Natascha didn't mind; she always lay on her bed when she was reading.

The next three weeks went well for all the students and particularly Natascha. She had managed to make friends with the receptionist despite the poor start. She learnt quite quickly that Ella was much more than a receptionist; she made things happen. The students required advice on all matters and she provided the answers. Ella was amused by Natascha whom she regarded as an interesting and charming girl who spoke some of the best Spanish from amongst the group. Their relationship grew and Natascha's quite different request to be allocated a community study place to be in the vicinity of Sierra de Francia was arranged by Ella. She admitted that she had a relative who lived in Béjar and Natascha could use one of the vacant holiday flats her cousin managed. 'You are lucky, Natascha, it is not yet the holiday season and my cousin will allow you to stay there for no more than the accommodation allowance that has been given to you.'

'Bless you, Ella, that is brilliant.'

'I have no idea why you would want to go there to study, there are so many other more interesting places to go.'

'Well, my great grandmother had a very close friend who lived there once and I want to oblige her by doing my best to trace her relatives. It's complicated; the person I seek information about was, in fact, my grandmother's godmother. I told you it was complicated; I hardly understand it myself.'

'But that was ages ago; she couldn't possibly still be alive.' Ella paused abruptly, being given over to her thoughts, and then her expression changed. *'Take care, Natascha, the time in which the godmother lived was very dangerous. Bad things happened then and some of the descendants of those who perpetrated those foul and brutal acts wish for a return to those days; sadly those who suffered are obliged to forget.'*

7

THE ROAD TO BÉJAR

Spring 2008

As the day of her departure approached Natascha started to feel nervous. Ella had pointed out that it was unlikely that any of the residents of the Béjar district would be able to speak anything but Spanish. 'But isn't this a good thing? After all, are you not here to learn Spanish?' said Ella trying to reassure Natascha. 'It would be no good running away to speak to someone who knew English or French whenever you had a problem.'

'Why are some of the mountains near Béjar called Sierra de Francia, then? Surely there must be French speakers living there?' enquired Natascha in vain hope.

'They're not that near to Béjar, anyway; maybe the French arrived at that place centuries ago and, if so, I suspect they had to adopt the local language very quickly if they had any hope of survival; how could they trade with the local people unless they spoke Spanish?' Ella gave Natascha a look that indicated that this was rather a pointless discussion. 'I know you are worried about speaking Spanish but it is a ridiculous concern; your Spanish is amongst the best I've heard from visiting students.' Ella stopped talking and looked at her wondering how else she might reassure the under-confident young woman. 'Yes, you do have a foreign accent

but, between you and me, Natascha,' she said in a low conspiratorial voice, 'all the boys will find it very attractive.' They both laughed, and Ella indicated that Natascha should go and get herself ready for her adventure.

Natascha left the room with a backward wave and then set about thinking what else she needed to do before her coach journey south. She strolled along the cobbles of Calle Libreros towards the Plaza Mayor and as she had done so many times before, looked about her at the wonderful buildings. She thought to herself how she would love to live in this beautiful city and how maybe it would be possible to come here and find work once qualified, but she would have to do well in her studies. Ella's words had lifted her spirits. She would take full advantage of what Béjar had to offer and come back to the university and prove she was one of the best students. She cut through a narrow street towards Plaza Carrillo where she stopped and treated herself to a café con leche and sat watching the world walk by. The bank would not be open yet, so she waited, this couldn't be a better place to wait, delighted that she had only her thoughts to deal with and that everything else seemed to be under control.

All the clocks and bells noisily threw themselves into action as they reached the hour, setting off a cacophony of discordant sound that shook her from her reverie. It was time to go and make sure her money had been transferred to the bank in Béjar and that she had enough cash in hand to set her up for the first few days. Within a short distance from where she had enjoyed her coffee Natascha walked through an arched entrance into the Plaza Mayor and stepping into the bright light that flooded the square stopped and stood still. She could not help herself; it was the visual impact of coming across such a magnificent space. The arcades fringed the royal plaza generating dense and welcoming shade and hiding little shops selling delightfully expensive items. She relished the thought of fabulous shoes, scarves, handbags and other girly things and made a mental note to get something for Mama before returning to France. She strode across the square aiming for *the far corner passing by the pavilion from where the royal family of the past would watch bullfights and other festival events. Moving swiftly in the hope to be at the head of the queue she entered the bank. It was quiet and it was cool inside and her sense of urgency melted away so she lingered by the counter until a young man approached and asked if he could help. 'I'm off down to Béjar very soon and just wanted to check that my request for money to be transferred to your branch down there has been completed.' She presented him with her best smile hoping to elicit his undivided attention. Her thoughts wandered a little as she thought back to what Ella had said; would this handsome young man find her accent attractive? She realised how silly she was being as she had far more important business to deal with rather than trying to catch this unassuming young man's eye. She looked away and waited.*

'Señorita,' he called to catch her attention. 'Señorita, you asked me about your transfer of money to Béjar.'

She had lost herself in her thoughts wondering apprehensively what difficulties she might have to overcome in this new venture when she realised the young bank clerk was trying to catch her attention. It was only when he mentioned Béjar that she woke up from her daydream and turned back to him. 'Oh, so sorry, I was thinking of something else I had to do.'

'I hoped that you were thinking of me,' the young man said with humour. He caught the surprised look on her face and suddenly felt he had overstepped the line. He cleared his throat and tried to recover a more distant and professional approach to his work.

Natascha was amused by his stumbling attempt to flirt but nevertheless felt complimented. Initially she had been thinking of him but certainly would not admit to it. He thought that he had gone too far and looked embarrassed and she started to giggle. 'I think we both should concentrate on the business of the moment,' she said forgivingly.

'I have checked and your money will be in the bank on Monday morning,' he said with an authority he didn't feel.

'Well, I hope so because I arrive tomorrow and need to pay some money to my landlady. What happens if the money isn't there, what do I do then?'

'Please don't concern yourself, señorita, get the bank to ring me here and ask for Enrique.'

'I will, Enrique,' she said coquettishly. 'Maybe I can speak to you myself?'

He recognised she was making mischief but he maintained his business pose. 'Here is the money drawn from your account to cover your earlier costs. Please keep it in a safe place because there are thieves around.'

'Of course, I know the very place,' she said as she turned towards him with a wide pseudo-innocent look. Laughing she left, leaving him amused if not confused. 'Don't forget about the phone call,' she called back to him over her shoulder as she passed through the swing doors.

Paying for her bus ticket was not as much fun and there was a bit of a problem about where the driver might stop the bus. It was a through bus from Salamanca to Plasencia with no scheduled stops in between. 'You're going to have to arrange that with the bus driver when you get on the bus,' informed a well-built chain-smoking clerk behind the counter.

'You have taken my money for the fare to Béjar and you are saying the bus doesn't stop at Béjar.'

'I'm doing you a favour, darling. I based the fare on what it would cost if you were taking next Wednesday's bus but you said you had to get there earlier.' He noticed a look of alarm pass across Natascha's face. 'Look, lady, this happens all the time, you slip him a small note and he won't mind stopping; ten would do it.'

Natascha left holding the ticket firmly in hand and was relieved to have had the good sense to have taken a reserve of ready cash for emergencies. She now needed to get back to her room to finish packing. She must also be sure her money was safely secreted within her clothes, apart from the bribe she had to give the bus driver, which *must be kept easily available. She chuckled to herself once again over the way she had teased the good-looking young bank clerk.*

She had agreed to meet up with her closest friends for an end of session drink but didn't plan to stay long as she needed a good night's sleep before the journey. How things have changed, she thought to herself as she sat down on a chair close to the door. She recalled the almost catastrophic start to joining the Salamanca study group and a little of the consequences of that lived on. Content she had caught up on the lives of others in the bar and done the required social bit she set out to leave accompanied by a few like-minded friends eager to prepare for tomorrow's journey, but as she approached the door the others arrived. She inwardly cursed as this could be trouble; this lot had a reputation for spiking drinks.

They insisted the girls should have at least one drink with them before they left. Some asked for wine but Natascha asked for a soft drink and watched them closely at the bar. She caught the sleight of hand as something was added to her soft drink. When it was handed to her she took it politely, pretended to drink then sniffed the glass. 'Raymond, I'm sorry but this orange doesn't taste as it should; will you try it and see what you think?'

The other girls giggled knowingly, revealing they were complicit with what had happened. She changed her mind and instead passed the glass to one of the girls. 'Here, you try and tell me what you think?'

The girl shrieked and tried to push the glass back to Natascha. 'I'm not stupid. I'm not drinking that stuff, you never know what's going to happen to you if you do.'

'I thought so,' she said. 'How sad.' Natascha left the bar alone; disappointed but content to think only of tomorrow.

The next day she walked to the bus depot situated across the river and was thankful that Ella had lent her a small rucksack to take the place of her broken one-wheeled case. She was twenty minutes early hoping to speak to the driver and arrange the unscheduled stop at Béjar. There were three or more buses in the area and none had *drivers attending them, nor any indication of where they might be going. Natascha hung about a bit longer comforting herself with the thought that she was in Spain and they always take their time when setting about any task. Even the office was still locked so she concluded all the lads must be having a chat and a coffee close by. There were plenty of cafes to choose from but it was the one that tourists would overlook being slightly uncared for and the look of a weary place that took her notice. And it was from which the enticing smell of rich coffee and freshly toasted bread wafted on the early morning air towards her; this had to be the place as she needed a fortifying breakfast.*

Pushing the door fully open she walked in and stood surveying the room. The loud conversations lost volume as the men looked up from their plans to save the world or how much better one football team was than another. 'Are you gentlemen in charge of the buses out there?' said Natascha feeling slightly intimidated by the all-male presence; there was general affirmation with much nodding of heads. 'Good, I see you are not quite ready to take off yet so I hope I have time for a little breakfast?' she asked less meekly.

'Which bus are you taking, señorita?'

'The one to Plasencia,' she replied. 'Will it be long before it leaves?'

'Time enough for you to enjoy your breakfast, young lady. Why don't you come over here and sit with us?' The driver pulled his red beret from his head and smilingly continued, 'We are good company and handsome, don't you think?'

Natascha laughed and said with false modesty, 'I am not clever enough to sit with men who have answers to all problems despite their good looks.'

'Sit where you want, young lady,' Red Beret said with a broad smile on his face. 'I'll have to leave in five minutes, though, as always I've got time to make up; I wonder how that happens?' His friends about him started to laugh.

'I'll be as quick as I can but don't you leave without me, will you?' She blew on her coffee, still too hot to drink then nibbled at the pastry.

61

'I hear you have a little request, señorita,' he called across to her indicating he had just been informed by the big man who sat with him; she recognised the bus clerk. 'I'll have a little chat with you outside when you've finished, OK?'

The driver said he was very happy to stop just outside Béjar and she was not to worry her pretty little head. No, he didn't want a tip as he could see that she was a student and not Spanish, so he was pleased to help her out. She thanked him gratefully. The driver suggested she keep the rucksack with her inside the bus rather than putting it in the hold. He could then let her off at Béjar with the minimum of fuss; he wouldn't need to open the under-carriage luggage compartment. 'Right, get on then.' She joined the other waiting passengers who then filed onto the bus.

The bus turned before the bridge almost a full circle revealing the magnificent views of Salamanca across the river. Warm stone and brick buildings oozed culture bearing unequivocal evidence of the grandeur of an historic Spain.

Natascha had settled back in her seat happy to have a double seat to herself. She stretched out with the borrowed rucksack on the floor giving support to her legs; the other hand luggage sat on the seat beside her. The driver had told her that Béjar wasn't much more than an hour away and that she wasn't to go to sleep because he was depending on her to remind him he had to make the unscheduled stop. She didn't feel like sleeping anyway; what happened last night in the bar left her feeling uncomfortable. She kept wondering if it was her fault. How was it she seemed to aggravate people and why did they always look for a way to embarrass her?

Her mind coursed through a list of possible reasons and then she remembered what Mamie had said to her the year before she started at university. She had been in trouble then with the company she kept which had almost disastrous consequences. "People will resent the way you so easily gain the interest of others, and being pretty makes them even more jealous." Natascha had looked very closely into the mirror after Mamie's comments and felt she had a long way to go before being classed as beautiful. She couldn't see it herself what with her nose and big mouth. *Never mind; I've got what I've got and must make the best of it.*

She stared out of the windows absorbed by the beauty of the broad care-tended "Tierra de Campos"; this great expanse of central Spain shimmered under the bright sunlight of mid-morning with distant shadowy mountains etched upon the horizon. Great fields of differing shades of gold made up the glorious patchwork interspersed with the moist green of later crops and walled gardens of neatly ordered vegetables clustered in the security of squat homesteads. The softer, kinder lands soon slipped into the past as the terrain hardened becoming stonier and less fertile. It was a land of rugged trees, shaped by winter winds, which seemingly out of desperation were anchored to the ground by muscular roots. Natascha found this landscape more captivating as the trees grew equidistant from each other defiantly defending their own plot but they spread their branches like lovers would, to reach out, touch and caress the other. Large weather-rounded clusters of rocks peeped through the rich green grass in the sunlight to be turned purple under the dense shade of the guardian trees. Her heart was lifted when she caught sight of black pigs scuttling beneath trees, seeking out acorns from the thousands upon thousands of holm oak trees that marched into the distant hills. There through the shimmering heat like distant somnolent monsters lay the brooding mountains, Sierra de Francia. A name on a map became reality. She crossed back to her seat and with the bus taking a long, sweeping bend to the right she caught her first sight of the Sierra de Béjar.

Natascha walked forwards to speak to the driver. 'I think we must be coming closer to Béjar, driver; am I right?'

'We've been getting closer to Béjar all the time, madam.' He glanced up at her from his driving and laughed. 'Yes, you're right, young lady, just about five minutes to go and we'll be there.'

Natascha smiled back at him trying to overcome the annoyance she felt with his silly remark. 'Thank you, driver, I hope this doesn't cause you too much trouble.'

'It's not a problem for a polite young lady like you. There are some who give me hassle and I wouldn't want to help them, particularly when they treat me like an inferior; there's a lesson in that, don't you think?'

He pulled the bus over onto the run-in at the top of the slip road that led down to the town making sure he parked clear of the entrance. Natascha struggled down the bus aisle towards the doorway. 'Look, young lady, you might be able to see Béjar from here but it's a long walk down there as the road has to traverse the hill to reach the river and the main bridge. Hitch a lift if I was you; you shouldn't have any trouble; people are friendly around here.'

'Thanks, driver, you've been very kind.' She rooted in her purse for a ten-euro note. 'Here,' she said, 'and thank you once again for being so kind.'

'No need for that, dear, it's been my pleasure. Put it in your purse for now then have a coffee on me.'

Natascha tried again but the driver was adamant and repeated again that it really was a pleasure to meet someone as nice as her. Natascha blushed and thought that maybe he did think that; she called out thank you again and then waved him on his way. It was not easy getting the rucksack on her back but once hauled upon her shoulders she started to follow the slip road down the slope to the town. The view was amazing as the highway was lifted over the valley by a spectacular viaduct and she could look down on the town laid out like an elaborate map. She paused and leant on the crash barrier looking closely at the buildings to see if she could find the church. Although you could not make out the river you could follow its course by the almost continuous line of mature trees accompanied by industrial type buildings that seemed to be at a lower level than the rest of the town. Those must be the old woollen mills, she thought, but where would the church be? She eventually picked out what she believed to be three churches. That was confusing because she was meeting Ella's cousin at the church; now which one would it be? She came to the decision that the church with the most impressive architecture would be the one to go for and she found that closest to what was left of the castle. She set off with purpose following the road; it seemed to be endless and she was already tired.

Within a relatively short time, a small lorry pulled up beyond her and the driver called back. 'You look done in, do you want a lift, young lady?' Natascha scuttled down towards the vehicle with the rucksack bouncing on her back afraid he might just take off without her. She reached him out of breath and he opened the door.

'Thank you for stopping. Yes, I am exhausted and would be grateful for a lift.'

'Get in then, throw the rucksack into the back of the lorry; it won't hurt there. Where are you going, anyway?'

'I've got a meeting with an estate agent in the main church square.' She looked at her watch. 'Very soon, in fact; will it take long to get there?'

'A couple of minutes; but it's difficult for me to take you up to the square as it's in the ancient part of the town and the streets are very narrow. They're always repairing the old places and that makes it even more difficult, but I will drop you at the roundabout; it's all uphill but only a short walk from there.'

He dropped her off at the roundabout just beyond a lovely tree-covered shady park and she thanked him.

Finding the church was easier than expected; there were signs everywhere that led her into a beautiful square where sitting like an immense geological feature was the church with rock-hewn steps leading to the main entrance. Natascha stood in the middle of the plaza and looked longingly at the shade cast by enormous trees. Nobody seemed to be around; it was still lunchtime for many. The only sounds she caught were the soft shifting of the leaves as the wind moved silently above and the constant and comforting trickling of water. Natascha walked towards the shade and sound of falling water to discover it was piped to pour into a collection of granite troughs; in fact, there were several troughs. She dipped her hand into one and in shock withdrew it quickly, not realising how cold it would be.

'Cold but it is perfectly good to drink, although be sure to take it from the pipe not the trough.'

Natascha turned quickly towards a dark-haired woman who was descending the steps. 'Are you Ella's cousin?' said Natascha hopefully. 'I hope I haven't kept you waiting very long.'

'Yes, I'm Maria, Ella's cousin, and you must be the mischievous Natascha,' she said broadening her smile. 'Here, let me help you with your luggage.' She looked quizzically at Natascha. 'There doesn't seem to be enough to meet the needs of a young woman like you,' she said with a chuckle.

'This might be true, but I couldn't carry any more. If I need something else, I can always buy it. You do have clothes shops here, don't you?' said Natascha anxiously. Maria laughed and told her that Béjar was famous for spinning and weaving so there was a tradition of providing things for people to wear.

'Now follow me, the flat I've set aside for you is no distance away, just behind the church; I hope you don't mind church bells being rung throughout the day.' Maria looked back over her shoulder at her. 'Don't worry, they don't ring out after Angelus which is at seven o'clock in the evening, but they might wake you in the morning because they call people to church at the same time.'

'I'm glad about that because I'm not very good at getting up in the morning. By the way, Ella said you had a few ideas about working here. I'm not expecting to be paid but it would be welcome if I was paid.'

They now stopped in front of quite a modern restored building. 'This is it, Natascha. My father, bless him, had these houses converted many years ago after most of the mills had closed down. We needed to get a little money back on the investment, so they are let out to tourists, most of whom are walkers or cyclists.'

'They look lovely but where have you put me?'

'There are not many people staying here at the moment and I thought you would like to be on the second floor because you can see more of the town and surrounding countryside.' She pointed upwards and said. 'Look, it's up there with the balcony.' Natascha warmly approved.

Before Maria left Natascha to settle in and after explaining how everything in the kitchen worked and the best place to buy her groceries and other items such as replacement gas bottles and bread for breakfast, she told her the name of the place she might find work. 'I have already spoken to the matron of the home and she assured me that if you have the qualities she is looking for you can work there.'

'What is it? It sounds like a hospital what with a matron running the place.'

'It is not a hospital but there is a need to have supportive medical staff on site. This is a residential care home for the elderly and infirm; it's a charitable institution funded by the contributions made many years ago by benefactors who had something to do with the old textile industry.'

'What would I be asked to do?' asked Natascha starting to indicate her concerns. Did she really want to work with old folk? She wouldn't have to take them to the lavatory or feed them while they dribbled, would she?

Maria recognised her concerns and smiled at her. 'Stop worrying, I think you are going to be asked to talk with them; show an interest in their lives. Some of them are very old and had an awful childhood being brought up at the time of the civil war.'

This immediately gripped Natascha's interest. She had made a point of coming down this way as it was somewhere around here that Mamie's godmother had lived. 'OK, that sounds very interesting. I hope the matron likes me enough to give me the job. Oh, and by the way, many thanks for all you've done for me; the flat is lovely and I'll pay the rent directly into your account tomorrow.'

Maria turned to go. 'Good luck with the job; I'll probably see you around at the weekends. My husband and I come down here when the weather's good enough for walking. Good luck, Natascha, I will see you soon.' She didn't leave immediately but stood looking at Natascha as if there was more to say but didn't quite know how *to say it. 'Natascha, I mentioned that some of the really old folk still suffer from what happened in the war; please know that there are some families who caused others a lot of pain and the justification for that has been passed down through the generations. Briefly, there are some people who still harbour those extreme views. Do take care; don't stir the hornet's nest.'*

Natascha watched as Maria walked away down the cobbled street and wondered at what she had said. 'Surely at these times and in a democratic state and surrounded by millions of lovely people I have nothing to worry about,' she mumbled to herself and then pushed it all to the back of her mind.

She set about the practicalities, putting her clothes into drawers but leaving out the items that needed ironing. Rucksacks are easier than stupid wheelie cases when travelling but they don't half make a mess of your clothes, she thought. 'Thank God there's an iron supplied in the flat; there's not much to do and I'll soon have this job done and my clothes in good order again,' she mumbled to herself. She looked around and was pleased to find a nice airy bathroom with a shower but no bath, but it was spacious. Her bedroom had a window that looked over the town to the densely forested hills and the mountains beyond with many of the peaks still covered in snow. The bed was comfortable with pretty bed linen. Natascha plonked herself down on it and smiled as she realised how fortunate she was. She made a promise to get in touch with Ella and let her know.

'It must be about time the shops were opening for the afternoon and evening session, so I must lock up my pretty little home and go exploring.' Natascha continued speaking to herself making a mental note to wander up to the retirement home and have a look at it from the outside. Then she needed to find the tourist office, if there was one, and get as much information on the area as possible. All so exciting; roll on tomorrow, she thought.

8

MATEO DÍAZ

Last Days of July 1936

He was not considered by his brother officers to be the challenging, thrusting type. He was no threat to those ambitious men driven by their well-placed families to seek higher office. Mateo joined the Republican army out of respect for the ideal that life should be fair to all God's creatures regardless of their circumstances. His selection into the elitist officer corps was a result of his family's position in society; his father was rich. The medium-sized industrial plant, to be more precise an engineering works in Valencia, was vital to the success of many small textile manufacturers scattered through Catalonia and up into Castilla y León. He was the eldest son of a wealthy family and was expected to take over from his father in the years to come. He regarded his father as a great man and a fine engineer, but Mateo did not see eye to eye with him over the management of the workforce. As far as his father was concerned he had an entitlement to the best possible profit and he was determined to get it. In his eyes, it would be just reward for a man of his standing, a fine designer with engineering skills that had been honed over the years.

His message to his sons was always the same; the workers should count themselves lucky to have a job despite the poor wages. 'Keep 'em hungry, they'll work all the harder just to get enough to eat,' he would say repetitively whenever the boys put to their father that being more considerate could provide better rewards.

'I don't agree, Dad. What you should do is to make them feel they belong here; develop a sense of mutual respect, listen to their ideas and if they're any good employ their ideas. Give them reasons to be loyal to you and they'll work all the better.'

'Poppycock, keep them hungry; they'll have to work then.'

The frequency of such differences of opinion brought Mateo to the conclusion that he and his father needed a little time away from each other hoping that over a year or two they would moderate their views. With his father's blessing he joined the army although he was not happy that the present-day army seemed to be propping up a weak government instead of being deployed in the defence of the land. It was beyond his father's comprehension how some of the general hoi polloi, the working class and women, were allowed to vote and decide what was best for his beloved Spain. "Only useful members of society should be allowed to decide what sort of government we have," was his monotonously repeated point of view. But the boys loved their father dearly despite their differences; he was a bit of a dinosaur and growled far more than he chewed.

'Proper governance, the way it used to be, will return again. I'm convinced it will happen and we'll all be the happier for it, mark my words.'

Mateo's brother felt like he did but stayed to help his father out with the completion of orders and despatching items needed to repair textile-making machinery up the coast towards Barcelona where much of this work took place. They also had good customers in the west towards Cordoba and beyond towards Salamanca. This was a result of Mateo's search for business a year or two ago and the business had grown, and profits had improved. Mateo just felt it was appropriate to share some of the profits with the workforce.

Mateo had made friends amongst like-minded officers but on this occasion, he wanted to sit alone in his shared room and contemplate the disturbing news circulating within the ranks. Some of the information received down the line had to be true; there was so much evidence to support it. He had spoken with his like-minded brother officers about his concerns but was careful not to share his views with the "elitists". There was certain to be danger ahead for those who backed the wrong side.

The talk of a military coup had been aired many times before, but there was menace in what was being discussed and the loudest voices siding with a rebellion were from the commissioned sons of the most privileged families. They spoke loudly, and certainty burned in their dark eyes.

It was disturbing that the colonel and a group of his sycophantic senior officers had left the barracks last night and not returned. The "hotheads" although of equal rank had taken control of the companies and many of the veterans within the ranks resented being ordered about by boys.

'What's going on, boss?' one experienced sergeant spoke to Mateo with annoyance. 'I don't like this one little bit; if they think I'm going to turn my gun on mates amongst the mines and elsewhere they'd better think again. I'd rather turn the gun on myself.'

'Look, Sergeant, I don't know what's going on but keep your opinions to yourself; talking like that could get you killed.' Mateo put his hand on his sergeant's shoulder in an attempt to console him. 'Miguel, we've been colleagues for a number of years now and remember it was I who promoted you.' The sergeant acknowledged his officer's comment with a nod of the head. 'I believe what's about to happen will be terrible and it will be chaos. Don't take my word for it, you can work it out yourself. Now listen, see which way the wind's blowing and if you don't like it, leg it. I'll turn my back.'

'Thanks, boss, but what are you going to do?'

'I'm going to have to put on a show pretending I'm something I'm not. I don't think I have any choice but to stay. There'll be too many of my men in danger; I must do all I can to keep the silly buggers safe. Do me a favour, Sergeant; if things go the wrong way take as many of your mates as you can with you. And your kit, I suggest.'

'Will do, boss, and good luck to you, too.'

Within moments of Miguel leaving to gather like-minded soldiers together Mateo noticed in the far distance a dust cloud on the road approaching the barracks. There was enough dust in the air to indicate quite a sizable convoy was advancing towards them, so it couldn't be just the returning colonel and his pals. There was something about the pace of the advancing convoy that disturbed him, unusually fast, and considering the number of rumours doing the rounds he could not ignore the possibility of it being a real threat. He knew he had to take some action that might give him and his men a small advantage over whatever the outcome of the advancing force might be. He didn't run but he moved as swiftly as he could towards the body of men lounging about at his end of the barrack room. Taking the initiative, he mimicked the way the "hotheads" strutted about and barked unkindly at his platoon. They looked about them in surprise. This was not the officer they knew; their boss wouldn't be that rude. Something was up, they knew it. They sprang to their feet and got into line quickly. He lowered his voice and spoke with urgency. 'Play the game, boys, play the game of your lives, our future depends on it.' One of the corporals caught on quickly and took charge of the impromptu parade.

'What do you want, sir?'

'Smarten them up, Corporal, and march them over to the barracks' gate and form a guard of honour for the bastards that are about to arrive.'

There was something disturbing about the way events were taking shape and particularly the secrecy the "hotheads" were demonstrating; whispering around corners and clamming up whenever anyone outside their clique came into earshot. They excluded those who were without so-called aristocratic blood in their veins. They were arrogant bastards, thought Mateo.

It was quite normal to come up to this summer barracks in July; the men were glad to get away from the dust and noise of the Cadiz garrison and the manoeuvres consisted of jogging through a tree-scattered landscape and learning how to build defensive positions amongst the rocks. It was more like a holiday than the serious business of soldiering, but Mateo didn't care. His term as an officer was due to end soon and he couldn't wait to get back home. Rumour had it that a rebellion had taken place and the African army was being shipped into Cadiz and, with help from the German Luftwaffe, many more were being flown to the airstrips north of Seville. It all seemed to be far-fetched as coups had been reported before and never came to anything. On this occasion, Mateo had a really bad feeling. It was the secrecy of the privileged and their unwillingness to include the rest of their brother officers in any of the reports picked up on the radio. However, Mateo, whilst being duty officer, had come across some papers left open on the colonel's table announcing changes in command at other barracks, far more than was normal. *Odd*, he thought. But it was yesterday that clinched it for him as he lost count of the number of aircraft that were travelling north and south. They were not any of the odd lot of planes used by their flyers; these were bigger with black markings. They were certainly not Spanish planes. *This isn't a failed coup*, he thought, *this is the real thing, God help us*. The advancing convoy had got to be the rebels and worse, he felt, they would be the ruthless bastards that made up the Spanish Army of Africa. Most of the troops would be Moroccan Regulares and the uncompromising ruthless criminals that made up the Legionnaires; no one messed with that group of cut-throats.

The corporal had lined up the men as if they were a guard of honour with two of them in a position to man the closed barrier. Lieutenant Mateo Díaz took his position by the barrier and called his men to order as the lead car turned and pulled up at the gate. He caught sight of his colonel sitting in the front seat beside the driver. This was odd as the colonel, by right, should sit secure in comfort in the back. The driver jumped out and opened the left-hand rear door allowing a barrel-chested pugilist-faced officer to leave the car. Mateo was taken aback believing all senior officers to be refined and well-dressed. Mateo came smartly to attention and saluted, noticing enough military braid decorating his epaulets to signify very senior rank.

'Lieutenant Díaz at your service, sir.'

'Díaz, eh?' he grunted. 'Ever seen blood spilled by this gate and into the sand beneath your feet?'

'Sir, no I haven't, sir.'

'Well, you soon will unless you move this fucking barrier right away, you effete, useless bit of shit.' The general moved back to the car then stopped; he turned back to Mateo and addressed him more politely. 'Get two of your best men to escort this traitor to a lock-up and make sure he's guarded well; there's a special event for him tomorrow.' He nodded to the driver who went around and opened the colonel's door. Getting out of the car awkwardly his commanding officer of yesterday walked forwards with his hands tied with wire behind his back. Mateo tried not to show his shock at what he observed as he ordered two of his men to take charge of the battered and bruised colonel. Mateo could not look at him; how could this pompous but honourable man find himself in this position?

'Take the prisoner to the lock-up and guard him securely.' He turned towards his men a second time. 'You four in the front rank, arm yourselves, rifles and fixed bayonets and accommodate the adjoining room. You will ensure that no unauthorised person tries to come close to our prisoner.'

'Well done, Díaz, better than I thought. Let's hope we get similar co-operation from the rest of this poor man's army.'

The convoy pulled up on the parade square and disgorged its contents. The majority were Moroccans distinguished by their looks but more easily by the maroon-coloured kepi-like headwear and puttied legs beneath their voluminous trousers. They looked confused and disorganised but before long the other unsavoury group started to marshal them like one would cattle. These big coarse-faced men wore the same badges as did their senior officer. Mateo walked up to the one in charge. 'What regiment are you and the Moroccans from? I don't recognise your badges.'

'Not surprised, sir, not unless you've spent some time in clink or you're a renegade murderer hiding with the *legionarios*.' He continued by pointing towards the North

Africans. 'We're a *bandera*; that nasty lot, they're a *tabor*, Moroccans, here for the crumpet and the money. Not us though, sir, we're honourable and wouldn't do anything naughty.' He laughed loudly showing stained teeth. The Moroccans looked confused, but the *legionarios* joined in enjoying the irony.

The resident Republican soldiers looked across the square at the unfolding drama. The *legionarios'* senior officer came into view again as he marched across the square to speak to Mateo who came smartly to attention. 'How can I assist you, General?'

'I'm not a general, son,' he said tapping his shoulder. 'I've been made up to lieutenant colonel just for this job. They don't make the likes of me a general; I'm far too good at what I do. That rank is left to useless buggers.' He examined Mateo's face looking for any sign of disapproval. Mateo made sure he gave none. 'Get the cooks out of their pits and into the kitchen; me and my men are starving and,' he said gripping Mateo's arm and squeezing him painfully, 'I don't want to see any of your lily-livered fairy boys anywhere near the food until my lads are full. Got it?'

'Certainly, sir, I'll see to it right away.' He saluted and marched away to his own confused troops to give them the good news. He indicated to the officers to close up on him and noticed that some of the most outspoken in the past were pale and deflated. *Extraordinary*, he thought to himself, *me of poor breeding might have to lead this lot*. He held up his hand to gain their attention. 'I don't know why but our newly acquired leader has fastened onto me as the go-between. I'm going to pass no comment because personal views might lead to extreme action taken against us. My advice to you, is don't make yourself a hero; what good will you be to the right cause and protection of your men if you're dead?'

'What's going to happen to the colonel? What has he done to be arrested?' Mateo had to field a number of questions to which he had no answer.

'I know as much as you do but I think I know the type of soldiers we're dealing with having spoken to some of the men and their senior officer.' There was an audible sigh accompanied by a discontented mumbling. Mateo spoke sharply to them. 'You can cut that out; you don't know any better than I do but I can predict they will take extreme action to ensure our loyalty.'

'How can they do that? We're loyal to our colonel and I think you should go to them and demand his release.'

Mateo was frustrated and only just managed to restrain himself from using much more colourful language in his reply. 'You pompous idiot, just try it and see what happens.' The dark-eyed, arrogant young man was angry at being addressed in such a disrespectful way and pushed forwards and grabbed hold of the front of Mateo's jacket. He raised his hand to slap Mateo's face but was held back by his friends. 'Do us a favour, back up your views with a bit of action,' continued Mateo. 'Let's see if my prediction bears fruit.' With that the young officer adjusted his clothing and brushed at the front of it making sure it was clean. He turned to those who had restrained him and with a return to character addressed the assembled group of soldiers.

'We are the ruling class; it is our duty to ensure the riff-raff there,' he said pointing towards the invading soldiers, 'them,' he said emphatically, 'masquerading as soldiers, are put in their place.'

Mateo suddenly felt responsible for the young man's life. 'Don't do anything, stay here; let us formulate a plan to make sure our men are safe and how we might be useful in the future. I beg you, don't go; it will end in pain, I assure you.'

The three young officers, ignoring Mateo's advice, marched across the square and halted close to the group of Legionnaires. The others could hear the raised voices but could not make out what was being said. Mateo admired their fearless naivety; he knew their courage came from an absolute belief in their lineage. They were untouchable. He watched as the most vocal one strutted about waving his arms, as would a triumphant matador taking applause. The appearance of the *legionarios'* colonel settled the matter.

He pulled his revolver from its holster and without a pause, shot the young man in the head. The other two turned to run away but stopped in their tracks as he called them to halt. They turned and as he walked up to them he lifted the pistol and shot each one in turn at close quarters. One dropped as if poleaxed, the other fell to his knees using both hands to hold his throat as his blood pumped out from between his fingers. His wide eyes innocent as a child reflected disbelief; with heavy lids they glazed as life mercifully slipped away.

The officer, unfazed by the action he had just taken, looked towards Mateo who was rigid with incredulity. Using the back of his hand he flicked his fingers as he moved his arm in a half circle indicating for the mess to be tidied away. With no more than a backward glance he then returned to continue with his earlier uncompleted task. The events had stricken all; there was no conversation. Each man turned in on himself and wrestled with his own thoughts. They were dumbstruck.

Mateo, with the aid of a few experienced soldiers, controlled the events for the rest of the day. He would not allow any action by the men that might bring about further brutality. He insisted that they carried out the orders to the letter and as night fell Mateo sent men to their barrack rooms to sleep as best as they could, but he stayed awake to ensure those on guard duty gave the mad officer no reason to doubt their competence.

Reveille was sounded just before daybreak and the events of yesterday ensured an urgency to comply with all instructions. The remaining officers gathered their men into good order and marched them to the area instructed. Mateo was given command of the remaining mainland troops and ensured they lined up neatly facing the latrines' outer wall. The new commander arrived, and Mateo called all to attention. This was not acknowledged so Mateo waited along with his men apprehensively. A group of six Moroccan soldiers were marched in and lined up in front of his soldiers standing in open order. Mateo caught a movement at the corner of the building and into view came their previous commander escorted by soldiers who instructed the proud old man to stand against the latrines' wall. The guards stood to attention alongside him waiting to be commanded to move away. The tension was brittle, and a saddened and tense Mateo listened to the sound of his own blood pumping through the arteries in his neck.

'Captain Díaz, come to me.' Mateo didn't move. He was Lieutenant Díaz. The officer called again. 'Díaz, come to me.' This time he did move but was unsure what might happen next. Mateo halted smartly in front of the lieutenant colonel and saluted. 'Díaz, you're promoted to captain and now you have an extra set of duties.' The man grinned. 'The first is to dispose of the prisoner. Do you know what to do?' Mateo looked out of his depth. 'No? OK, you order the most junior commissioned officer to command the execution squad. Once you've done that, I'll tell you what else you're going to do.'

'Sir.' He acknowledged the order then marched over to one of his officers he thought might have the steel to control and carry out the execution. Tears sprang into the eyes of the young man he had selected for the task and he realised it would be the same for any of the remaining officers. Mateo turned on his heel and called out to his commander that he would take on the duty. The brute grinned knowingly and indicated with a jerk of his chin for him to get on with it. Mateo wasted no time. He marched forwards to the prisoner and spoke gently to him. 'I will do all I can to lessen the pain your family will suffer as a result of this unjustified action, Colonel. May God care for you and all who love you.' The man said not a word but turned away from him disdainfully as Mateo tried to comfort him. The blindfold was offered but the brave old man shook his head denying any comfort it might bring.

Captain Mateo Díaz walked clear of the field of fire as the colonel shuffled his feet and lifted his chin to look his executioners in the eye. Mateo called them to take aim then dropped his arm and they fired. He walked back to the fallen man who was still moving and had opened his eyes; Mateo recognised he was still conscious and in pain. He cursed the incompetence of the marksmen and with all his emotions in turmoil drew his revolver and delivered the *coup de grâce*.

Later that day the Spanish officers were distributed amongst the foreign troops taking charge of the mostly Moroccan squads. Captain Díaz was not an exception and his orders included the clearance of a group of mountain villages in an area east of the Gredos Mountains. They were commanded to destroy the enemy: Socialists, union leaders, Jews, freemasons and other troublemakers. Mateo felt an almost physical pain in his chest as he realised that these were from the same group of people whom he had previously advocated a better life. Mateo had no idea who they were; he had no names and no official document that would give credibility to their actions, if you could call it that. He decided to contact the lieutenant colonel on this important point. 'Sir, I am conscious that you provide me and my fellow officers with the authority to set about our tasks but surely we will run up against some official resistance along the way, therefore should we not have an order issued at the highest level to confirm our authority?'

'Don't you worry your pretty little head over such trivialities, Díaz. That's my problem to worry over and I'm sure I'll have a few sleepless nights struggling with my conscience.' His cronies laughed and Mateo smiled unconvincingly. He felt sick to his stomach; this went against everything he believed in but it became worse as the colonel informed them that every company would have the privilege of a *Guardia Civil* escort who would provide all the information they needed and make sure none of them failed in their duties.

The very thought of what he was being ordered to do and all that under the watchful eye of the *Guardia Civil* filled him with self-disgust and worse, a sense of hopelessness.

9

PASTORA AND SEBASTIÁN

August 1936

Pastora Ruiz moved from a district in Seville many kilometres south of Santo Domingo after her marriage to Sebastián just a few years ago. From the very start she attracted keen attention of these inquisitive mountain village folk. She was different. The local people were conservative in nature drawing a sense of security from the customs and traditions promoted by the village elders directed by the church. Her husband, Sebastián, had grown up in Béjar, a local mill town, in the valley beyond the northern slope of the mountain. Although not born and bred in Santo Domingo he knew many of his generation who lived there. They were workmates from the "Carding and Fulling" part of the cloth-making factories that lined the riverbank in town. It was said that Sebastián's parents were disappointed that he'd gone off to somewhere south to find his bride when he could have had his pick of the best of them from around here, he being the tall and handsome lad he was. Pastora, taller than most Andalusian women, was slender and eye-catchingly beautiful. She was elegant and walked as all dancers do bringing to Sebastián's face the broadest of smiles whenever he was with her; he loved her, of that there was no doubt. Smile as he did when with Pastora, he was not known by others as an easy man. Many of his colleagues could verify he would not tolerate unfair treatment of himself or his friends by anyone, especially those in authority. Sebastián never used obviously threatening or insulting language when in a disagreement with others but there was menace in the clarity of his logic and the manner in which he delivered his words. From his height he would lean towards the recipient of his wisdom and in a soft but deep base voice inform them how they might improve their performance. His close friends often warned him that the bosses had the upper hand and could sack him at any time; and what would he do then? He was a good worker and could move the heavy bales of cloth with relative ease. He was tall, had good arms and nobody cared to challenge him; he was one to fight alongside rather than against so all, including the bosses, wanted him on their side. Since the appearance of Pastora he became more tolerant of others' nonsense; she had softened his generally uncompromising attitude and he had developed a greater sense of humour. He was an easier-going person now; he recognised this in himself and justifiably credited Pastora with making him a better man. She made him happy. Any sign of injustice still stirred his capacity for annoyance, but now he responded with cool logic and discovered how much more effective his new-found strategy was.

Pastora loved her life as much as she loved Sebastián. She adored and admired this tall and handsome man who had whisked her away from the complications of her busy life. He was a breath of fresh air. Seville was the centre of the world to her but family rivalries and the unsavoury expectations depressed her to the point of sickness. It seemed, then, as if her life was being sucked from her by the demands of the elders. It was no longer hers to rule; no longer could she dance at fiestas unless instructed and she was often commanded to dance in seedy back rooms for money of which she saw so little. Old men in well-cut suits, smelling of stale cigars, sat holding brandy glasses inflicting discomfort by the intimacy of their gaze. The line of her *traje de flamenca* had been tailored by her dresser to make her more alluring, so said her seamstress. Pastora did not like the changes, not because she might be more alluring, but this was a start to something that might corrupt the elegance of flamenco. She was instructed to be unafraid to involve the clientele, something she would never dream of doing when dancing properly. She loved to lose herself in the dance listening and responding to the anguish portrayed by the cantor driven by the amazing rhythms and evocative sounds of the guitar. It was personal. But they demanded she carry her dance almost into the laps of the clientele thrusting her dress towards the *caballeros*. She smiled as they insulted her art, suppressed the anger they generated but was very careful not to let them know how she really felt. Climbing up from their table they came to stamp their feet with intoxicated incompetence, to whirl and stumble into her and destroy the mood she had created; she hated them. This was never dancing to her, it was an imposition that diminished her and her art; she wanted her life back and would work in the tobacco factory to get it if necessary; dancing was for the fun and joy it could bring to all, not a means to amuse dirty old men. Sebastián, the man from the mountains, with a smile as wide as the sky, stole her heart and rescued her soul. He had an active mind and a strong body that supported his determination to extract fair play from a prejudiced world and he called her beautiful in a way she knew to be true. He changed her life. Here she was in the clean, cool air of the mountains with her new son, the delightful Bartolomé, a toddler big for his age and so much like his father. She might be a little poorer, but the purity of her happiness bubbled within her. It was a childlike innocence she shared with those around her. Yet little did she know her contentment and her popularity aggravated the small-minded and the envious.

Pastora became a friend of Juana at their first meeting. They had left the church together as both Rodrigo and Sebastián had slipped away to have a few words with a group of men who needed to recover the will to live after yet another lengthy sermon by Father Jaime. They had been subjected to the usual comments. Once again, the priest had predicted that hope of the Kingdom of Heaven was well beyond the reprobates now seated about the coffee table; there seemed little point in going to church any more. Maybe they should take up the ancient art of poaching instead? Laughter always made them feel better despite the difficulty many of the men had in getting enough food to put on the family table. Everyone knew Sebastián well and admired his courage in challenging the bosses over conditions at work explaining to them that they couldn't afford to lose any man through illness or injury. They had agreed to make the conditions more reasonable but they couldn't do much about the pay.

'Surely they make enough money out of us, anyway? They always have food on their table, not like me; just look at the difference between my kids and the factory boss's kids,' Jorge spluttered feeling angry. His friends warned him to keep his voice down as there were plenty of little sneaks around.

Rodrigo took up the theme. 'I know what you say about the bosses is right, Jorge, but they are not the owners of the factories. The bosses do get more money than you but they have to do as they're told, just like you.' Rodrigo held up his hand indicating he wanted to say something else. 'Our friend Sebastián is not just courageous, he is clever. You can't just demand something and expect them to give in to you. The art Sebastián employs is based on knowledge of what is possible; the military call it intelligence.'

'What do you know about military intelligence? Sounds a bit dodgy to me.'

'Well, like most of us, or should I say, some of us who got caught up in the shambolic recruiting process, we had to do a bit of military service whether we liked it or not. I was required to do my bit by gathering information about certain people just to make sure that they wouldn't cause trouble for the country in the future. I hated it. I hate spying on decent people.'

'I didn't do any of that military stuff. Did anybody else?' called out a newcomer from behind his well-established beard.

'Well, I did for a short time,' said Rodrigo. 'I was designated as a clever peasant,' Rodrigo grinned. 'So I was conscripted into helping out some of our prestigious leaders who seemed to demonstrate a woeful lack of basic knowledge in anything useful apart from being able to act important.'

There was ribald laughter from around the table and Jorge spoke up once more. 'I hope you served up the silly sods a bit of misinformation too, not that they would know what to do with it.'

Rodrigo leaned into the table and lowered his voice. 'You can't help picking up information from those back rooms; stuff you're not supposed to know about. Let me tell you, there are some very clever blokes that hold high positions in the army. Not that I got to meet any of them.'

'Come on then, what did you learn that would be interesting to us?'

'In those days there were rumours that some general or another was going to take the government down. So many of them hated the way the Republican Government had got control. Apparently all the aristocrats, big landowners and the rich bastards that controlled industry hated the way things were going and I'm sad to say that included the bigwigs in the church.'

'What do you mean, the church? Aren't they supposed to look after us; you know, the poor and the meek?'

'You're not meek, Sebastián. Anything but meek, I would say; especially the way you hassle those poor buggers unlucky enough to pay your wages.'

Everybody laughed again enough to attract the attention of Alfredo Cortés, who had come out of his house unnoticed and happened to be leaning against the closed door of his home smoking a cigarette. 'You lot making fun of me? Just take care; you might regret rubbing me up the wrong way.' He growled at them through the trails of cigarette smoke and spat upon the ground.

Jorge loathed this man who had married his wife's cousin, a simple lass with nothing much to recommend her apart from a kindly and forgiving nature. 'We wouldn't waste our time even thinking about you, Cortés, let alone speak about you. So clear off and if I hear you've thumped my cousin again I'm going to tear your bollocks off and shove them down your throat.'

Rodrigo took hold of Jorge's arm pulling him back into his seat. 'OK, Jorge, enough said.'

He sat down heavily into his seat and rested his head in his hands, a face like thunder. Rodrigo lowered his voice again as he didn't want what he was about to say to carry to Alfredo Cortés. 'Look, I hear quite a few bits of news from parents who come to see me about their children and, as you know, I have a radio. I've occasionally picked up the news from Cadiz and Seville and most of it is worrying. It's not very clear some days but it was my job in the army to make sense of scraps of information and I believe some interesting things are about to happen or maybe have already happened.'

'The worst has already happened,' said the newcomer from behind him. 'Let me introduce myself as none of you has asked and Jorge hasn't bothered.' He grinned across the table. 'I'm Jorge's friend and have been for a long time. I've recently released myself from military service. The generals don't know yet; well, not all of them, but my immediate boss knew and helped me; he's a decent sort. He was a lieutenant when I knew him but I've heard the new regime have made him up to captain, Captain Mateo Díaz.' He waited for some response hoping someone might recognise the name. There was none. 'The reason I'm here and not with my troop is that everything has changed for the worse. I'm not prepared to turn my guns on the people I joined the service to protect.' There was no comment from anyone around the table, but uncertainty was palpable. 'I'm Miguel, by the way.'

'But you've already said you haven't done anything military,' said Sebastián.

'I was lying. I needed to find out a bit more about you guys before committing myself but we're short of time, that's obvious, so I've told you now,' he shrugged.

No one spoke but all looked hard at Miguel wondering what to believe. Jorge also was silent sitting at the table hiding his head in his hands. This did not seem to be a vote of confidence in Miguel. The men eventually turned back to Rodrigo hoping he would go on and tell them what he thought. They looked towards him as he picked up his cup and sipped at his coffee. The continued silence disturbed Cortés and he sidled towards the table; he hadn't heard what had been said but was certain it was about him. The men transferred their attention to him as he moved closer. Rodrigo put down his cup and raising his head said, 'Well, *Señor* Cortés, how can I help you?' He couldn't keep the sarcasm out of his voice as he addressed him.

'I know about you, schoolmaster, and your clever ways, but you aren't clever enough by half so let me advise you to crawl back under your books and remember there's a group of us making our way up the pecking order here and we know best. By the way, pretty little thing, that wife of yours, Rodrigo; very nice. We've got our eyes on her, too, but for different reasons.' Cortés laughed coarsely whilst the others waited for Rodrigo to react.

He had grown pale and his eyes revealed his anger. However, his words were quietly spoken. All could feel the contempt he had for this man. 'Alfredo, since you have lived amongst us in Santo Domingo you have never taken the opportunity to assist any who needed help; in fact, you despise them when they fall on hard times.'

'What are you saying then?' Cortés looked uncomfortable. 'You're saying it's not their fault? Don't you think they deserve it? It's because they have too many children; too much time spent on the nest, I say, and not enough time spent working their arses off.'

The men about the table groaned in unison some calling out insulting names; it didn't bother Cortés who just grinned. 'I don't wish to humiliate you through an intelligent and logical argument, Alfredo, but can you explain to me why you need to comment so coarsely on the despair of others? Being poor and in many cases starving are conditions commonly found in these times of general poverty; it is not the dying who are at fault, it is the avarice and greed of others who have nothing but contempt for the landless.'

'I've got money and I won't go without; I'm different. I'm not lower class like them; haven't you heard the lower classes are just the same as Arabs and Jews? Franco said that and the church says you lot should be kept in your place.'

Sebastián cut in on Alfredo's commentary. 'Enough of this nonsense, we know you're in the pay of the gentry, you're out here to spy on us and make the existence of us poor sods even more difficult than it is at the present.'

'We know how you get your money. You get paid for every tasty morsel you can deliver to the ones who keep us down and I know you're making up a hit list for when the time's right. There's a bonus for you with every name you give; right? I know it's the truth cos I got it from a reliable source.' Miguel was starting to slap the table to emphasise his words. Rodrigo leant across the table and tried to restrain him. Miguel shrugged his hands away. 'How do you feel about selling our lives for a few pesetas? Does that make us closer to God, only cheaper? He was worth thirty pieces of silver, wasn't He? Maybe you should ask for a raise, you treacherous bastard.'

Voices were getting louder and their little Sunday morning chat was getting out of control. 'Enough, lads, this sort of argument will get us nowhere. Calm down, please.' Rodrigo looked around the table for acquiescence and then turned back to Alfredo Cortés who was now leaning against the wall well within earshot of the friends. 'Alfredo, can I say, first of all, we are all the same; the masters are not a superior race to us and I include you. You are close to the church and understand the Gospels but nowhere does it say that some men are superior to others. Secondly, you are being used. Once you have done what they want you to do they won't even give you the time of day. Your future lies with us; you are not rich, you may have a few coppers now but you're poor like us; our only strength comes from standing together as a group. Come, join us.'

Alfredo sneered at the thought. 'I've got my own group of friends. I don't need you. I'm close to the money and that's where my future lies.' He pushed himself off the wall and threw his cigarette on the cobbles and ground it out with his heel. Pointing at the extinguished cigarette he turned to them and said, 'That's what's going to happen to you lot and very soon.'

They all looked at his retreating back as he walked away and were visibly shaken by the menace of his threat. Rodrigo could see the anxiety on their faces and knew there was no point in continuing their chat. 'Time to go home, boys, and give thought to what is going on. Don't frighten your women folk but talk to them and gently let them know that things might get nasty in the near future.' He turned back to Miguel. 'Do you mind if you and I have a little chat? I think we may need some serious military advice in the near future and maybe you're the man to give it.'

10

SEBASTIÁN BRINGS BAD NEWS

September 1936

Rodrigo and his friends had crowded into the small space set aside for the storage of school documents, books and surplus bits of equipment, to hear what Sebastián had to say. They were concerned that those who sympathised with the rebel cause, particularly Father Jaime, would think they were plotting against what was happening so they needed a plausible reason to mask the real purpose of their meeting. The school had been chosen as a cover and the men had brought with them their hand tools on the pretence they were going to repair some of the school furnishings.

Earlier Rodrigo had picked up some details of what was going on down south on the radio broadcast from Seville and wanted to let the others know the details. Seriously disturbing action was reported from there. He also told them that much of the style of broadcasting news had changed; in his opinion you could sense there was nervousness and undoubtedly an uncertainty affecting all because nobody seemed to give support to one side or the other. Many of the music programmes had been shut down leaving space primarily for news bulletins but mostly it was just white sound or military music. Rodrigo looked around at the men who had gathered in the school; there were not as many as he had hoped for with one surprise omission: Jorge. Miguel explained he was forbidden by his wife, Miranda, to be seen with them too often. 'But he is the one who drove Sebastián to Plasencia when he picked up the details of what's been going on down there,' said Rodrigo with feeling.

Sebastián reassured Rodrigo that Jorge was not changing sides but Miranda couldn't sleep and was crying a lot and he didn't want to make things any more difficult for her. 'Don't worry, he's well committed to our side but doesn't like to advertise.' Rodrigo looked more comfortable because he had always valued Jorge's support. Sebastián continued, 'Let me tell you what has happened since you got the news from the radio; it's not good and I have no reason not to believe it, but, boss, I think you should give your brief first so we can keep it all chronological.'

'Big word, Sebastián; school couldn't have been that bad when you were little, if you ever were little.' The others chuckled and someone said that Sebastián not only had the biggest muscles but also the biggest head. Whereupon he gripped the comedian's shoulder and squeezed until he squeaked.

'I see what you mean about muscles and I concede that he is clever,' said Rodrigo smiling with mock concern. 'Now let me tell you what I learnt from the radio; I'll try and make it brief.' Rodrigo cleared his throat and glanced down at a scrap of paper in his hand.

'If those are notes, boss, I suggest you burn them as soon as you have used them; there are a lot of nasty people out there who would just love to put you up against the cemetery wall.' Miguel spoke with the usual directness and perception developed over the many years he had spent in the army.

'Point taken, Miguel, but I just want to get what I heard to you and not forget anything important. Right, here I go and stop me if you need me to repeat anything.' He set off recounting what had happened across the water. 'First, you know that it was General Mola who sent the orders by coded message to the troops in Morocco to start the uprising, and any poor devil who opposed the rebellion was done away with and that included the big man, General Morato; not that he was much good to us anyway.' Rodrigo paused knowing that the scraps of news would be confusing.

'Worse than the loss of Morato, nearly 200 loyalists including Franco's cousin, whom Franco personally approved to be executed, were slaughtered. On that basis we should expect no quarter from that bloodthirsty bastard. We should prepare. What made it easy for the rebels is that they used the Foreign Legion, *Legionarios*, and we all know that is made up of criminals; yes, murderers and rapists, who boast their savagery. Probably more frightening are the Moroccans, *Regulares Indigenas*, to whom General Queipo de Llano has told the lie that Republicans wanted to abolish Allah. Although based on an untruth, it has given them good enough reason to come over here and kill infidels.'

Miguel interrupted and seemed to be very agitated. 'Forgive me but I am prompted by what Rodrigo has just said to elaborate on what I was really involved in during the last few days I was in the army. I need to do it now before we are sucked into a dangerous mess. I've hinted at this before, but I've met them. You know who I'm talking about; those bloodthirsty buggers, Moroccans and *Legionarios*; I've seen them in action; they are ruthless.' Miguel paused as the others wondered why he had interrupted and looked at him sceptically. 'OK, I'll be straight with you; I didn't retire from the army, I deserted because I couldn't bear the thought of what I might be asked to do.' They all looked at him with open mouths unable to believe that a good man such as Miguel could be a treacherous deserter. 'Wait before you judge me. I've told some of you this already; we were going to be asked to turn our guns on the likes of you and worse. I have met the beasts of Africa. I've seen what they can do.' Pausing briefly he looked towards Rodrigo. 'Forgive me for interrupting, boss, but what I tell you is important. When I deserted I left with the blessing of my officer who also wanted to escape from the Nationalist control but stayed to try to keep his men out of trouble. Those criminal *Legionarios* bastards would kill you on the spot if they doubted you. I've seen what they can do, vicious sods; innocent men's blood spilled without them blinking an eyelid. The Moroccans are seriously bad too, but the cruelty dished out by the criminal corps is worse.'

'I think we all had an idea that they were ruthless killers, and we take the point "know your enemy" but what advice can you give us when facing up to them?' asked Sebastián looking really concerned.

'This is the best answer I can give you,' said Miguel looking about his colleagues and making a mental note of their number. 'Have good "lookouts" and if we pick up the slightest clue they are coming our way run and hide our children but especially our women because that is what those beasts live for; they have been given the right by their senior officers to abuse women as a reward and then slit their throats if so inclined.'

'All this could be just exaggerated propaganda from someone who is trying to find an excuse for being a cowardly deserter,' someone at the back of the group mumbled.

Miguel, incensed, jumped quickly to his feet. 'I've been ten years in the army and as one of its most respected sergeants and you, what do you know, boy?' Miguel breathed deeply knowing it was no use losing his temper. He continued speaking, but quietly. 'I have seen two, no, three young men, no older than you, son, shot dead in front of me for saying something the African officer didn't like.' He held up his hand. 'Wait, let me finish; they were the sons of "*Aristos*". Yes, they were sons of some of the most important people in the land. Not dispensable nobodies like you and me.'

'We support you, Miguel, and don't doubt your integrity in the slightest,' said Rodrigo trying to draw a line under the unpleasant argument. 'Now let me just finish what I was saying before Miguel's warning interrupted me, of which I am most grateful and will take very seriously.'

Rodrigo turned back to his notes and picked them up once more and smiled. 'Don't worry, Miguel, these are going in the fire as soon as I get home; now, let me continue? The Republicans have lost the African colonies to the rebels but they saved their ships from being commandeered by the rebel forces all except one, the *Churruca*, which has carried nearly 3,000 men and all the heavy guns they need to Cadiz. So things aren't looking so good for us. You also need to know that the ships our side managed to hang on to are being shadowed by German battleships so they had no hope of stopping the *Churruca*. Anyway, they have already landed in Cadiz and, I think, in Algeciras and, if that isn't enough, the Germans are flying Moroccans in Junkers 52s into an airport north of Seville. Thousands have been landed and that misogynistic monster, Queipo de Llano, has taken control of that enterprise. I'm a bit out of date and I leave it up to Sebastián to fill you in on what has happened since.'

Sebastián continued with the news. 'I have nothing good to tell you from my little venture south with Jorge. He, by the way, had a bit of business to do down there supplying fencing posts to some bigwig who's got a lot of land bordering the river. He dropped me off at a bar where I met up with some of Pastora's relatives. They had a few of her belongings; furniture, would you believe, and heavy stuff too. Just as well Jorge had plenty of space on the back of the lorry. Anyway, they were having a bad time down south and planning to scarper and find somewhere safer to live. Her lot, I mean Pastora's family, look like gypsies and that is good enough for the boys in blue to bump them off. Nice world we live in, isn't it? I have been told that many people in the surrounding villages are really confused. Local bosses have joined up with the *Guardia Civil* and armed themselves as they thought they were going to defend the country from the rebels. But it was just the opposite; the *Guardia Civil* took control of villages in an underhand way. They had all the guns and they used them on anyone who complained, supported the government or had anything to do with a workers' union. There weren't any trials, they just shot them and did nasty things to the women. They shaved their heads and made them swallow litres of a gunge made up from olive oil. I didn't see anything like this but I was told about it in a way I believe it to be true. Worse, and I confirm what we've just been told, they kill women too, but not before they've been raped.' The men were dumbstruck. They couldn't believe that anything like this could be happening in their own country. 'I blame it all on that sick-minded bastard Queipo de Llano. Look, I've got a paper here and it reports on what he has been saying. I didn't believe it at first so I asked one of Pastora's cousins if it was true and he said he heard it on the radio himself. And another thing I have to tell you is that bands of horsemen are being formed by the sons of the big landowners and are used to harass people who continue to work on land they've earmarked for themselves; they also attack columns of refugees even when innocent people try to get out of the way. These fun-loving little gobshites swoop down on them like fucking cavalry. If you ever go down there just look up into the skies and you'll see plenty of vultures circling in the thermals in and about the countryside.'

The men talked amongst themselves for a moment or two asking who Queipo de Llano was and how foreign troops could be allowed to perpetrate such atrocities on people in their own country. Rodrigo picked up from where Sebastián had left off. 'Franco has given the job of securing Seville for the Nationalists to General Queipo de Llano and he's all about making a name for himself. Did you know he was for the Republic before Mola started the ball rolling?'

'A lot of this news could just be propaganda but I fear it nevertheless,' said Sebastián in an understated way, not wishing to cause too much alarm. 'But we do have to make provision in case there is more truth in the story than I think.' He looked about the group hoping someone had an idea how they might do that.

Rodrigo agreed, 'Well, I take seriously everything that Sebastián has said. It seems to confirm the message given out over the radio and I'm sure it is the Nationalists who've taken over the radio stations so there's a good chance we'll be dished up with a load of lies.'

'Of course it is, you wouldn't have that vile man Queipo de Llano being given a spot on the show if the radio station was still in the hands of the Republicans,' commented Miguel with some scorn.

'That being the case then things are worse than we thought; we do have to make a few plans. The first is to tell our wives without alarming them too much but, and this is a big but, don't let the opposition know that we know what's going on; warn our families not to ask the priest any questions and certainly don't talk to Cortés or any of his thugs.'

'What if the rebels send the African corps to our village? What can we possibly do to stop them?' This seemed to be uppermost in Miguel's mind. 'I don't know how many of us have got a rifle or a gun of any sort. I've got a rifle and a good supply of ammunition; happened to find it amongst my kit when I got home.' This brought some laughter to the disconsolate group.

'I'm more worried about what may happen to us if we have to evacuate the village,' said Rodrigo, 'not about defending ourselves with the pathetically few weapons we've got. If we find out our village is about to be attacked everyone at risk must leave, because any of us who is known to support the Republic will be executed. I think that was the point Miguel was making earlier. Don't think of surrendering; there is no hope.'

'What do we have to do then?'

'I will arrange an alert system using runners if the attack is imminent. I'll let you know how this will be done later. You must go to your families and plan what you would do. Please tell others who are in danger but make sure all plans are kept a secret. I will be in touch soon; now go home and prepare.'

The men got up to leave gathering about them the tools brought in to support their pretence of carrying out a few repairs. Sebastián then asked the men to hold on a minute. 'Look, we've been repairing shelves and fixing a few hooks on the backs of doors if anyone asks.'

'Well reminded, Sebastián, we need to protect ourselves with a plausible cover story; for certain that nosey priest will quiz a few of you in the street and the confessional box, or should we call it the inquisitional box? So, take care.'

When all the men had left Rodrigo turned the big key in the lock of the main door and made his way home to Juana and the joy of their lives, Alicia.

11

THE TROOPS MUSTER

October 1936

The horses had been released from the claustrophobic conditions of their boxes. They were skittish, energetic and more than a little excited by their newly found freedom. The hours of tediously winding through the lower hills towards the target left them ill-tempered and their wards had difficulty keeping them under control. Hernando struggled with Captain Díaz's gelding as he also had to hold tightly on to the reins of his own horse which tossed its powerful head in frustration; at times he was lifted off his feet dangling like a marionette. His *Guardia Civil* colleague, Felipe, laughed openly as he came to the rescue. It was not long before the three animals were under control. Exhausted they admitted contritely it was more a result of hungry horses being enticed by sweet grass growing in the shadows close at hand than their skills as horsemen.

The Moroccans, also unused to such prolonged journeys in confined spaces, were equally relieved to be released. They scrambled eagerly from the high-sided vehicles, which had previously been used to transport sheep; the strong smell of animal urine had made their bone-shaking journey even more unpleasant. No amount of hawking and spitting seemed to release them from the all-pervading stink. Their clothes smelt not only of their own unwashed bodies but the stronger smell of animals. These men, veterans of hard-fought military conflicts, complained bitterly of their unpleasant experience grumbling that the enemy was now trying to kill them off with the smell of filthy animals but conceded, with gracious thanks to Allah, they did not have to suffer the filth of pigs. Still complaining they shuffled into line on the same verges as the feeding horses making sure to keep their distance from the white-eyed, flat-eared stances that warned close proximity would not be tolerated. They now seemed to hate all animals particularly big bastards like these.

Tonight's objective was Santo Domingo. Some of the more senior soldiers who had been given access to a map of the district recognised Santo Domingo to be by its very size hopefully a more affluent village than others raided, thereby promising them richer pickings. They were quick to spread the word. There was more to this place than the previous collection of poor men's hovels they had ransacked as they searched for anything worth taking. They couldn't understand why the previous insignificant places needed their attention and amongst themselves they agreed it would be hard to find such destitution in their own country; they never expected to find such abject poverty in the glorious superior Spain. These people were poorer than themselves, living on the edge of life; flat bread and the poorest cuts of home-butchered meat eaten from cloths upon the earthen floor would constitute the rarest feast. There was nought there, little that took the plunderers' fancy making the pain of the incursion hardly worth the effort. Let us not forget the degenerates, despised by the majority of their colleagues and supported by one or two less discerning soldiers who forcefully took advantage of the terrified women. Poor souls, decrepit and emaciated, whose femininity had been stripped from them by the misery of their lives, were driven like cattle to the slaughter and raped upon the God-forgotten earth. Spirited intervention by sons and troubled husbands, not held by bayonet at the throat, added spice to the actions of the perverse. Frail-boned mountain men with the courage of lions failed to protect their women as voyeurs of this disgusting spectacle, resentful of intervention, drew bayonets and swung rifle butts despatching them as one would persistent flies about a plate of sweetmeats. The *Guardia Civil* knew of what had happened but did not witness how the men died and intent on keeping the truth from Captain Díaz simply added the names to the lengthening list of executed enemies of God's renewed Spain. But Mateo Díaz sensed some foul act had taken place.

'You've got to play the game, sir. The only way we're going to cover up these savages' misdemeanours is to make out those poor sods resisted our legitimate action.'

Díaz shook his head, growled angrily his disgust unable to put his revulsion into words.

Hernando continued, 'Look, sir, we're at war, a lot of bad things happen in war and we haven't got the time to charge these bastards with crimes; anyway, we'd soon run out of soldiers the way things are going.'

Felipe's laugh was cut short by the look Captain Díaz directed towards him. The soldiers looked on darkly not quite understanding what was said but knew they were on the wrong side of their officer. He wasn't happy with the liberties they had taken which they considered to be legitimate compensation for a pointless journey; can you really blame the boys for the bit of fun they had with those skinny old hags? They concluded he was a mainlander too soft by half when dealing with the enemy but still there was something dangerous about him when dealing with them. Warily they kept clear of him and his iron-shod horse. Resentment smouldered in his eyes, but what did they care? He wasn't a general and they weren't following the captain's orders anyway; he was just a lackey so they didn't give a toss what he thought.

Two days had passed since that shameful episode and Díaz still felt sick. It was important the next action would be carefully thought out with no room for errors, he thought. He was determined to maintain control throughout and approach the village cautiously by keeping the men in a tightly disciplined group.

For the convoy of vehicles to have continued to approach Santo Domingo by road would have been a mistake as the steep and winding road would have been slow and noisy with the lorry engines eliminating the element of surprise. The locals knew the Nationalists were in the area and no one in their right mind who had anything to do with politics of the Left or an elected member of the council or even a member of a workers' group would hang about to argue their case. Díaz concluded that surprise was critical to the success of the next action; they needed to capture as many of the opposition as possible. Little did he know that the villagers had also made plans to reduce the element of surprise. If any on that fateful list escaped, it would bring relief to his conscience. He did not want to find them.

12

THE WATCHERS

October 1936

Twelve-year-old Pepe had fallen asleep as he had on other occasions. His father, Alejandro, had told him not to take the blanket as being chilled would keep him alert. But he had taken it without his father knowing; nothing had happened in the past and he didn't want to freeze to death up the mountain even though he was not expected to keep guard for much more than an hour.

He had awoken quickly and became alert within less than half a minute. He knew in that moment that the noises were not animal made; it sounded like a lot of men stamping their feet as they do when trying to keep warm while watching a local football match. If they had been speaking normally he would not have been so frightened but what was worrying was the way they whispered to each other and the sounds they made as they shuffled around like pigs in a pen. He couldn't see them so they couldn't see him; a little comfort, he thought. As he listened there were metallic sounds like the buckles you find on horses' bridles and snorting that sounded like horses too. They were no distance away, just below him, he thought. He looked hard into the darkness beneath the trees and could make out the angular shapes of some lorries parked on the other side of the road. Just then the back of a soldier's head came into view and it was clear to Pepe that he was mounted on a horse. He could not work out who was speaking but the voice used Spanish to talk to the others standing out of view on the road. He then picked up a different voice speaking a different language after the Spanish speaker had finished. He suddenly came to his senses. What on earth was he doing here eavesdropping? He should be away to tell his father and Rodrigo that the worst was about to happen. But he needed to get as much information about the invaders as possible; it was expected of him. Rodrigo would want to know numbers, who were they and if they were armed? Pushing himself forwards along the ground towards the ridge he peered through the undergrowth. *My God*, he thought to himself, *they are soldiers and not the ones you see walking around Béjar, these ones are armed to the teeth with officers on horseback. That's enough*, he concluded, *I've got to get back to the meeting*. Pepe was frightened. He must not be seen or heard but he may need to throw caution to the wind as he was already late. Pushing himself backwards until the officer's head could no longer be seen he stood up carefully and backed away at a crouch keeping his eyes on the area where the soldiers had mustered. He must turn soon and run but he couldn't take a chance; he was still close enough for them to be alerted. No more time for delay, it was time to turn and run like the wind to make up that which was lost when he had been asleep.

The meeting had been taking place in an outbuilding near the school and Pepe arrived without ceremony bursting through the door startling the occupants. He was hauled to the floor by Miguel who held him tightly about the neck. Alejandro quickly came to his son's aid gripping Miguel tightly and demanding he let the boy up. 'Oh, God!

Alejandro and Pepe, I'm so sorry,' he said brushing the boy down.

'Never mind, I'm OK,' he said feebly through his tears, then more forcibly, 'Never mind,' as he pushed away Miguel's hands. 'They're here, they're here,' he repeated very much more loudly despite having run up the hill through the forest.

'Right, calm down, Pepe, and take a deep breath. Just tell me what you have seen; no fabrication, right?' Everyone was still as Rodrigo held the small boy's arms and waited for him to get his breath back.

'They're very close. I missed them first of all but they're already starting to come up the track from the Béjar road.'

'Who is, Pepe? Who's very close? What are you talking about?'

'They're soldiers; twenty, thirty, I don't know and three on horseback. They seem to be in charge. It's really strange as the soldiers I think speak a different language.'

'How long did it take for you to reach us?'

'I don't know but it was the fastest I've ever run; I'm really scared; they've already started to come up the track and they've all got rifles just like Miguel's.'

'Listen, there's a dog barking. I recognise that vicious little blighter. It's my neighbour's dog,' Alejandro interrupted. 'God, they must be close to my house and nearly in the village.'

'It's too late for us to do anything. We must make a run for it. If they catch us they will kill us and if we're not here they may leave without doing any damage.'

'Not a hope in hell,' said Miguel. 'There is nothing we can do except the intelligent thing and that is hide. We'll get the bastards on our own terms later. Now we retreat and then regroup.'

'Well, I'm going back; I can't leave my wife and children to face this lot on their own.'

'Don't, Alejandro, you being there and on the "wanted list" will draw attention to your family.'

'If they recognise you, they'll kill you and God knows what will happen to Eva and the children,' warned Rodrigo.

'I'll take my chances; you do what you think is best but Eva is troubled enough with her nerves and can't cope with any more bad news without me.' With that he ran through the door, sprinted across the square and he plunged through the half-open door of his home and slammed it shut.

'Go,' is all Rodrigo said. The men slipped out of the window that looked out on the forest helping each other with their belongings. Tonight's meeting was to look over what equipment and supplies each man felt he would need if they had to operate from the forest and by good fortune they had all the basic needs with them. 'Spread out now,' he spoke to them in a heavy whisper. 'And we all meet up at point "A" as arranged. We then search out the best place to make a base camp.'

13

THE ATTACK

October 1936

There was not much he liked or admired in his charges and there was not much he liked about himself as he recounted the events of the past. He cursed himself beneath his breath over and over again, trying to dismiss his confused thinking, believing he was unduly influenced by colour and creed. Nor could he shake off his resentment that they were invaders but knew his survival depended on his Republican roots being well and truly hidden. Hand and boot assisted them into line but amongst them was a frisson of excitement that Captain Díaz had never experienced before. He found it disturbing in the light of what had happened recently. None of his Spanish soldiers had ever behaved in this way before conflict or even exercise; to a man they were quietly apprehensive about what the immediate future would hold, but not this lot; they behaved as if they were going to a *feria*. How he hated his job. He should have died at the barracks when the rebel invaders had taken control of his loyal troop, not be fighting with a side opposed to his principles; but he recalled, that at the time, he had good reason not to aggravate the *Africanistas*. He needed to keep his men as safe as possible and the only way he could do that was to play the role of a supporter to their foul cause and his troops to do the same. To his great disappointment and continuing anxiety his company had been dispersed, scattered amongst other units. He had lost them anyway only to be given this motley crew; a bunch of unruly savages, intent on gross mischief. Mateo Díaz understood why this had happened. His new masters were no fools; they were never going to take unnecessary risks with mainland soldiers, many of whom harboured justifiable resentment and might yet turn against them. He had set out to save as many as possible of those targeted by their cruel actions but it was almost an impossible task particularly as this callous bunch of unfeeling mercenaries had no affection or respect for him. He knew himself to be a failing officer who would become more and more dependent on his accompanying *Guardia Civil*; God help him. How he hated his diminished self; he was no longer honourable and he cursed and hated those he once respected, those who gave these godless orders. How could cultured and refined gentlemen born within the most noble families in Spain be set on destroying their own people? Furthermore, how could they consider ideological opposition and poverty threatened the state with Communism? The poor were desperate and would seek out any opportunity to improve their chances of life, within or without the law and so few knew what Communism was, anyway. A label given by the cynical, who, at this time of the emerging power of propaganda, learnt to play to the fears of others.

He called them to silence, pushing from his mind the horrors of past events and explained the importance of a stealthy approach. 'We do not wish to lose capturing any of the renegades. We cannot afford giving them notice of our arrival so be silent all the way through the forest. If they know we are coming, they will slip like ghosts into the trees and we'll never find them. I will lead and you will behave with decorum. Sergeant, if you please, get the men into single file to follow.' He turned towards the mounted *Guardia Civil*. 'Guardsmen Hernando and Felipe will make sure the stragglers keep with us by bringing up the rear; but do it quietly, gentlemen.'

They approached their target by following the goat track that cut through the densest part of the holm oak forest from the valley floor to the centre of the village. It was a steep climb but for those who travelled on foot or horseback it was the swiftest way home under normal circumstances; however, for them of evil intent, thieves and murderers, it was unseen and the quickest way to their prey.

On foot and breathing heavily the soldiers traipsed up the steep hillside. The cumbersome vehicles had been left behind parked along the verges and where possible, hidden by overhanging branches. Each man was responsible for his personal belongings but he was required to take particular care of his rifle, which was inspected regularly by their superiors ensuring cleanliness and function. They knew any failure to meet standards resulted in an unpleasant punishment. As far as the officers were concerned the rifle was more important than the man.

They moved with care, almost soundlessly, avoiding low-hanging branches and keeping their rifles from scraping through the dirt. Occasionally loose stones from the rough surface of the track moved and rattled downwards towards those following or a horse snorted in its efforts to move on up the hill. Captain Díaz, mounted on a sleek chestnut gelding, maintained his position towards the front of the group with the two young, mounted *Guardia Civil* officers bringing up the rear. As they approached the village from the darkness of the forest the military order had lost some of its cohesiveness; the boulder-strewn track had done that, but one could still feel the collective apprehension, an eagerness born of lascivious intent. Díaz sensed their excitement knowing these corrupted men, enticed from the moral guidance of Islam by Spanish generals, brought with them a menace infused with evil; he knew no good was to come from their arrival.

Evening approached and the sun slipped its face behind the high mountains with a swiftness equalled only by an unwilling witness leaving the scene of some horrible crime. Shadows deepened but light from the reddening sky stained the west-facing houses a soft pink. It was a sight that had already welcomed the workers home, its beauty enhanced by the enticing smell of woodsmoke. It was a century's-old comfort to bone-weary peasant labourers; the sweet scent of promise ensuring that good food and a caring family were ready for them. Life was hard, more it was harsh but the comfort brought by their devoted families and the collective selfless dedication to each member gave purpose to living. Family and the church gave succour to the present and vague hope for the future.

The soldiers entered the village from the stand of oaks that over-covered a collection of poorly constructed buildings that smelt and appeared to house goats but may well have been barns when the roofs had been watertight. Animals bleated plaintively and a dog began to bark as it strained against its chain trying to reach with teeth the puttied legs of passing Moroccans. A soldier, using the butt of his rifle, delivered a killing blow to the back of the dog's head; it collapsed and twitched, its legs racing to get purchase on the ground pitifully elusive. The killer lifted his head and grinned through bad teeth amused by the result of his actions and the others laughed at the cruelly comic sight of the animal's pathetic efforts to stand as life faded from its eyes. No point in trying to be quiet now; one or two continued laughing, others spitting heavily upon the ground. Unknown to them by being so preoccupied with the vanquished dog they missed the chance to claim the first of their promised rewards for fighting in a foreign land. The wide-eyed, terrified face of a young woman looked through the broken shutters of an adjoining ramshackle house. Díaz high upon his horse looked down on her and although surprised that anyone could be living in such a building knew at that moment what might happen if the soldiers knew her to be there. She caught the movement of his hand as he indicated for her to hide. Within a heartbeat she understood. His expression of that moment conveyed fear for her life. She slipped swiftly below the window and crawled across the earthen floor making her way back to the bed where her children soundly slept. *Where in God's name is Alejandro?* Eva thought. *He should be here now when needed most.* Her husband and their son Pepe, who in her view was too young to be included in the group, were with the others who were at that very moment planning the defence against such an attack. It was all redundant now, all far too late. More people were disturbed by the sounds of the marauding men moving with unchallengeable confidence and many realised their lives would never be the same again.

As the soldiers shuffled into the square the sound of doors being shut and steel bolts firmly driven home rattled about the village walls. Then silence; all stood still and looked about them in the unwelcome vacuum created by the end of sound. Soft-feathered birds tumbled from surrounding black-limbed trees lifting swiftly into the air to glide unheard towards sanctuary within oaks clustered on the lower slopes. Hope had abandoned all who once lived in harmony just as she had deserted the men named upon the fateful list. They too like soundless birds had taken to the trees seeking out the darkest shadows to hide their shame and weep in fear for those they'd left behind.

More and more soft-shoed strangers moved menacingly into the square to assemble untidily about the man high upon his horse. He looked sullenly towards the stragglers shepherded in by the *Guardia Civil*. Villagers waited and watched anxiously through partly opened windows and through gaps between the panelling of the firmly closed doors. Dark-skinned mercenaries peered slyly from within their shadowed faces as predators do seeking out the weakest for their prey. About the dusty bodies of the invading militia hung munitions in heavy canvas packs, some carried rolled blankets tied about their shoulders with red kepis tucked into their waist belts, but hands never left their rifles. The Spanish officer looked despondent, slumped untidily in his saddle as if weighed down by the unpleasantness of life; there was no arrogance, no certainty and no pride. Old women, with the wisdom of age, tried to read his mind. Did he hate his work? Would he be kind? Would he be at least lenient or maybe even merciful? What could they read within that darkened face? It was a vain hope; all knew for certain he would carry out the will of his generals, close his eyes and like all the others turn his back on the cruelty to come. It was said they all callously turn away once the job is done but this one already hides his face for the cruelty to come. What hope had they?

The priest stood in the porch by the partly open door of the majestic church, hidden within its impenetrable shadow; he too read the signs of what was yet to come. He put his trust, not in God, but in the bishop's communiqué from Salamanca; the rebel army, supported by the brave army of Africa, was to consolidate the church's rightful position within the Christian state of Spain. "This is paramount so do your duty", an unchallengeable call from those so distant from the people.

'I could do both.' He spoke out loudly to himself hoping to bolster his courage. 'I can be loyal to my church and save my children.' With that he set off swiftly tripping down the steps holding his black cassock clear of the ground and across the cobbled square to intervene. The hero sent by God to intercede, here to prevent slaughter, He will be remembered.

The officer drawing himself up in the saddle, stiffened his spine to play the evil role demanded by his generals, prepared to give the fateful order for the guards to direct his men to go about their business. His head was turned by the interruption created by the priest running towards him from the church with his arms and cassock flapping about him like some ungainly bird. Father Jaime pushed roughly at the surrounding Arabs to get as close to the officer as he could.

'No violence, I beg you; I can give you the names of the enemy. Not many here, I assure you, just a few. Most of my parishioners are good men.' He called out with fervour and then he grasped the officer's leg to gain his full attention and so doing startled the horse. It whinnied in fright taking a few short steps backwards before the officer regained control but not before two of the soldiers had been knocked to the ground. The senior NCO turned quickly on the priest driving his rifle into his stomach and followed through with a blow to the chin. Father Jaime crumpled within his black vestments and dropped without a sound upon the cobbled square. The watching villagers called out in protest from behind their feeble barricades; outrage reverberated about the village and chased the remaining creatures from the trees. Manolo Barthez burst through his front door leaving his family screaming at him to stop in fear for his life as he charged towards the soldiers. He was a bull of a man but God-fearing and the priest needed aid.

'Halt, stay where you are; stop, stop, I say,' Captain Díaz called out ineffectually over the sound of protesting villagers. Doors opened, and people beat upon the ground long-handled hoes, staves and tools of their trades. Díaz feared he would lose control. Outraged, the fearless and the simple shuffled forwards menacingly as did Birnam Wood advance on Dunsinane.

Two shots, fired almost simultaneously, struck Manolo in the chest throwing him backwards to slide and settle in appalling stillness. His children screamed in horror and with the same blind courage as their father broke from behind the protective arms of their mother and raced towards him. Eleven-year-old Maria did not stop and with hardly a glance at her father launched herself at the nearest soldier determined to claw his face. Carlota, older, dropped to her knees beside the lifeless man and sobbed helplessly with hands entangled in her hair. The widow, frozen in the doorway, soundless with open mouth, rolled eyes in wild confusion. The soldiers held onto Maria's flailing body and they in number pushed forwards with grievous intent to touch, fondle and push hands beneath her clothes. Father Jaime, upon his knees, looked up to witness the gross abuse as they carried the writhing child away through the doors of the great barn. The bloodied, defeated priest took advantage in the cover of their crime and scuttled, a black-backed beetle, to his church to tend wounds and fabricate excuses to qualify his shame. Mateo, in an attempt to bring order to this terrible event, wheeled his horse in front of the rapacious mob calling them to come to order but nought would stop the madness, driven by an insatiable urge. Carlota, snatched from her father's lifeless embrace, was swept by eager arms, lifted into the air with her limbs akimbo, to be carried as a trophy justly won. They struck out at the officer's mount forcing it back and making it buck, kick and twist in white-eyed panic. With his stirrups gone Mateo clung grimly to the mane cursing himself for being unable to master their indiscipline and shamed by his impotence to save his people. Their mother stumbled before them unresisting as they pushed her towards the open doors.

Lost in her grief she moved oblivious to the danger and crimes to be perpetrated upon her children.

The *Guardia Civil*, with swinging cudgels on those who broke the ranks gained control and assured the remainder there was much to be lifted from a place like this. They could have the pick of the treasures now that half their mates had gone and there would always be women but not always sewing machines.

Captain Díaz tried to recover some dignity by calling the group to order. They shifted listlessly, begrudgingly knowing he still had powers to punish harshly. The guards, Felipe and Hernando, sidled up to him each mounted and stopped on either side of him; too close, he thought. He felt intimidated and turning with angry face feared that they too were rebellious.

'Easy, sir, together we can sort this out.'

Felipe then spoke, 'You know, sir, what General Mola said before we set out on this adventure? Well, he didn't say it to us in person, but we all saw it in the dispatch; you remember what it was?' Díaz nodded. 'Yes, sir? I think you know; well, it's made a great difference to the way we conduct ourselves in war and I'm not sure it's for the better. Now to the point. It said: "extreme violence to shock the Left into paralysis". And it's listed quite graphically what they should be encouraged to do and that includes stealing what they want, beating up anybody who's a nuisance and shagging the women. Well, that's what those animals are doing, so get over it and let's get on with the rest of the job.' He walked his horse forward of Mateo and yelled at the senior NCO who had a good understanding of Spanish. 'Get your men together over here and stop drifting about like farts in the wind.'

'Now, sir, do you want to tell them how to go about sorting the wheat from the chaff, or do you want me and Felipe to do the business?'

'I'll do it; we don't want a repeat of what has just happened.' He cleared his throat and tried to regain some stature. 'What happened a few minutes ago is shameful and it removes honour from our proud unit.' The translator looked at him askance then translated only to be jeered and laughed at by the assembled troops.

His voice was drowned out by the disapproving voices and jeers from the ranks.

'That's enough.' Captain Díaz tried to make himself heard above the noise ineffectually.

'Yes, that's enough, sir,' interjected Felipe. 'You are sitting on a powder keg here. Let me do the business.'

He knew they were right, he had lost all respect and felt further shame seep into his being; he wished to be anywhere but here. With barely a thought to the consequences he conceded his responsibility to the *Guardia Civil*. 'I'm sick to my stomach over what has happened. How can we allow these disgusting animals to kill our people and violate our children and what do we do? Just stand by as if we approve?'

Turning his horse away from the ranks of men he was supposed to be leading he walked it towards the church. He could not suppress the churning, gut-wrenching pain as he passed by Manolo's barn made worse by the sound of a child's distress. He dropped his chin upon his chest, suppressed a sob and passed beyond its painful reach. With hands grasping his head and directing his horse by using his knees he moved towards the great shadow of the church. He had tried and failed to extract himself from a hell of his own making.

14

THE SOLDIER
AND THE PRIEST

October 1936

Dismounting by the church gate and slipping the reins around the post, he collected anything that might be pilfered from his saddlebags. With his arms full he made his way into the church where, in the stillness of the shadows, Father Jaime met him. They stood at arm's length both distressed by what had just happened. Each examined the other for something that might bring a morsel of comfort; there was nothing. Father Jaime was bloodied and earlier tears had coursed through the still bleeding face cutting pale skin trails through a ravaged countenance. The eyes were confused verging on insanity; they were wild, excited as if possessed. Captain Díaz stood hunched with his shoulders heaving; he could not control that which emanated from the pit of his being. Both recognised the failure of the other; they were creatures diminished by their inability to protect the innocent. Their wards had been slaughtered and they would now have to live with the consequences. The priest took the soldier's arm and gently led him further into the church. They moved slowly impeded by the heaviness of their guilt towards the altar where they knelt at the rail.

Mateo clung to the woodwork to steady himself and hoping to regain his moral self; was he closer to God? Would he gain comfort by being here? Father Jaime called upon the Almighty, his God to forgive him for his failure to save the girls. The soldier turned to the priest. 'Ask for me too, Father. Surely I am the greater sinner, I am the defender of weak and I should have saved their lives but you are here to save their souls.'

'Not true, my friend. These are my children, I am here to guide them to live lives according to edicts of Rome, and through that I can save their souls. You understand?'

Mateo shook his head in confusion, then dropped it onto his arms and closed his eyes. Some comfort seeped into his being from the hollow silence of the deserted church. Seconds, timed like minutes, eased a little of the agony buried deep within his guilt until the demented priest failed to muffle laughter with his cassock-covered arm. Mateo peered towards the darkened face; half-closed eyes glowed, insane or possessed but the laugh was real, throttled as he thrust fabric into the offending mouth.

He paused and then continued speaking rapidly under his breath. Mateo looked towards him with growing concern. *Is he taking refuge in insanity?*

The priest searched his enfeebled mind for excuses; he could not take the blame; he should not take the blame for what had happened. No, it was the fault of the women themselves; they had means to entice, to seduce, he had felt their power as it drew him irresistibly to fall beneath its spell. 'Weaker men cannot resist the wiles of devil women,' he spoke up loudly to himself. 'And the church gives strength against the struggle to keep the demons at bay; but I'm captured, my heart races, breathing is difficult whenever that scented temptress stands too close. She is the Devil. Honour is suspended as my eyes control my will. I try not to look but they seek the most intimate of places and I yearn one small glimpse of perfection. Soft moulded, stirring with each breath, the sweetest of all fruit, honey to lift the captive mind to ecstasy.'

Mateo watched as the priest used his tongue to moisten his lips as he continued to mumble but he caught the words. *To whom can he be speaking? Surely not the Holy Father; such language is for the Devil.* Confused, he continued to listen. 'These cursed creatures, with their hair like silk sashaying in the softest breeze turn their knowing eyes on me and understand the agony. They smile, oh, how they smile but should they not favour me with more than just the smile. They move like ripe corn in a summer breeze as breasts and swaying hips provoke deep stirrings with every stride they take.'

He emerged from his inner thoughts and spoke with certainty. 'Wait, my son.' Moving his face closer to Mateo, his eyes bright with the power of his belief, he lifted his hand demanding all the space in which to speak. 'Did you know that God did not intervene at the crucifixion of His Own Son? Was He not more innocent than any of us, and certainly more innocent than those young temptresses who now justly suffer? So think no more of them; they are as one grain of sand in a vast desert.'

The soldier was horrified by what the priest was saying. *Is this the church's message?* 'I don't understand, Father. Are you saying that those children are without innocence, even at their tender age, and worth nothing?'

'Those girls are sinful, soldier. Look how their bodies draw the most holy of men away from the straight and narrow. This may be a test but what I know to be certain is they are guiltier than Christ. God moves in mysterious ways, my son; we don't always know what he has in mind for us.'

'They are children, Father, just children with their God-guided life ahead of them.' Mateo was sickened by the priest's implications. 'Father, wait, don't speak, you listen to me,' he continued, pushing at the priest's hands as he moved them across the soldier's face. 'God is all-loving. I don't believe he would not have saved them if He could.'

The priest continued as if the soldier's words were unheard moving his hands towards Mateo once again. 'Some believe all women are born into sin. Look at Eve; wasn't she the first temptress? You can't deny it, it's in the Bible.'

'Father, I beg you, think about what you say; this is wrong. It cannot be the truth; you are misguided. Escape this Devil who has you in his grip.' With that he raised his voice in anger and shrugged off the priest's hands. 'No, take your hands from me.'

The priest continued, ignoring the pleas from the angered soldier. 'Did you not see those girls? Do not be deceived by their beauty, their scented, silken hair, eyes deep as pools and lips soft as the summer air; they are the daughters of Eve and as the Moors held them aloft, did you not see? Were you not moved by what they revealed to you?'

'Priest, you are a man of God, have you lost your mind? They are children as innocent as the day they were born.' Mateo was angry. *This man should never be a priest, he is sick and taken by the Devil.* 'You cannot lay the blame for your failure at the feet of those innocents; they are children, not like the whores of Triana.'

'They are all whores, all temptresses here on Earth to corrupt man and all men are not strong; I am one who's weak, I am corrupted, God help me to resist.'

Turning sharply to Mateo he once again gripped the soldier's arms using both hands. 'Did you not see,' he paused to draw breath and shape his thought, 'that soft skin tender, perfect limbs lean and slender?' He sighed dropping his chin upon his chest.

'Stop this, Father, this is madness.' Mateo shouted above the monotonous ramblings of the man agonising over the images of his depraved mind. 'What possesses you?' He awaited an answer but there was none. The priest was lost in a churning of confused thoughts. 'You are no longer a man of the church; would Christ have you speak this way?' He paused once again to no avail. 'Listen to me,' he spat out in frustration and taking the priest by the shoulders shook him. 'You are as them,' he said thrusting his chin in the direction of the door. 'Those pigs, those disgusting creatures we call men, those who at this moment rape and murder our children; you are as them.'

The soldier rose up from his knees avoiding the priest's hands. 'Stay away, Father, do not touch me again; you're poisonous.' He shuffled backwards stooping to pick up his belongings from the tiled floor.

'But you brought those beasts here, soldier. Without you we would have been safe and I would not be mad.'

'Don't blame me for your weakness, Father.' Mateo twisted away beating his clothes with his free hand as if to remove an infestation. 'How could I have called you Father? You are a mad man. You are the Devil,' he spat out angrily but winced feeling many of his words he had used accusingly could be directed at himself.

The priest turned and lifted his head to peer into the soldier's eyes. 'Save me, soldier, save me. I am a weak sinner, not the Devil.'

Mateo looked into the tortured features and feeling no sympathy he swept away the hands as the priest tried, once more, to take hold of his clothes. 'Recover yourself, you will find yourself in hell unless you do. Pray for your salvation, you are dangerously close to the flames, sinner priest.'

Mateo Díaz staggered towards the great door that led him to the outside; the sultriness of the approaching night and evidence of the horrors perpetrated in his absence emerged from the shadows. Horrified, he looked down upon the results of his inability to control the excesses of his men. He did not know them; he knew nothing of the violence of their lives. But what was certain, they had been given licence by Spanish generals to kill, rob and rape Spanish innocents. These Moroccan victors, who brought the formidable Rif tribesmen to their knees, now found women and children such easy targets, just playthings. 'Shame on you, you vicious bastards, and shame on me; once a decent man, now useless, diminished, all my rights to an honourable life squandered.'

15

THE END OF INNOCENCE

October 1936

One of the cottages burned and the drifting smoke formed a backdrop paled by the light of fading day. Dark figures scuttled with urgency splashing water on the glowing embers of the destroyed home. Mateo ran towards the fire and stopped short of its entrance noting there was little that was burning beyond the door. It was then he turned his attention to the door and looked closely through the smoke towards that which was burning. What remained caused him to step back in horror; he was unable to draw breath. There, wired to the frame, were the smouldering remains of some creature he could not tell whether it had been man or woman. Trembling with rage and spinning on his heels he turned towards his men and within three strides grabbed hold of the nearest, striking him with a clenched fist. The soldier fell to the ground and in the time the others had realised what had happened he had drawn his pistol from its holster and they scattered. He discharged a shot at their retreating backs. No one fell and before he could take more careful aim he was held from behind in a powerful grip.

'Hold your fire, sir; you're in enough trouble already; you don't want to go adding to it.'

'Let me go.' He spoke with a voice choking with rage but, feeling the weight of his responsibilities, struggled to gain control forcing it to disperse as quickly as it had arisen. 'What do you mean I'm in trouble already; what have I done?'

'Well, that's the problem. You haven't done very much.' Felipe looked steadily at the officer, unfazed by the crisis. 'If you had been here maybe this operation wouldn't have been such a shambles.'

'But you and Hernando had taken control of the operation, don't you remember?'

'Well, I don't know about that, sir. What choice did we have when you disappeared into the church?'

'And don't blame the Arabs for that poor bastard nailed to the door. That's a result of action taken by those low-life bullies who have turned up from somewhere local. They're "Blue-shirts", unofficial supporters of the big man; they'd do anything to curry favour amongst our glorious leaders. They'll get his blessing soon, that's for certain.'

Mateo looked towards them in disgust. 'That scruffy lot don't look as if they've got a brain cell between them. Where did they come from?'

'I don't know, but they follow us like jackals at a kill. Come to practise being shits, no doubt.' With that Felipe spat heavily on the ground then looked up at the captain with a smirk upon his face. 'That, sir, is because of the smoke not what I think about the pretty boys; I wouldn't want anyone getting the wrong idea about me.'

Not wishing to believe what he had been told and certainly not wanting to be lending support to the

Falangists, Mateo still had a duty to perform. He pulled himself up to his full height, pushed his pistol back in its holster, straightened his clothes before clearing his throat. He turned towards the two men. 'This is what we are going to do to try and put things right.' He fidgeted, adjusting his hat and pulling down on the hem of his tunic, clearing his throat once more and set about thinking. It was hopeless. No ideas would come. 'Get the men together, now,' he demanded trying to put some authority into his words.

'We're not going to have one of your little chats again, are we, sir? Because that's not going to get us back on an even keel. Just look around you, it's a bloody disaster.'

'I know, I know,' he called out in despair, waving his arms in frustration in the direction of the clustered groups of soldiers. 'They're the bastards I want to kill, our own men; can you believe it? My own men! They're foreign scum. Why are they here?' He strode towards them with murder in his heart screaming obscenities as he went.

The restraining arm of the guard held on to him once again. 'Take it easy, sir, this is our job and remember they're doing our dirty work. You go get your horse, mount up and park yourself close to where we've tied our horses. Make yourself distant from this shambles and concentrate on regaining your authority. Do it, sir, and get some dignity back.' Leaving him open-mouthed the guards abruptly turned away shouting coarsely at the soldiers as they started to drift about aimlessly. 'Pick up your kit, smarten yourselves up and get into line. Now, I say, and don't dawdle or it'll be worse for you.' They picked up the message and moved swiftly about their business knowing what may happen if too slow.

Captain Díaz had remounted and peered curiously across from his saddle to the men being brought to order. Once assembled they stood in ragged ranks clutching onto newly acquired possessions. The inquisitive officer walked his horse towards them. He looked about taking in the evidence of their destructive raid, then switched his attention to the looters who stood awkwardly holding onto the most unlikely objects. 'Whatever do you want a sewing machine for and you, with the bucket and the rolled mattress, what are you going to do with them?' He looked around hoping someone had an explanation. 'We've got a war on our hands; how can you possibly do your job hauling that crap along with you?'

The Moroccan spoke rapidly to his NCO who then turned back to Captain Díaz and in accented Spanish explained what had been said. 'These are our rights, sir; we didn't just come here for the fighting. We wouldn't have left our homes just for the fighting. What interest have we got in your squabbles?'

'What rights have you got?' questioned the incredulous captain. 'You're in our army, you're paid by our country, more than you are worth, I suspect.'

The *Guardia Civil* looked on in frustration.

'This isn't getting us anywhere, sir. Let me explain,' cut in Felipe with barely disguised annoyance. 'Our generals didn't find it easy persuading this group of bandits to come over here to do our dirty work. What swung it was the freedom to shag who they want and take what they want. We even promised to deliver the goods to their homes in Morocco.'

Everyone stopped talking and listened, turning their heads towards a different sound. 'Here they come, Captain, not before time I'm glad to say. And now, sir, do you mind stepping back out of the way and letting us do our job?' The vehicles struggled up the last steep slope into the village square; the sound increasing and reverberating off the walls of the closely packed dwellings. It now became obvious why they had no choice but to advance on the village through the forest. Had they approached by lorry the chickens would have been well and truly warned and flown the coop to hide forever in the forest.

Mateo turned to the *Guardia Civil* officer. 'You've recorded the number of the enemy accounted for and their names?'

'Yes, sir, all the names on this list have been recorded but sorry to say a goodly number of them were not at home; we can't put 'em on the list. Somehow, they must have got the message we were on our way. How, I don't know.' Felipe registered his disappointment with a look. 'But to compensate for lost numbers I've added a few more names, ones not on our official list, but if nobody notices it'll make it look better than we deserve.'

'What do you mean a few more?' he responded, dropping swiftly from his saddle but maintaining a grip on the bridle. He handed the reins to Felipe.

'Look, sir, there were a few who got in the way, you know, tried to protect their man or, in some cases, their dad. Collateral damage, sir, collateral damage; it always happens.' The guard cleared his throat in embarrassment. 'There were the others, sir, the ones the Moors had their fun with, it was too much for them; some of them were quite young, you know, and those left still breathing they shot.'

'Jesus Christ,' he said with a burst of anger.

Mateo then turned back and looked long and hard at him for a moment in silence; he shook his head as if denying that which he knew to be true in an attempt to expel the horrible images now crowding his mind.

'What, those children, those girls and others too?'

'Well, some were more like young women.' Felipe broke off suddenly venting the fury that had built up in him during this ugly, ignoble event. 'Do you think I like it any more than you do, sir?' he yelled disrespectfully. 'But it's happened and we haven't gone beyond our brief, God how I hate it. I've done some bad things in my time but this beats them all. I'm hellfire bound no doubt.' He pulled himself together clearing his throat again. 'There are no names on my list other than the ones we set out to get but it is difficult to account for everyone in a shambles like this, so you can rest easy, sir. Let's get out of here.'

'Get them in the lorry then.' He turned to look upwards towards the church. The soft light of candles flickered somewhere beyond the great door but nought else; it was barren, salvation lost and no place for hope. 'Let night cover all that offends the day,' Mateo mumbled to himself. 'May God be in the soft breeze of morning to ease the pain of the living.'

Mateo Díaz walked across to the guards loading the horses. He took the bridle from Felipe's hand and led the chestnut gelding away from the ramp. 'Let me keep my horse, Felipe. I will ride behind and reach you later in the evening.'

Hernando gave Felipe a knowing look. 'It's not far, sir, but are you sure you know the way?' Mateo nodded, and Hernando continued, 'I can add you to the list of casualties, Captain. It will only take a minute and it will give you the freedom to do whatever you need to do.' Mateo looked closely at the young man and believed him; he nodded his appreciation. 'We could put you down as "Missing presumed dead".'

'Thank you, Hernando, but there will be no need. I said I would be late so don't make a fuss; I wouldn't want you to take the risk of helping a pathetic officer. Just delay reporting me missing in action, if you please; that's if I don't turn up, of course,' and he smiled wryly.

'Forgive me for saying this, sir, but you were not cut out for this sort of shitty campaign. You think too much and you're a bit too soft.' Hernando held up his hand to stop Mateo interrupting. 'I don't want to know what you have in mind, sir, but Felipe and I think you're a decent man; good luck and may God go with you.'

'God bless you too and thank you for understanding my horror of all this.' Mateo mounted his horse and walked it past the stationary lorries. He did not look towards the Moroccans nor did he look back towards the church but he gave much thought to the child Maria.

16

FRANCISCA

April 1937

The winds that coursed across the arid plains from distant seas were lifted by the south-facing wall of these brooding mountains, only to sweep downwards between the ice-covered slopes and fall upon the moist air of the darkening valley below. An area of sweet repose rendered uninhabitable. In daylight this is a place that brings comfort, a purpose to life, warmth to the soul even on the hardest day when persistent rain soaks every stitch of clothing. Fertility is in the ground, the air and the calloused hands of the generations that turned the well worked soil that was once their master's. Now it is land that they can call their own. Fortune has smiled thinly upon this community. This privilege to the underclass lies undiscovered by those who would steal it back when sheep have more value than God's children.

The early spring caresses the tender plants encouraging pale leaves into a new world; a world that becomes harsher with the months when an unforgiving sun climbs higher in the sky, shrivelling the weak and fiercely demanding the survivors to bring forth their fruit. It is here that crumbling soils give life to the pastures and pocket-sized plots growing asparagus, pimientos and potatoes. Fruit trees mark out the allocated spaces with figs amongst the rocks and black-branched almonds pregnant with hope, waiting in line to unfurl the first petals of spring. Spaces in the barns need filling and larders restocking for the bleaker, leaner months that lie ahead. But it is not a place to be when darkness falls and the steep, uneven path home is treacherously unseen.

It was late and she had been there too long. The moisture had condensed in the falling temperature and the valley mist had come so quickly she had hardly time to gather up her tools and the meagre fruits of her labour. She would have chosen the longer track home for two reasons; it was easier on tired legs and, of more importance, it passed at a greater distance from the hunting lodge, now the meeting point of those she despised and hated with poisonous vengeance. But on this fading day she was late, so it was the shorter, more difficult, route she struggled along, pausing only to draw breath and rest her weary back. The sound of the men's voices was carried on the air as she pulled the coarse blanket more closely across her shoulders, lifting her head towards the sound of revelry. Oil lamps glowed deep orange in the dense blackness of the night silhouetting the twisted forms of ancient trees. Holm oaks shuffled leaves above their dense shadows. Impenetrable pools of darkness hid secrets, some more foul than others, and pale pools of the fleeting moonlight feebly illuminated the rocky hillside.

She stood still beneath the swaying branches paralysed by the memory of that treacherous day. Their voices carried with them a return to the brutal event. She knew them; these were the men who stripped from her husband not only his uniform, but also his dignity. These were the men not only satisfied with his death but who also revelled in the preceding cruelty. The handling of José was cruel. He was a man of honour, respected for his fairness and compassion for those who had fallen on hard times. They showed him neither respect nor compassion. Were they less than human?

Someone cleared their throat and spat onto the ground. The moon shifted its gaze and there, urinating against the outside wall, was the despicable Alfredo Cortés, squat, broad, needing a haircut and useless. A foul man, a wife beater suddenly elevated in life by a blue shirt. The hatred she felt for him was as steam upon the skin, the intensity of its pain choked the words cluttered in her throat as she struggled for breath. Unable to move she stood as still as the night, wishing him dead. He turned in the process of redressing; paused as he caught the strength of her gaze then leeringly he smiled, 'Not for you, old crow, but I don't mind you looking.' He turned and pushed himself through the door. There was a surge of drunken laughter cut short by the slamming of the door.

Cold penetrated the fabric of the blanket she had pulled closely about her shoulders and once again, leaning heavily upon the hoe, she struggled forwards up the rocky track. Tears were in her eyes and she had no idea for whom she wept. Was it for her or José? José was dead and at peace; he no longer suffered the indignities of a world so brutally changed. How she wished to be with him; she had grown weary of living with grief and corroding anger.

She lifted the latch of the small, boarded door that led her into the single room she now called her home. With José's death and the unwarranted disgrace they poured upon him, she had lost her official home on the outskirts of the town. All officers in the *Guardia Civil*, particularly those of José's standing, had allocated houses. He was not a vindictive man as many were encouraged to be in the later years. He was different from many of them; he cared for his fellow man and understood their frailties, the law was important, but justice and compassion were equally so. The cynical manipulation of the law by those with the power to do so was to him just another awful, demeaning crime. His support of the innocent and rejection of the demands of the manipulative power brokers was to them his greatest "crime". He was a tough officer, uncompromising to lawbreakers but also known for doing his best to support those who had fallen on hard times. There were many fathers who would do anything to feed and bring comfort to their families despite the risks they took and where no one was harmed by the action, José did what he could to solve problems before they came to court. The master's response was always extreme in the victim's view but beatings by those on the estate's payroll were easier to take than beatings by the *Guardia Civil* who sided with the wealthy. José despised the association forged between the privileged and some elements within the *Guardia Civil* and had often spoken out against it.

Francisca closed the door; it was cold inside the house but she was now out of the icy wind. There was still a glow coming from the hearth and before long, with the help of a little kindling, it would be warmer. She knelt before the fire holding out her hands, seeking to bring back life to her frozen fingertips. The pot was ready and the kettle filled and now she waited for the smoke and flames to subside before pushing them in place on top of the embers. The blanket she had removed and placed on the back of the chair to air. It needed to dry out before being added to her bed so she could be as warm as possible throughout, what promised to be, a very cold night. Francisca stayed kneeling in front of the fire but had unbuttoned her coat to allow the warming air to pass within her clothes. This always took a while, leaving her enough time for contemplation and painful memories. On most occasions she wrestled with what she might do tomorrow or that which she may have failed to do at her garden plot. But these trivial issues would not aggravate tonight. Seeing the blue-shirted monster in the forest had taken her back to what happened to José. That man, she had been told, orchestrated the incident that ended with the death of her husband. Bad news always travelled quickly and it had taken less than a day for her to learn of José's death; whereas the manner of his death filtered through to her over a period of several days. There were different versions, depending upon which side you supported. The official report, which took more than a few days to compile, declared that her husband had been executed for treachery. He had taken action against the interests of a liberated Spain and the church. The truth of what had happened was revealed to her in whispers; moments snatched whilst at the market or returning home from church. They were brave women who associated with her because the official line was the only permissible line and any diversion from that would result in serious repercussions. When challenged by Nationalist sympathisers, the women would spit back at them that all widows deserved sympathy regardless of their husband's misdemeanours.

Having pieced together all bits of the information and confirmed as much as she could by talking to others, Francisca believed she had the full story. There were still a few details that she would have liked to have been certain about. Who did what first and was there anybody who tried to help him? From what she understood it all happened so fast that there was little anyone could have done to save him.

José should not have been in the village that day, but he had said to Francisca that he wanted to check on the two new firebrands recently recruited into his cadre. He said, before he left that day, that they were competent young officers but felt they had been posted to his unit to "give it a bit more steel" as the very self-confident young Hernando had quoted. He told her that, in his view, the *Guardia Civil* had changed for the worse and seemed to be becoming the private army of the aristocrats. He had ridden into the village on the bridle path through the oaks, passing the ramshackle old house that Juana had been forced to occupy since the disappearance of Rodrigo, and into the square. Everybody could hear the raised voices and many villagers stood in their doorways taking a cautious interest. One of the guards was leaning down from his saddle holding the tall Sebastián by his clothes with one hand and thrashing him with his riding crop held in the other. Sebastián called out in pain and as he tried to pull away from the beating, the other guard moved his horse against him pushing him back into the punishment zone. This was accompanied by shouts of derision from the scruffy group of five men holding cudgels and calling out to the guards to kill the Red.

'Whoa, whoa, stand back and cease the beating,' José called out over the shouts and screams. 'You, *Señor*, stand still.' Then turning to the group of Blue-shirts he growled, 'You lot keep your distance; I don't want to see any one of you near our man.' José turned his horse and rode up close to the prisoner and leaning forwards in his saddle demanded his name.

'Sebastián Ruiz, *Señor*.'

'Ah, you are Sebastián Ruiz. Do you know you are in trouble?'

'Yes, I know so now; have you not noticed what these officers have done to me?' he continued, pointing across the square. 'And that collection of scum over there wants me dead. I need protection not a beating.'

'Are you not married to the dancer Pastora?'

'*Si, Señor*, and I'm pleased to tell you she and my son, Bartolomé, are not in the village today.'

'Yes, I have noticed the way these officers have treated you and I'm pleased that your wife is not here to witness it. For the present you will be safe with us, but did you know there is a warrant for your arrest?'

'What?' he exclaimed in astonishment. 'Why; because I reminded the authorities that they must protect us, do fair by the peasants, you know the ones who are treated with less respect than dogs?' He continued in confusion. 'The law is supposed to be fair; it shouldn't take one side or the other. Do you know that patch of earth that was allocated to our families, you know the bit that's been promised by the elected government so poor folk can grow a few vegetables? Well, the grand master in his big house, who already has a thousand hectares, can't survive without having it back, the greedy bastard.'

'That will do, Ruiz. You cannot stand there and insult our superiors. Say another word of that nature and I will bring another charge against you.'

'That's right, charge him again, officer,' called out one of the blue-shirted ruffians. 'It's not going to make any difference, we're going to castrate the big, ugly bastard anyway.'

José turned his horse towards the group. 'Hold your tongue, this man is in my charge now; he is in my care and nothing will happen to him whilst he is in my care. So you watch what you say or you will join him.'

As José turned back towards the mounted guards, Sebastián Ruiz shrugged off the grip of the young guard who had administered the beating and took several steps towards the mob. Hernando moved his horse swiftly on him and knocked the prisoner to the ground. As Sebastián struggled to his feet, Felipe called out, 'Do it again, Hernando, trample him. This useless old codger can't stop us doing what we came here to do.'

José turned his horse towards the *Guardia Civil* and before he could confront the man, Felipe had taken his turn to trample the prisoner but misjudged his charge and crashed his horse into the mounted José. Caught unawares he struggled to keep his seat. Taking advantage of this opportunity, the group of cudgel-bearing Falangists rushed in to haul José from the saddle. He managed to draw his pistol and as he tried to regain his feet and bring his pistol to bear on his attackers, a swinging cudgel knocked it from his hand and the continued swing caught him on the side of the head. He crashed senseless to the ground.

Consciousness returned in less than two minutes, and as he peered across the cobbles he noticed, close to him, the bloodied and lifeless form of Sebastián. His head was deformed and one eye seemed to be resting on his cheek. It was a brutal sight. A pool of blood continued to seep over and between the cobbles from between his thighs with his trousers tangled about his left ankle. It was then, as his head cleared, that José noticed that he too had been demeaned by having his uniform stripped from him. His boots had gone and his trousers, shirt and jacket too, leaving him in just his underwear. He had been stripped of all that signified his authority but determinedly he would not accept that they had taken his dignity and struggled to his feet.

'Hey, look, I thought the old bastard was dead. Who was it who said that they'd mashed his brains? Come on, who was it?' No one admitted to the failure. 'Well, whoever it was is useless, they didn't do a good enough job.' With that, the self-appointed leader, a short, stocky man, marched with purpose towards the wriggling José.

'Wait for us, Alfredo; you can't have all the fun.'

Alfredo Cortés turned about and waited with some relief for his colleagues to join him. This gave José just enough time to search around for something with which he might defend himself. There, lying on the ground close to Sebastián's body, was the knife they had used to emasculate the poor soul. He picked it up tentatively as it was sticky with Sebastián's blood, but he felt empowered by the evidence of their cruelty; he turned and strode fearlessly towards the oncoming brutes. Enrique was stopped in his tracks by the determination on José's face, someone bumped into the back of him making him stagger forwards, but he tentatively held his ground fearing the advancing man. Others shuffled forwards towards the comical creature in his bloodstained underwear. José ploughed on, driving them back into Alfredo's arms. He buried the butcher's knife into the soft belly of the first man; the scream tore at everyone's nerves, and Jose's second slash cut deeply into the face of another. Felipe and Hernando were quickly on their feet and ran towards the disturbance with pistols drawn. Alfredo swung his club catching José in the neck who dropped to his knees unable to draw breath. Kneeling on the cobbles with his head dropped forwards onto his chest, José wheezed; the knife fell from his hand as he stretched his arms forward of his body and spread out his fingers as if feeling for some invisible object. Lifting his head with his eyes firmly closed he sighed deeply, 'God help us and all good men.' It was then that the guards, with pistols drawn, fired destroying another decent man.

17

FALL FROM GRACE

April 1937

Francisca stood by the window looking out at the small group of officials and civil guard officers as they milled about in an agitated way. The raised voices and waving about of arms indicated they were obviously engaged in some heated discussion. She was not surprised to see them; their visit was inevitable but she had expected them some days earlier. She knew why they were there and understood the embarrassment felt by her slaughtered husband's long-term colleagues; they had been complicit in the destruction of this honourable man's reputation. José had never been swayed by the promises of rich rewards for using his position to assist the powerful to become more powerful nor would he engage in unlawful actions that would further work against the interests of the poor and dispossessed. Sadly he was in the minority. Loyalty to the powerful became the dominant purpose of the *Guardia Civil*'s role in society relegating their sworn responsibility to the elected government as inconsequential. Francisca had packed bags in preparation for this day and they stood just inside the door. The few sticks of furniture she could call her own were easy enough to carry outside and deposit on the cobbles for the move to somewhere else. Her wait for them to make up their minds was over, they turned towards her little house and strode purposely towards her. The two *Guardia Civil* officers held back a short distance from a small, rotund man in army uniform wearing wire-rimmed glasses on his pallid face. He was clearly the authority as he held the clipboard and sported the most miserable expression. Francisca sighed deeply. It was now her turn to be humiliated and she was glad her children were not here to witness it. Their absence always concerned her; she had no idea where they might be and the execution of their father might well have compromised their lives. She hoped that the incident was not widely reported. There was enough casual killing going on throughout the country for his to have been overlooked.

Major Morán went to strike the door with his swagger stick but was taken by surprise when the door was pulled open before he could he do so. Francisca was tall for a Spanish woman and the additional height of the front step gave her the advantage; she looked down on him. '*Buenos días, Señor*, I have been expecting you. Please enter my simple home; perhaps I can serve you a coffee?' she said with affected courtesy.

'This is not a social call, *Señora*; I am here to ensure that family members of the traitor Savater are disengaged from the advantages they enjoyed before his treachery was discovered.' He went to push past her to enter the house, but she held her position.

'You have been misinformed, Major; my husband was an honourable man who served his country with distinction. His only fault was to support the right to justice for all people, whatever awful circumstances they should find themselves in. He would not give in to the corrupt masters who bribed his brother officers.' Major Moran held her gaze; he could not help being moved by the despair and sadness in her voice but he was resolute; she must go. 'Never fear, sir, I am going; I assume you are an honourable man and not in the pay of the criminal class?' she said unkindly.

He felt compelled to respond but could not find the words. She unsettled him; this intimidating woman empowered by great dignity made him feel inadequate. He was unable to meet her gaze in his embarrassment as he felt the colour rising in his face.

Francisca moved aside and let him enter, she then picked up some of her belongings and stepped outside the door putting her bags down on the cobbles. As she prepared to return to the house to collect more of her possessions Major Morán, with a need to feel he had recovered a degree of dignity, denied her access. '*Señor*, I have other things to collect. Will you also take those from me?'

'The administrative procedure instructs me that once you have left the building, *Señora*, you cannot re-enter.' He smiled as if in sympathy, then waved a piece of paper towards her. 'It's all in here and there seems to be no allowance for uncollected luggage.'

Francisca stood as if in shock; her world was collapsing around her and she seemed not to have a friend in the world. Sadness overwhelmed her and the tears came as she dropped her chin on to her chest. There was no sound but her whole body trembled as she lowered herself on to her knees and softly wept. Morán had won.

José's ex-colleagues had until this moment kept themselves in the shadows. They knew the truth behind the killing of their old friend and felt ashamed. They had not spoken up for him but had to be cautious and think of their own families. There were evil forces at play and the only way to survive was to keep your head down. However, the way that miserable little toad was behaving towards Francisca needed some response. '*Señor* Major, is there anything in your instructions that prevents me and my colleague from entering the repossessed building?'

Major Morán cast his eyes over the document in search for something that might make life even more awkward, but without success. 'Sadly, there is no exclusion of others with authority from entering.'

They both strode past the bespectacled officer into the house and started to collect the rest of Francisca's possessions. They came to the door marching past the major to deposit them beside her on the cobbled square. 'Is this all that you have, Francisca?'

'Yes, pathetic, isn't it? All the years we lived here as man and wife in service to the state and with never a stain on his character, these are my sole possessions.' The old colleague leant forwards and touched Francisca on the shoulder as she then started to speak softly to herself. 'José, I have let you down, I don't even know where they have put you; have they just thrown you away like all the other poor souls?'

'I know this will be of small comfort to you but we have ensured José will rest undisturbed in consecrated ground at Santo Domingo. The priest was not keen as he had made a pledge that any who opposed Christian Spain would never be allowed to rest in sacred grounds.'

Francisca lifted sad eyes and thanked them. 'So much for the dead,' she said, 'but where am I to rest my weary bones?'

'We have made arrangements for you, Francisca, not what you deserve but all we can manage.'

The major pulled the door closed with a flourish and locked it with the large iron key. He turned to the officers comforting Francisca and advised them to leave her to her fate. 'We have no place in the Christian Spain we have rescued from the godless for the likes of her or her treacherous husband. If she lives or dies it is of no consequence, she is now underclass. Leave her be and let her find her own way.' He marched a few steps to the civil guard officers and passed one of them the key. 'Have more care to whom you allocate this house in the future; we don't want any more mistakes.' Nobody said a word but they hoped their thoughts would do him mischief as he strutted away down the hill.

They lifted Francisca to her feet and collected up her meagre possessions. 'Come with us, we have a place you can use as your home. Please don't expect too much, Francisca, it's a place abandoned by a family that's fled north.' They led her away to the back of the adjacent building where they had parked a car. 'It's a very small house in Santo Domingo, not in the main village, but tucked away just on the edge of the forest.'

They drove the car over the crest of the hill and pulled it under the trees on the lower road. 'I don't want to drive into the village as it will draw too much attention to what we're doing; they're not all friends there, you know; so we have a bit of a hike up the goat track.'

Within twenty minutes they had arrived at a small stone-built building. There was a small window beside the door to the front and a larger window to the back. It was a single-roomed dwelling but someone had been in and lit a small fire in the ancient hearth. It had been cleaned and made quite cosy. There was a small table and one chair but no bed. The officer apologised and hoped Francisca could manage one night on the straw mattress by the warm stove. 'That pompous idiot made a mistake by giving me the key,' said the guardsman. 'Before I pass it back I'll get you a bed and a few other things to make you more comfortable some time tomorrow.'

146

'Your kindness is a comfort,' said Francisca as she searched in her baggage for blankets and other warm clothing. 'Who has done all the cleaning? The place is spotless.'

'Our wives came here earlier to see what they could do. They have always admired you, Francisca, and they've looked up to you even though you frighten them just a little.'

Francisca laughed, 'Oh, I'm sorry, yes, I suppose I was unnecessarily fierce but that is my age and maybe I was a little jealous because they're both so pretty; please give them my love and thank you.'

The young officer continued conveying his regret for all that had happened to José and the distance they were obliged to keep from her from now on. 'Francisca, sadly we cannot be seen helping you or even being polite to you in the future; our lives depend on it, we will help if we can but we mustn't be seen.' She nodded knowingly and acknowledged the inevitability of need for such caution. 'We must go, but by dark tomorrow I hope you will have a bed to sleep in.' Both men turned away and left quietly to return to the hidden car beyond the well-used track.

18

JUANA AND RODRIGO

Spring 1937

Night, like ink, seeped into the torn fabric of the fading day as the shrouded sun slipped away, a tired guest to sink behind impenetrable peaks. Clouds moved in from the south absorbing the last remnants of reflected light cutting short both the evening and the working day prompting the closing of doors to confirm the day was over. Heavy bolts were pressed home. Within the cluster of squatting houses simple food was prepared in the glow of wood-burning stoves whilst the yellowing light of oil lamps illuminated small rooms. On the fringes of the great forest small creatures, more comfortable in the deepening shadows of the approaching night, scuttled in the undergrowth. They burrowed deeply into the multitudes of leaves stripped cleanly from wind-blown branches of century-grown oaks. Their skittish behaviour reflected an affliction born recently from the loins of paranoia; a neurosis, tumorous within a nation, whose innocence has been superseded by unsurpassable cruelty. This once contented place, poor yet happy, is sickened, stricken with a rational fear. And men from across the water, predatory creatures, armed by false premise, seek out their weaker fellows, swat them aside and that which was forced to be abandoned is claimed as rightful reward.

Juana had lived here for some months now, since Rodrigo's escape on the night of the attack and the consequential closure of the school. The schoolhouse had been taken from them. She had learned that the sound of the forest, constant during the day but increasing with intensity with the fading light, was not something to be feared; it was as normal as stars brightening in a blackening sky. But recent events had corrupted the purity of that knowledge. Those sounds, were they still the black-footed pigs that brushed against the outer walls? Was it them that snorted like Moros hawking phlegm from their throats and spitting heavily upon the ground? Each heavy sound chillingly recreated the fear that was born during the blood-soaked events of that awful night. These were fears she must suppress for her daughter's sake. In the same way Juana must make light of so-called evidence manufactured to dissemble her character by ignoring foul comment and laugh off the molesting fingers. How the world had changed since her arrival here with Rodrigo such a short time ago. It was blissful then; it was the time of her life; it was a time in which Alicia grew into a beautiful child. Those days early in her marriage had been filled with joy and an undeniable promise that the simplicity of these events would enrich the soul. Had she been blind to the realities of an uncompromising world? Did not birdsong, first flowers of spring, fruit upon the trees as leaves grew golden in autumnal air and neighbours who cared, helped and laughed against the petty annoyances, all enrich her life? It was not so long ago she saw no reason why the years ahead would not bring anything but happiness and love from all around her. The day of their arrival was full of hope with

Juana clinging to Rodrigo's arm in happy embarrassment. She had been taken aback by the enthusiasm of the villagers and the warmth of their welcome. Whilst mothers crowded in upon them with a thousand questions, sturdy men stood at a respectful distance, curious but not wanting to be involved. However, from that very moment, she felt watched. He stood just outside her line of vision and Juana was moved uncomfortably by the intensity of Father Jaime's gaze. It smouldered, intruding on the warmth of welcome by the mothers, leaving her wondering what she was doing here. Was the welcome as genuine as she had first believed? His gaze was more than inquisitive, more than disapproving; it was intimate. She remembered clinging even more tightly to Rodrigo's arm, causing him to turn and look quizzically at her. She smiled weakly in the hope she could put him at ease and making a point that would effectively discourage the priest's attention. To this very day she had never felt easy when close to the Holy Father but she must show him the respect his position deserved. Was he not the reason the school was here and not elsewhere creating the wonderful job that Rodrigo once loved so much? She put aside the uncomfortable feelings, hid them with a smile and never let her husband know. Not every village had access to a teacher and Rodrigo and his family were the fortunate ones to be chosen. He had come home.

He could not believe his luck in having landed this new job. However, this did not stop him querying the reason for having a school here in so small a place as Santo Domingo, whereas other villages in the vicinity, of a greater size, had none. It puzzled them both. The church was magnificent and adorned with riches way beyond the means of the folk who worked the land. It had to be the possession of holy relics of some long-dead saint, they thought. It was Saint Domingo, of course, Rodrigo had pointed out to her. The fragments related to Domingo were kept well-hidden until the saint's day when there was a surge in the number of pilgrims who passed by on their way to somewhere else. Those were great days for them both and the school flourished becoming every bit as important to the villagers as the church. Despite its success Father Jaime lauded his position over Rodrigo who responded respectfully, unemotionally and with quiet acquiescence. They were not the best of friends but they rubbed along together each convinced that what they did was more vital to the community than the other. The brutality of later events split the community; it had changed everything with Rodrigo on one side of the rift and the priest on the other. Juana pulled herself back to the here and now and thought of what Rodrigo had said to her time and time again. Think only of now and just a little of tomorrow, yesterdays are too distant and too painful to contemplate.

Nowhere in Republican Spain, however remote from the centres of unrest, felt safe. Santo Domingo could feel the ripples of discontent move insidiously within its close community. The pillars of society comforted the nervous dismissing much as unfounded rumour. Anxiety welled up painfully from within the breast. Some dismissed the tales as nonsense yet took themselves home sickened by the faintest possibility there might be a grain of truth in what was being spread on the southern airwaves. They found themselves unable to eat their meagre rations and took to their beds to lie restlessly through the blackest of nights.

The wiser and better informed who had access to the radio transmissions picked up by the office of the *Guardia Civil* knew more. Arguments had broken out as to which of the two versions they should give credit and to whom they should give their loyalty. The young guards were excited by the chance of action and Franco's propaganda stirred a passion in them to be part of the revolution. The elders reminded the young guns of their loyalty to the state, the democratically elected government dedicated to helping the destitute and creating a fairer society. But it became obvious as the heated discussion continued that several of the senior officers had compromised their status by having already served the interests of the wealthy for money; of this they would never be allowed to forget.

Juana was indecisive: which way to turn, who was right, who was wrong, what was right, what was wrong? *Will harm be brought to our doorstep and how can I be sure to save my children? Will we lose our home?* A million questions to be answered and left unanswered because no one knew the answers. "Cadiz and Seville are such a long way away. What happens there surely has little to do with a small town in hills so far from the centre of conflict?" unwisely spoke the elders to comfort nervous villagers. They told them this had happened before in Asturias. It was brutal up there amongst the miners but nothing happened here. It was just words, frightening words no doubt, but words all the same with many of the reports grossly exaggerating. *How wrong the village elders were*, thought Juana. They should have listened to what Sebastián had told them after his visit to a town near Seville. The wise ignored Rodrigo also. He was sure that Santo Domingo would not escape the rebels' attention; he had picked up clues from the radio.

The generals had vowed to seek out all who opposed them leaving none declared as the enemy unscathed. So in came their foreign soldiers to do their bidding on that most horrible of nights. Pastora and Juana and other young mothers survived by hiding in the darkest places. The infirm, the brave and the foolish suffered the worst. Young lives were destroyed and many so needlessly taken. All of which had left Juana deeply depressed with no Rodrigo to share her concerns. Her life was now further threatened by a priest who should have brought spiritual comfort at this time of uncertainty but brought nothing but the fear of lascivious intent.

19

IN THE CHURCH

Spring 1937

It was a hot day; an extremely hot day but not unusual for this time of year. The fierce and penetrating heat from the sun nettled exposed skin. Her arms smarted from the radiant heat as she scuttled into the patched shade spread by the overhanging vines hanging from blistered buildings on the southern aspect of the plaza. Pilar, her neighbour, cared for Alicia as Juana made her way to the church where she sought solace and God's help in keeping Rodrigo safe.

The church was an unusually large and elaborate building for this small town but it settled comfortably and regally into the eastern slope of the plaza from where it dominated all other buildings. It was the quiet time; she needed to be alone to seek help and to ease the almost intolerable anxiety she suffered for her missing husband. Will it be this time she is granted spiritual support, she thought, and how will she know she has received His grace? Perhaps through her prayers she'll gain comfort, and does it matter whether she speaks to Him in Spanish or English? It matters not as long as Rodrigo comes home safely to her.

Ever since that horrible night when Rodrigo and his Republican colleagues had fled into the deep shadows of the forest her world had turned upside down. The blindly optimistic group, who believed they could save the poor from suffering further, scuttled through back doors and windows scattering like startled deer before the huntsmen. Where were they now? Had they regrouped, and would they ever drive the invaders back into the sea?

The school had closed and the mothers, who were once united in the interest of their children, had broken into factions that mirrored their husbands' political alliance. Her friends had dispersed. Light-hearted chats by the school entrance, jokes about their men folk, many bawdy in their nature, were a thing of the past and had to be abandoned in fear of reprisals. Eyes averted contact, new alliances formed, whispered words soft as the breeze but lethal as a hidden razor cut to bleed unwitting victims of any hope of peace. She tripped quietly across the uneven surface, fearful of being seen, then up the short-stepped pathway to the great and ancient door. It lay partly open; she squeezed through the space into the porch making sure the rusted hinges failed to announce her arrival. The cool and darkened air of the porch brought relief but an even cooler place lay beyond. Juana glanced briefly over the notices announcing times of the masses and the hand-scrawled news of the coup. The message was clear; God was on the side of the invaders, soon to be our masters. "The Jews, killers of Christ and the Reds' evil methods to bring the church and Spain to their knees are being defeated. Franco's liberating army of Africa will crush all who do not fully support the saving of our glorious country." Then it warned, "All the children of God must join the cause." She was confused; of course, she wanted God on her side and why would God need the Moroccan *Regulares* to do His work?

With immense care she pushed against the inner door and slipped into the vast space held secure by towering columns and a magical, arching roof of stone. Her eyes adjusted to the dimness bringing Christ and His saints' faces into focus as they emerged benevolently from the blackness where they had hung for centuries upon the internal walls. She relaxed a little but still her eyes nervously swept the pews and all corners of the great church. He was nowhere to be seen. However, she still moved with caution slipping into a space at the foot of a great column. Juana moved forwards in her seat seeking out a small cushion. She knelt, her shoulder resting against the cool stone of the huge support. She started to feel more comfortable, more at ease and the durability of the stone columns and the oaken pews seemed to guard her with benevolence. Perspiration cooled and she sighed; a small shiver rippled beneath her clothes. Her lips moved imperceptibly as she went through the ritual of her prayers. Once God had been praised for His great goodness she formed in her mind the impassioned words that pleaded for help. Was He listening to her as she whispered Rodrigo's name over and over again? It was a chant that took her deeper into her misery then lifted her in the belief that God was listening.

Within the darkness of the confessional Father Jaime strained to hear what she said. He fought the urge to call out to her that Rodrigo was dead whether it be the truth or not. He wanted to tell her that he loved her, he would care for her; *so give yourself to me*, he intoned. *The schoolmaster is gone; he is a fading shadow, a ghost with no part to play in the brightness of today.*

He had seen her coming from the opening in the great door as he moved to leave the church. He faltered and stopped, shuffling back into the deeper shadow to be hidden and secretly to watch. He was irrepressibly driven to look at her; tormented by an urge to let his eyes feed upon her graceful form. Forbidden fruit is all the sweeter for being tasted unobserved.

He had been about to go home but was delayed by the arrival of the latest news bulletin and as he pulled the great door open he had caught a movement in the far corner of the square. It was Juana. She had come up from the lower track that led back into the oak forest; the same one taken by the African soldiers in their attack on the village. She seemed to be hurrying to seek out the cooler parts of the square. He was convinced she was making her way to the church. His heart surged with pleasurable anticipation; of course she was coming to the church; no housecoat, the apron had been removed and the dress was one of her best. She most always wore that in the church and on sun-filled mornings he could make out the revealing form of her lovely legs shadowed behind the lightweight fabric of the skirt. But it was his secret, for his eyes only and he smiled in the comfort of such intimacy. There was little he did not know about her but there was so much more he needed to know. He watched as the light cotton dress moved with every step that she took. It swung evocatively as she made her way up the hill moving rhythmically with her hips. Father Jaime drew in a breath sharply as a gust of wind folded the delicate fabric against her thighs. Was this a sign? Had the demons that possessed him ever since her arrival hinted at what lay ahead? Should he demand of the demons, "Get thee behind me," and leave the church as he had planned; to travel home uncorrupted? He must not surrender to the weakness of the flesh and place his soul in jeopardy; God trusted him. He must not put at risk the promise of eternal life, it was his just reward, and yet this devil woman had turned his will to liquid. Sighing deeply and leaning forwards to relieve disturbing abdominal pains he shuffled backwards into church without thought to what was happening. He must not be seen, he must hide; never in his life had he experienced such feelings of indecision; was it panic? With the overwhelming guidance from God his life was sound and incorruptible, but now all that was good was corrupted. Was it the lean-limbed child in the arms of the Moroccan rapists that had turned his mind? No, surely not, it was this woman who tumbled his world; it was she who created this confusion and she was not just any woman, she was Eve.

Where to hide? Should he run to the enrobing room to the side of the great altar? No, from there he could not see her. This was a God-given opportunity, or maybe not; he did not know. Unable to think clearly, he found himself drawn into the deepest shadows seeking and finding security in the depths of the confessional. From here he could peer out on her unseen.

She pushed through the door and for that brief moment the light illuminated her delicate form. He watched, barely able to breathe, as she turned her head this way and that searching for anything that might disturb the solitude she so desperately sought. With due modesty Juana held on to the shawl that covered her head and shoulders pausing as she looked intuitively towards the confessional boxes. Father Jaime stopped breathing for those long seconds until she moved her gaze into the furthest corners of the building. That brief glimpse confirmed his state of mind; he was lost, nothing could save him from her. All that was held most dear to him was in jeopardy. His religion, beliefs, responsibilities and standing in the community were being eroded by desire for this temptress, this beautiful woman. There was no one to tie him to the mast and save him from the Siren. He could not lose himself in her and still be safe within the church.

He watched. Hair fell from beneath the shawl, a few strands trailing across a lovely face and he knew the large, anxious eyes sought him out in the darkness. She feared him. He knew now she was vulnerable and, in his madness, it empowered him. He watched as she knelt. Her soft whisperings provided him with the rhythms of prayers so confidently known to him and he followed every unheard word. She finished with the chants proclaiming adoration and seeking absolution then with a voice, broken with emotion, appealed for God's help to find Rodrigo or at the very least keep him safe. The priest could no longer bear the sound of the man's name; he needed to go to her, bring her comfort, release her from the bonds of this man and show her something more worthy of her attention.

He moved stealthily from the confessional but she picked up the smallest of sounds as the curtain fell back into place; she knew not what it was. Her consciousness alerted she sat back firmly into the pew as his last step sounded on the flagstones behind her. He was breathing heavily through open mouth and, unable to control his advance on her, blew softly on her slender neck lifting dampened hair from pallid cheek.

'Be at peace, child,' he whispered moving his hands beneath the shawl and placing them on the bareness of her shoulders.

She froze.

'Still, child, you are safe,' he breathed into her ear.

Every sinew strained within her frame holding her as if gripped by death; she was caught, held in the monster's grip. He moaned softly into her hair aware now of the moisture that lay as nectar upon her skin. Ecstasy was at his fingertips. With closed eyes enhancing the image, his fingers moved beneath the straps of the cotton dress and forwards and beyond, intimately to settle on the swelling beneath her throat.

Too much for Juana, she thrust her body forwards to the pew in front and turned in to face him with anger coldly kept at bay.

'No, Father, no,' she said emphatically. 'You are too close,' hissing both in fear and rage. 'Stay back and let me be.'

'You are alone, child, you need me; what can you do?'

Without a second's thought she threw herself over the forward pew moving behind the great stone column as if to hide. He could not see her and moved to his right to block her escape. Anticipating this she spun on her heel reversing the expected direction. He had failed; she was gone, running swiftly towards the great door and out into the blistering heat of the sun-drenched square. She flew down the path almost bowling Francisca Savater over as she carried flowers towards the cemetery. They gripped each other's arms and the tears in Juana's eyes told Francisca a story. She lifted her head looking towards the priest as he clung to the doorpost of the partly open door. The older woman transferred her disgust in a glance. Shame overwhelmed him as he turned away to hide once again in the darkness. He collapsed within the confessional box holding his head in his hands. 'Oh God, what have I done? Can you find it in Your heart to forgive me?' He stopped short in his prayers and lifted his moistened hands to his face, then pressed them close beneath his nose. Not all was lost; a reassuring sense of calm descended as he breathed deeply to inhale the sweetness of her scent. The images returned.

20

REPUBLICAN MILITIA

Early Spring 1937

On Miguel's advice they had established their base camp high up the mountain slope but still well covered by the forest. Many of the deciduous trees had given way to conifers but it was still possible to find pockets of mixed birch and ash providing more comfortable quarters than the barren needle-strewn spaces at the feet of pine trees. Miguel said that the higher altitude camp was a much safer place to be, away from foot or horse patrols, so to stop whinging about being cold and make the best of it. They set up their simple bivouacs on the windward side of a convenient rocky outcrop and covered the floor of their shelters with fine green branches cut from distant undergrowth, bracken and then copious amounts of leaves. They lay their under-blankets on top of the vegetation then wrapped themselves up with whatever they had to keep them warm at night but they were still cold, very cold.

'No doubt we're safe from the bullet or the bayonet, Miguel, but we're going to freeze to death up here and save them a job.'

Miguel smiled at the young man knowing he was half joking. 'Look, you're sleeping in pairs. Think of your partner as someone special who loves you. Cuddle up and you'll keep each other warm.'

Rodrigo laughed as he picked up scraps of the ensuing conversations. 'You're not getting into my bed until you've cleaned your teeth, you hairy bastard.'

'No, and you're not coming anywhere near me unless you're handcuffed. I can't risk you dreaming I'm that luscious sweet-smelling one Miguel talks about.'

Despite the horrific events of the recent past and the desperate situation they found themselves in today, Rodrigo and Miguel had managed to keep their spirits in good order. Because of the low temperatures at this altitude it was normal to take to their beds after eating; it was the only way to keep warm. Having a fire to bring an element of comfort under such difficult conditions and to keep the coffee hot was out of the question as it would only draw attention to their presence. Planning the next day's events had to be done as quietly as possible whilst wrapped up in the relative comfort of their bedding. The diminishing warmth from a setting sun gave way to the bitterness of the bone-chilling winds that swept down from icy peaks. The knuckles of the Sierra de Gredos catching the last rays of the departed sun shone cruelly pink in the glacial blue sky of advancing night; beautiful it may be but it was brutally cold. In breathy whispers the planned action was explained whilst frozen fingers drew into the dusty ground mapping the route to be taken. Aspirational plans of counteraction masked despair of yesteryear and unkindly hope perpetuated self-deception. Deep in their hearts they recognised their limitations; courage was not enough but they had very little else. The rebels had the upper hand. They had more troops and despite them being foreigners, as much Spanish weaponry as they could wish for. What went against those who were loyal to the state and the democratically elected government was their inability to organise any effective resistance. Republican leaders refused at first to arm their loyal subjects, and this critical inaction would bring about the death of half a million of their subjects. The mainland Spanish army had been decimated by the actions of the controlling generals, many now enemies to the state, and what was left for the most part was brave principled junior officers and inexperienced soldiers. They were not short on passion to defend their land but without the means to do it. Small breakaway groups of local Republicans formed militias, of which Rodrigo's group was one, and they adopted as their duty action that would disrupt the advance of the invaders through guerrilla action.

This cadre of loyalists consisted of seven combatants and two boys no more than fourteen years old. They looked up to Rodrigo to make them effective soldiers and keep them safe. He had been their schoolmaster in Santo Domingo in the hills beyond Béjar and had some experience in soldiering but had learnt much about intelligence-gathering as a conscript. He relied on the military experience of Miguel. As a teacher he had always preached pacifism to his students telling them that all problems could be solved by intelligent discussion. But his world had been turned upside down and his ideals crushed by the messages received over the precious radio; a present given by English friends to him and Juana on their wedding day some years ago. It had saved his life. The reception was never perfect but by leaning close to the radio and cupping their ears they could pick up most of what was being broadcast.

What had shaken Rodrigo and other militia commanders was the speed at which the rebels moved.

The landing of the African corps in Cadiz by battleship and the rebels being flown into Seville did not feature strongly in the Nationalists' propaganda campaign, or maybe Rodrigo had just missed it. The credibility of the rebels swift mastery of all that southern Andalusian coast, at first, was treated as an unbelievable fantasy. There had been other attempts before; all had failed. The Republican government had put down earlier efforts at a military coup but sadly ineffectively. Some of the main players they put in jail, others the government demoted, and some quite influential senior officers were posted overseas to get them out of the way. For them it could not have been a better move. There they enjoyed the company of other eminent like-minded thinkers; a treacherous group.

When the radio stations in southern Andalucía had surrendered to the rebel army the normal programmes were quickly replaced by military music and the wild exaggerations by General Queipo de Llano. The boasting of this man was extreme, spreading raw fear amongst the common people and causing some to succumb to the rebel cause with sullen acquiescence. Others, foolishly brave, were determined to stand alongside those who had no future. Men like Rodrigo who had vocally supported the reforms that went against the interests of the wealthy knew they must flee. They would be on the death list. What choice did he have? He hated leaving Juana and his beloved daughter, Alicia.

Tomorrow's plan was ambitious: it was expected that the Nationalist's column, that caused so much destruction locally, was moving north to start another offensive elsewhere. Senior officers would be travelling under the escort of the main body of troops. Rodrigo had received the information via the local network. An excited Miguel jumped at the opportunity, determined to do the bastards some real harm. 'Assassinate the officers on the road when they're supposed to be guarded by the whole force.' Miguel's enthusiasm bubbled over affecting all the men who growled their approval. 'That'll be a kick in the teeth for them.' It was a dangerous plan, against all the odds and without the cover of darkness to make certain escape.

Moroccans never liked to travel in the dark for fear of ambush; they preferred to subdue a village in the fading light of day, steal what might be useful to them back in Africa and sate their basic needs. Quite a lot of good stuff could be found in the so-called wealthy villages to be sent back home to the delight of their expectant families; but it was the fun of rooting out the women from their hiding places that was the driving force. The Spanish generals said they could take the women of "infidels" as reward for their triumphs, but for certain none of their adventures would be shared with those who awaited their return.

Taking Miguel with him, Rodrigo turned back to remind those who stayed behind what they had discussed. They were to wait until his return and remember that if danger threatened simply to retreat and hide. 'This is the action of an intelligent militia and that is what we are,' Rodrigo insisted. 'Take on the enemy on our terms and only when we have the certainty of a safe retreat.' Miguel and he knew that their planned action was going to break this basic rule but they had no choice. His last words were directed at the young men. 'You two are to keep yourselves safe, listen to your seniors and obey what they say; you are our future.' Unknown to Rodrigo at that time, their future as young Republicans was very bleak.

They left the lower slopes of the forest by a known path. It had already been cleared of obstacles so they could move at night without drawing attention to themselves. Light lingered in the atmosphere illuminating the top branches of the alder and beech guiding them down towards the chestnuts growing on the fringes of that land cultivated by man. The domain of the wild beast was left behind and that of the free-running black-footed pigs was to the fore. The tangle of competing trees and safety of the higher slopes were now left behind. But Rodrigo knew his men would be safe if they stayed in that place; a place no horseman could hope to ride.

21

THE AMBUSH

Early Spring 1937

Both men had lain hidden within the fringes of the forest until the evening's full moon had lost its revealing intensity. So bright was the night that the risk of being observed became too great when crossing the open ground that took them to the foot of the rocky outcrop. They were behind the schedule they had set for themselves and now must make up for lost time. They didn't feel the tiredness generated by previous actions as the chilled air kept them alert and the importance of tomorrow's engagement kept them keenly focussed. It was designed to have a real impact upon the enemy's morale. This, they hoped, would make the invaders reassess the belief they were invincible. Although quietly confident they would succeed, fear for their chances of escape was real. Rodrigo turned and looked back to judge how far they had come and noted how dark and featureless the mountain had become as morning broke in distant places enfeebling the blackness of the night. It was time to go and use the lengthening shadows to hide their intentions. They had heard the sounds of the forest, most of which, by their normality, eased their anxiety. They were tuned into the sweet persistence of a nightingale and the contented mellowness of owls but not all brought comfort. Black pigs still scuffled in the undergrowth as they did throughout the day following their leader as they bulldozed on cloven feet down past the hidden men to gorge upon the scattered acorns. Such sounds drew their attention as did the unsettling death call of hunted prey, a hare or snared rabbit.

Howsoever, it was the soft snort of a horse and metallic sound of bridles that struck fear into the hiding men's hearts. How far away were the horsemen and what was their purpose? Minds were racing as they discussed their options in low tones. Sound travels great distances at night, so hopefully not much to fear at present, but it warned them to be cautious. Rodrigo was puzzled for this was strange; mounted huntsmen do not risk the cover of darkness where the assassin can wait unseen and unheard. It is they that are at a greater risk than those they seek. It is not possible to hunt stealthily on horse and certainly not at night which demands cautious movement and fear of broken legs. Everything is different in the brightness of the day when the noise and pounding hooves strike fear into the fleeing prey. Rodrigo could feel the apprehension building and a look towards Miguel told him he suffered too. Were they the prey and were the volunteer police here to run them down? Rodrigo knew these men; the private army of the masters, made up of poor men who had sold their loyalty to the rich and led by the arrogant, merciless sons of the great estates comfortable astride nimble-footed polo ponies.

'The sounds are above us, Rodrigo. We must ease away from them to further down the slope.'

'Lead the way, Miguel, you know this terrain better than I do; I suggest we move obliquely to that cluster of young holm oaks.'

'Exactly my intention, boss. Try and keep close together; we must move as one now. Two movements flitting amongst the trees attracts the eye more easily but we might get away with it by moving as one.'

'Lead on, soldier. I'll hang onto your jacket but move slowly; much better than a quick movement which is also easier to pick up. I'm ready when you are.'

They scuttled together through the widely spread chestnuts towards the safety of dense shadows and lower foliage of the young holm oaks. The run left them breathless more as a result of the prospects of being pursued by the horsemen than the difficult posture they were compelled to use.

They paused beneath the young oaks and lowered themselves upon the pig-churned ground scattered with small acorns and struggled for breath. Rodrigo put his finger to his lips indicating to Miguel not to say a word. Miguel put out his hand and touched Rodrigo's shoulder then pointed up the hill. They were no distance from the edge of the natural forest which they could see easily in the paleness of the moonlit night and there, as they watched, came a group of horsemen guiding their beasts into the shadows cast by the trees. Each man turned his horse to face down the slope then backed up to place themselves further into the forest. They were difficult to see now and only someone who knew they were there could pick them out. With his finger still pressed firmly to his lips Rodrigo indicated they needed to go and go soon. Miguel, eyes wide with concern, nodded his head then rolled to lie on his stomach ready to crawl. He was about to set off but turned back and indicated to Rodrigo to leave a goodly space between them before he moved. Running together was not the action to take now; everything had changed. They slithered, well spaced for safety's sake, like serpents towards an outcrop of rocks that marked the edge of a steep falling away of the hillside. They were now hidden from the sight of the huntsmen. On they moved as quickly as the ground would allow them, regularly checking their position against that of the enemy. The dense foliage of the holm oaks and chestnuts hid them for a great part of the journey as they moved towards the prearranged observation point; but the last part across the open ground gave no cover at all. The sky was brightening so no time could be lost as they took a chance and sprinted towards the higher ground. It was a steep climb to the top and they concentrated solely on the task in hand. The first part was relatively straightforward, following a well-used goat track but soon it became a serious climb. Miguel carried the rifle across his shoulders and climbed easily and fluidly up the almost vertical rock face. Rodrigo watched him and carefully followed the hand and footholds that Miguel took but without the grace of a well-practised climber. On reaching the top they made sure they did not present a profile as the sky had brightened and their silhouette would have been easily seen. It was essential that their presence was not known. Amongst the rocks, pockets of soil accommodated tall bushes and scrub-like trees giving the men sufficient cover in which to hide. Both rested for a while enjoying the relief of not being found. Rodrigo got up onto his knees not wishing to use up any more time resting as the urgency of the task in hand gripped him. 'Miguel, stay here and keep a lookout off to the south and west; if the rebels intend to travel north the road below is the only route they can take.'

'Bloody obvious, boss, easy targets for us, fish in a barrel, don't you think?'

Rodrigo smiled and sighed at the directness of his colleague. 'You know best, Miguel. Anyway, I'm going to see if anything is happening towards the east and more importantly I'm going to find out what those horsemen are up to.'

'OK, but take care, this is an obvious observation spot those horsey-bastards would love to use; great place to pick out refugees. Anyway, the easy way up is from the roadside; hope the horsemen don't know that.'

Rodrigo pushed through the bushes and cautiously moved back towards the cliff edge recently climbed. He slipped his pack off his shoulders and took out the telescope. This also was one of his most treasured possessions, a wedding present received when he married Juana in Burgos. How important it had been since the escape from Santo Domingo all those months ago. The sun was now climbing beyond the Gredos peaks and lighting the lower slopes of the sierra. Rodrigo polished the lenses and slid the sleeves apart. It would be difficult to pick out the enemy hidden in the shadows of the forest, but he had a good idea in which part they had secreted themselves. Lying on his front he rested his elbows firmly on the ground and putting the extended telescope to his eye he adjusted the focus. Even though the forest edge was in shadow he was surprised how much detail he could pick out. He scanned the border of the forest in the area he had seen the cavalry enter and within a short time he could make out the shape of a couple of horses but only because they had been allowed to shake their manes.

It puzzled Rodrigo why this group of predators had come to hide themselves in this remote spot. What could they possibly wish to gain? There was no forest track that might be used by the opposition and, more extraordinary, this group of hotheads had never been known to show such patience. They were opportunist aggressors. It did not take long before the reason for their patience became obvious. Two women had moved into an open space below the forest and away to their left. They demonstrated clear signs of anxiety; creeping forwards with carefully placed feet. They kept together, stopping frequently and looking intensely into the surrounding trees; they stopped and leant towards each other and whispered with cupped hands to discuss what they had seen. He could see from their body language that they had reached a conclusion. They then walked less furtively back into the forest. Rodrigo hoped they would stay there believing there was danger afoot and not move in this direction again today. He kept the telescope focussed on the area where the women had re-entered the forest. He waited, hoping the women folk would not return and just when he had relaxed in the belief they had gone somewhere else he caught sight of small movements. A group of children came forwards one or two steps into the relatively open space beneath great chestnut trees. They were joined by a collection of adults; the majority were young women but scattered amongst them were elderly men and women quite a few of whom leant on poles or walking sticks. To Rodrigo the women appeared to be young mothers who moved amongst the group ensuring hands were held and that the children kept close together not allowing stragglers to be left behind. It then dawned on Rodrigo that these poor folk must be refugees from the village that had been attacked last night; escapees who had been able to retreat into the forest before the rebels had completed their search. He counted them quickly noting there were about ten, maybe twelve children, definitely four or more elderly men and women of a similar age escorted by five or six young women, probably wives of lost men, he thought. They were moving steadily down the slope but keeping fairly close to the lower forest edge walking in the shadows but the early morning sun brightened the day and no one could fail to see them. Rodrigo vainly hoped the horsemen would overlook them; maybe they had more worthy opposition to wait for. In his heart he knew this was not the case.

He turned back towards where the cavalry was hidden. They had not come out into the open but he could see movement within the forest; hands tightened straps and adjusted their grip on home-crafted clubs. He could not make out any firearms but he knew for certain that their leaders would carry, at the very least, shotguns. Sons of the wealthy landowners would not be short of weaponry.

As he continued to watch them through his telescope he picked up signs that they might be ready to move forwards. An elegant young man with oiled black hair swept neatly over his head from brow to nape sat tall in the saddle with legs outstretched into the stirrups; he swept the ends of the poncho that had kept him warm for most of the night over both shoulders and with a wave of his right hand holding a pistol signalled his men to move forwards.

Rodrigo involuntarily called out a warning to the distant group. He sprang to his feet and jumping up and down and waving his arms vigorously to draw the attention of the women he screamed as loudly as his lungs would allow. All to no avail as no sound against the wind could carry towards them. The sad little body of people tottered on down the hillside unaware of the imminence of the danger. Miguel arrived spitting in anger his annoyance at the attention Rodrigo had created with his noise. Rodrigo gripped Miguel's arm fiercely and pointed towards the escaping group. 'What can we do?'

Miguel loaded a round into the chamber of his rifle. 'This will be a long shot but with God on our side we might make a difference.'

'Hold your fire, Miguel; if you look across to our left you can see they are not in a hurry.' Rodrigo pointed out the static line of horses just clear of the forest. 'They will make their move soon but the closer they come to us the better the chance we have to bring one or two of them down.'

'OK, boss, good point. So when do you think they will make their charge?'

'Look down below the children,' said Rodrigo pointing with his telescope. 'Do you see, a marshy area with tussocks of reeds and below, water in muddy pools?'

'Difficult for me to see as I don't have a telescope but I can see the ground is all cut up; that will be hard for little legs to manoeuvre.' Miguel continued to look. 'Yes, I see, that means they will have to turn right away from the marshy bit and sadly any hope of escape into the forest.' The awful truth dawned on him. 'That will be the time when the volunteer police will attack, when they can hit them side on; the children will have no chance.'

'Exactly, but that does us two favours. One, they will be closer and two, if the horses pass the children they will find themselves in the marshy land, very difficult for horses; they will be slower in turning about and may even unseat one or two of the cowardly bastards. That's the time when your skill as a marksman will be called into action.'

'OK, boss, let's be patient then; you know me, I can't wait to get those shitehawks in my sights.'

Both men moved urgently settling Miguel into a position set for action. They used Rodrigo's pack as a support for the barrel and packed whatever clothing they could under Miguel's arms and chest to stabilise him on the uneven rock face.

Rodrigo kept an eye on both parties. It would not be long now as the first of the children had reached the marshy area and waited for the others to catch up. The horsemen walked their horses in line down the slope but were still unseen by the escapees who were now concentrating on not getting the children wet. The children and their escorts had wheeled to their right and once again set off in a column moving steadily across the field. Rodrigo thought they were moving painfully slowly but realised that some of the old men were having real trouble in keeping up with the children. It was such an easy target for a cavalry attack and there was little he and his colleague could do about it.

The horsemen had now cleared the area of holm oaks and must be visible to all, thought Rodrigo; surely someone would see them. With that, a scream went up from one of the women as she turned towards the men. They charged, sweeping down the slope and in a flash bowled over any in their way breaking through the children's line. The women called the children towards them as the old men feebly struck at the passing horsemen. A swinging blow struck an elderly man across his shoulders and knocked him to the ground; a following horseman pulled up beside him and as the old man struggled to get to his feet the sadist walked his horse forwards to trample him back into the ground.

It was then that Miguel fired his first shot. The horseman had spent too much time in the same area unaware of any danger as the bullet struck him high on the shoulder passing through the bulk of the muscle close to the neck. He was hurt but thought someone had hit him with a heavy stick; he wheeled his horse to look behind. There was no one there except, to his right, two women holding on to a terrified group of wailing children. Anger surged through his body and he drove his beast at them; the women pushed the children out of immediate danger but were struck down by the horse with one falling dangerously under its feet. Nobody had heard Miguel's first shot as the noise of the children screaming and snorting of horses drowned all others. It was the visible effect of the second shot that drew the attention of those close by. As the man turned his horse to make a second run at the women, he paused again for far too long. He smiled at the terrified faces, enjoying the horror he raised amongst the innocent, and with club raised above his head spurred his horse forwards. The second bullet took him in the face and blew away the back of his head. The horse swerved to the right into the waterlogged ground and stopped abruptly depositing the remains of his master amongst the reeds. It was apparent to Miguel and Rodrigo that only some of the women and children had been aware of what had happened. All other attackers were too busy with trying to haul young women onto their saddles to notice; others beat the old men to the ground as they attempted to save their daughters' lives.

Miguel turned his attention to those who were wrestling with the struggling young women. He had no clear shot as the horsemen were surrounded by the children who not only held on to their mothers but beat at the horses with the sticks dropped by the defeated elderly. The horsemen's heads were above those on the ground but the slope of the hill and the angle from which Miguel fired, placed children in danger of being hit.

One of the horsemen broke free from the melee and after a short gallop up the hillside turned and raising his shotgun fired one of the barrels into the air. Action was brought to a halt and all faces turned towards him. Rodrigo and Miguel could hear him shouting as he reloaded the discharged barrel but they could not catch what he was saying. The women withdrew from the proximity of the horses pulling the children with them and they stood in two small groups.

Rodrigo and Miguel discussed in whispers what was about to happen next. There was no purpose to be served by drawing attention to their position if the immediate danger to the women and children had ceased. Miguel reloaded and was ready for anything but Rodrigo looked sharply at him fearing his friend was about to throw caution to the wind. Putting his hand on his shoulder he asked him to wait. 'We're going to be needed again, no doubt, and let us make the best of the opportunity we've got next.' Miguel nodded but was still boiling with anger. 'Be ready but let's hope we're not needed: I doubt it because the bastards have not yet noticed one man's missing.'

A sudden increase in the weeping from the children and women drew the snipers' attention back to the drama immediately below. The man with the shotgun had started to shout again and his comrades aside him were whooping and laughing. The women had appeared to have responded to some shouted instructions and had moved up the slope towards the men. They held on to each other and one or two tried to move even further towards the horsemen but were being resisted by others from doing so. Suddenly one of the women broke free from her friend's hold and turned to face her group of friends. She spoke. Some of the women were clearly upset by what she had said, hiding their faces in their hands; others stepped forwards and tried to get hold of the solitary woman and pull her back into line but to no avail. She called out to the children and old men who looked confused but slowly responded to what she had said. The old men went along the line making sure the children turned away and looked down the hillside. The most vocal young woman, who seemed to have had the role of leader thrust upon her, turned back to the horseman and called out angrily towards him. He answered and she shook her head vigorously refusing to do what he wanted her to do. He called again to her and in so doing waved his arms towards the children; she turned, calling out to them. With that, the children, guided by limping old men, turned right and started to move as swiftly as possible across the open space before a left turn down towards the road.

The women's leader spoke emphatically to her colleagues and Rodrigo noticed there was much disagreement, with some of the women collapsing to the ground. One young woman was screaming in her face hysterically and pulling at her clothes; their leader slapped her and spoke firmly to her through her tears. Rodrigo did not like what was going on; these young wives, or maybe they were widows already, were being forced to do something against their will, it was obvious.

Miguel was restless and kept muttering under his breath; he was itching to kill again but Rodrigo held his arm to prevent him carrying out his wishes prematurely. 'I am certain I know what is going to happen, but if you fire now they will use their horses to escape us.'

'I've got such a clear shot at that snotty rich boy; when he's gone the others will make a run for it.'

'Right, but let as many as possible dismount; you'll be able to pick them off as ducks later as the noise of your first shot will scatter the horses.'

The two men watched as the first young woman undid her dress and then stepped out of it, and then she removed her shift and stood facing the men with her head held high. 'And the rest of your bitches,' called out the leader. His cruel laughter was joined by whoops of approval from the others.

She turned towards her weeping friends but focussed on the disappearing children. It was eerily silent and Miguel heard what she said to her friends. 'Our children are not safe yet, do what they have demanded; the longer we delay these monsters about their foul business the better chance for them to escape.' She then went along the line comforting the most terrified as they removed their clothing. Suddenly one young woman broke away from the group running for the forest. The leader fired. The shotgun pellets struck her in the lower back dropping her heavily to the ground. Her inertia carried her forwards and she rolled into the swamp. The others, in horror and silence, stripped away their clothing to stand awkwardly hiding behind their hands as the men dismounted. All that could be heard was their whimpering and the soft moans of the wounded girl as she lay bleeding amongst the reeds.

'Now, Miguel, get the bastard now.' With that, Miguel fired and struck their leader in the throat. He went down instantly, blood splashing on those who had been standing beside him. The men turned and foolishly raced back to their mounts but they had gone, spooked by the crack of the rifle. A second man went down hit between the shoulder blades as he scuttled vainly towards the trees. The women started screaming and running towards the safety of the rocks but Miguel was not distracted. Firing with precision he dropped a further two men. The remaining unhorsed men had scuttled off to hide in the folds of the land with some sprinting for the forest. Those hidden in the fold of the land were unlikely to cause more trouble because unknown to them Miguel still had sight of their bodies as they lay thinking they were safe. Buttocks made an appealing target. Miguel chuckled to himself as he fired and Rodrigo looked quizzically at him. 'Got the cowardly bastards in the arse, boss. Won't be riding any horses in the near future; I guarantee.'

The women had now realised that their saviours were on the top of the rock and they called up to them to help. Rodrigo spoke with Miguel. 'I'll go down and help them organise themselves and send them on their way. They must catch up with their children. But first, I must see to the young lady who's been shot; I've got first aid stuff in my pack.'

Rodrigo knew the almost vertical slope they had scaled earlier would take him too long to descend despite it leading directly to the distressed women who crowded in under the cover of the rocks. 'I'm taking the easy way down, Miguel, over the front slope leading to the road then I'll cut back and find them on this side.' He climbed to his feet, instinctively keeping his head down so his profile could not be seen above the foliage. 'Keep your eyes skinned, Miguel, the escapees may reinforce and make their way back.'

'I doubt it, boss, their paymaster's dead; no point in working for nothing.'

'Good point but keep a sharp look out when I'm gone.' It was then that Miguel stood and walked towards Rodrigo asking him to wait. Not a word was spoken as the men clung to each other for a brief moment. They were aware of the fragility of their situation. He then left. Rodrigo pushed through the bushes on the reverse slope and was about to run swiftly down the hill when he noticed a small dust cloud on the distant road. It took him a microsecond to realise this could be the main force of Nationalists in a motorised convoy making their way towards the north. He watched for a moment trying to confirm his assumption.

Once off the exposed slope he stopped and focussed the telescope on the advancing vehicles. There was no doubt about it; leading the convoy was a limousine and he could see clearly through the side windows men in uniform with enough gold braid to indicate seniority. He was reminded that this was the reason they had come here and their targets were less than three or four minutes away. The women and the children had compromised their objective but it was just as well they had been here to save them.

He called the women to gather around him. 'First, if you haven't collected up all of your clothes do so now.' No one moved. 'OK, you're going to leave here very soon, that is in the next minute, because the enemy is driving up the road behind us.' One or two of the women started weeping, calling out, 'What about the children?'. Rodrigo had to be firm. 'Stop this noise; we have no time for discussion. Get together in pairs and stay together in pairs, because two brains are always better than one.' Suddenly a shot rang out and everybody froze. 'That was Miguel from up there,' said Rodrigo pointing up to the top of the hill. 'He is slowing them up; they must be very close. Now, you lot, make your way following the marshy ground up to where it turns into a river. Once you get there check you are still in the shadow of the hill. That's very important.'

The tall young woman who had taken on the role of leader when they were forced to remove their clothes stepped forwards. 'My name is Maria, what is your name?' she demanded emphatically.

'Rodrigo,' he replied wondering why she should want to know.

'I know of you, Rodrigo, the schoolteacher from Santo Domingo. You are a brave and honourable man. We thank you and will never forget you.' Rodrigo tried to reply but she held up her hand to stop him. 'I see you have no weapon and your friend has only his rifle and you are going to fight over 200 men. I think you had better have this.' She passed to him the shotgun and a handful of cartridges. Rodrigo tried to speak again but once more she stopped him, pre-empting his next action. 'It is too late; you cannot help her. Our dear little Ali is dead and we have made sure they will never find her.'

'Go then, time is running out,' said Rodrigo as Miguel fired another shot. 'Last word of advice, always look ahead, pick the next hiding place ahead of you before you move and make for that each time; get into the forest as soon as you can.' They left at a crouched run following the watercourse as a third shot rang out. Their first target was the broadening of the reed bed where the water lay in shallow pools before emptying into the softly flowing waters of the infant river. It was less than a hundred metres distance but they ran with a renewed energy; less than halfway there the sounds of intensive gunfire drove them even more fiercely to the relative safety of the densely packed reed bed.

The enemy had wisely split into two groups each advancing up the roadside slope from widely set angles giving Miguel real difficulty keeping them locked in at the bottom of the hill. One group would advance whilst the other gave covering fire. This required Miguel to sweep across his field of fire from one extreme angle to another. Each time he had to move his body across the ground to get comfortably behind the rifle butt and ensure a half decent shot. He had taken down five men already but they were closing in on him and it wouldn't be long before they made the final charge.

Rodrigo waited anxiously for the troops to advance on his position; they seemed to be ignoring him or maybe they didn't know he was here. He could hear Miguel firing and he picked out the different sound of the returning fire. The enemy fire was intensive but it didn't mean they were any closer to Miguel than they were at the commencement of the attack. The longer Miguel kept firing the more hopeful Rodrigo became but he knew it was vain hope.

He heard them before he saw them and it became obvious to him that they were unaware of his presence. They were concentrating on the steep slope that he and Miguel had scaled at the beginning of the venture. He watched them closely as they started their climb and now Rodrigo understood they intended to attack Miguel from the rear. He had a dilemma; should he fire at the climbers or save his limited ammunition for the ones that stayed behind and threatened him most? He could do both, take out the ones below first then concentrate on the climbers.

He waited until the small group of climbers had scaled to a dangerous height and were awkwardly placed to return fire. This was the time; he stood up unseen by those encouraging the climbers. He was no further than ten metres from the group and with his first shot aimed at the three clustered at the base of the climb. The buckshot spread only a little and was concentrated enough to cause severe injury. The men fell writhing on the ground and trying to reach their weapons which had fallen from their hands. Rodrigo only had three cartridges left but knew Miguel must be given the best chance. The climbers were moving as fast as possible away from danger but not fast enough as Rodrigo's second shot struck both men. One hung desperately to the rock face, clearly not critically injured, as the other soldier fell heavily amongst the wounded below. Rodrigo moved quickly back behind his defensive rocks as he picked up the voices of the enemy reinforcements; it had not taken them as long as he had expected to gather their force together. He waited for the worst to happen; they would come at him from both sides. He looked back over his shoulder as the second group advanced noting it would pass closely to the women's first hiding place. He could not see them but imagined the light might not be reflecting off the pools of water but from the fabric of light-coloured dresses. In his sadness he realised that Miguel and himself could not be saved but he gained comfort from knowing the women and their children would survive the day.

They fired on his position without real hope of hitting him; it was more an action to keep his head down whilst the others advanced from the rear. He knew he had to move so he took them by surprise as he sprinted to a new position; they fired to no avail. No sooner was Rodrigo in position he stood and fired into a group of newly exposed enemy soldiers. Bullets flew past his head and one nicked his left arm; he hadn't felt it at the time but it was starting to hurt now. He wrapped his handkerchief about the wound and chuckled to himself at such a pointless action.

There was a yell from above him and the men below called back. Rodrigo did not understand what was said as they spoke some North African dialect or was it Arabic? The meaning was obvious when they hurled Miguel's body from the cliff top to land heavily not more than two metres from Rodrigo's new position. For a moment he just stared at his friend's bloodied corpse. Overwhelming sadness gripped him. He was surrounded and he didn't care. He'd had enough of killing; they could do what they liked. In his grief he looked again at his dear friend and with a sharp intake of breath he noticed in horror that Miguel's nose had been sliced from his face; he felt a surge of anger that became incandescent when he noticed his ears also had been cut away. In an explosion of rage, screaming obscenities he had never uttered before, he stood and charged the concealed men. They were advancing on him from the rear now but he didn't care; he fired his last shot at those who advanced from the side then threw the gun away. His left arm was useless but he had drawn his hunting knife with his right and was determined to do some damage. All his hopes evaporated in the briefest of seconds as he ran onto the bayonet of one who emerged quietly from behind a tree. Others who were closing on him from behind ran in their bayonets through the small of his back. They pierced his kidneys, his intestines and everywhere else about his waist and the others joined the humiliating laughter. Light faded as the pain intensified. Pierced by their steel he was lifted off the ground enough for them to move him into the open space where all could see. Even Maria from amongst the reeds in the pain of her despair witnessed his suffering. Rodrigo died to the sound of the Moroccans' laughter as he struggled to breathe. Images of his beautiful Juana and Alicia brought fragile comfort and with his last breath the vision crumbled into the vortex of rapidly failing light.

22

CARE HOME

Early Summer 2008

She managed to get him into the car and sitting comfortably. It had been difficult, partly because of his disability but more particularly it was his height. He was an unusually tall man when compared to the rest of the community in which he had grown up. He had told Natascha that his father was a big man, too; his grandmother had come from Galicia and had met and married a Dutch sailor from a trawler which regularly called into Vigo. The great majority of the people, who had lived all their lives here, in this community tended to be small in stature, lean and tough. This was a toughness based on the resilience of the sinews rather than muscular bulk; these folk were members of a breed who made a virtue of hardship. They relished the challenge of a demanding life and their environment prepared them well for the future. The town, following the river, was built above the winter floodplain on the outside of each of the sweeping bends; the first to the right with the second to the left, leaving the alluvial soils deposited on the inside of each bend rich in minerals and ideal for the growing of crops. This area of well-ordered vegetables growing in neat rows and fruit and nut trees, was the domain of the women. It was they who tilled the small and valuable plots which were one of the essentials of life in this rural community, particularly during hard times, and there were plenty of those. The women lovingly tended, watered and harvested the seasonal crops. They gathered in the roots, seeds, plump fruit from the trees and leaves that spiced and balanced the diet of butchered flesh harvested by the men as was their due. This quota, pathetic as it may have been, was from the animals they managed, grazing the higher slopes, and this distribution of cuts of meat was overseen by the meanest of managers who had the right to claim what remained. However, this was supplemented unofficially by the wild creatures hunted in the shadows of the dense forest despite the best efforts to prevent poaching. Living here in such a steep-sided river valley ensured good exercise, indeed extreme exercise. Men laboured in the forests, not only coping with the density and weight of the felled timber, but they were also required to haul it up the steepest of slopes. Those tending the livestock may well have had even more difficult terrain in which to work as they kept safe the cloven-hoofed animals in high pastures. Demanding it might have been but as a consequence they became tough and hardened workers. Most died in harness having given no attention to the persistent aches and pains whereas in other communities such ailments would have set the alarm bells ringing. These were the consequences of unremitting work and a body enfeebled by age. The general attitude was "So what? We all die in the long run and hopefully move on to a better place, leaving the aches and pains, including life's disappointments, behind".

Those of a certain age having survived a shameful period in Spanish history try to shake the horrid memories from their consciousness. They are still haunted by the events that shamed their youth. Mindless acts of savagery and blooded imagery relentlessly disturb their sleep, and throughout the rest of their lives the guilty live fractiously unable to undo their dreadful deeds but as they approach their final days comes hope. A promise of relief from the consequences of their crimes will be fulfilled, the priest would see to that.

It had taken Natascha three visits to win Bartolomé's confidence. Most of the other elderly men and women were cautious in their responses to her enquiries and she did not feel it fair to press old folk too firmly about a time which, it was becoming apparent, was too painful to remember. There was a tangible resistance from the care staff to admit to anything that happened such a long time ago. This she could understand; after all, there was a degree of confidentiality that came with such work. Had she not met up with a cleaner, who had been struggling with buckets and a collection of mops and brooms at the end of her shift and who had accepted her offer of help, she might well have concluded there was nothing further to be gained by more visits. Bartolomé liked her and seemed to welcome her attention but he would never respond to questions about the past.

"I can't really remember that far back" was the often-said response. "You know, I was quite young then and didn't really take much notice."

This was very unlikely. What was rumoured to have happened was so awful that Natascha felt it was impossible to forget, whatever age he happened to be at the time. She believed she knew his real age because she had bought him a present on one of her visits after he had hinted it would be his birthday this time next week and she made a connection with this and what she had learnt from the care staff. She was convinced he did know something from his early years but felt she would never get past his reluctance to speak about it.

As Natascha helped the cleaner to wash out the buckets and rinse through the mops in the sluice room the lady felt obliged to show a little friendliness asking her directly what she was looking for. Natascha replied she wanted to know what had happened to her grandmother's godmother who had lived nearby with husband Rodrigo and daughter Alicia.

'I happen to be down here as part of my university course to improve my Spanish,' Natascha explained. 'You see, my grandmother, being very elderly, wanted to tie up a few loose ends. You know, she really loved Señora Juana. She was my grandmother's godmother who was really close but behaved more

like a friend; she was caring, generous and kind. Mamie just wants to know what happened to her.'

'Look, I'm not from around here, I'm from a place closer to Salamanca,' she said excusing herself from helping Natascha with her enquiries, 'but I can tell you people don't like to bring up what happened during the war and worse, what happened afterwards. Actually, nobody likes to talk about it in any part of Spain.'

'I know, I've gathered that already. My grandmother's quite an old lady now and all she wants to know is whether her godmother Joan lived out her life normally after the war or whether she was just another victim,' she said, doing her best to explain the reasons for her enquiries.

The cleaner looked at her in surprise. 'Oh, she was a victim all right if she had the name Juana; I've heard people speak about her with the old man who has bad dreams; you know, the noisy one,' the cleaner remarked with some feeling. 'You know, old Bartolomé, the fat one, who can't walk properly? Well, he saw what happened; apparently it was horrible and left a lot of people terribly upset.'

'Bartolomé is not fat, he's just big; maybe a little fat.' Natascha did her best to side with Bartolomé but was visibly shaken by implications of the cleaner's casual comment. Did some murderous action take place? She needed to know more.

'Do you know, it still upsets him?' continued the cleaner oblivious of the impact her words had on Natascha. 'He has horrible dreams.'

'What do you know?' she asked.

'Well, not much to be honest, it's only from what others have told me. He used to make such a noise, I asked the nurses what was wrong with him and that's when they explained it to me.'

'Why won't he talk to me? You would have thought old folk would want us to know.'

'Oh no, they don't; some of them don't, anyway. From what I've gathered a few of those sweet old darlings, butter wouldn't melt, were really horrible way back then.'

'What about Bartolomé when all this was going on; was he also horrible?' enquired Natascha.

'Oh him, I don't think so, he was too young then. Don't be deceived by his looks; he's one of the younger ones in the home. You wouldn't think so to look at him, would you?' she drifted on.

'Is that all you can tell me? There must be more.' Natascha stated being cautious, not to press the lady too firmly.

The cleaner moved around the small room collecting up her belongings in preparation to go home. 'Not much really, but I've been told his mother was one of them that got done.'

'What do you mean, "got done"? What does that mean?'

'I can't tell you any more, I've said too much already, go ask somebody else.' With that she turned on her heel, shrugged into her coat and left the building.

Natascha followed the cleaner from the retirement home and took a short walk past the cemetery to the centre of the town. Most of the residents found the shops, bars and other facilities within an easy walk, but her man and others relied on wheelchairs and friends to push them. As she walked swiftly back to her flat to collect her notepad and writing materials she gave thought to what she had learned about the people of this area and the place in which they lived. Her conversation with the cleaner had shaken her, the growing complacency had been blown away by a remarkable chance meeting. She tried to place in her imagination what life must have been like living through those awful events. She admitted to herself, that although she listened to her lecturers she had not really heard what they had said but she could not deny the impact one history lecture had had upon her. It had really disturbed her, having conjured up the most horrible images in her mind, some of which had kept her awake at night. Initially there had been only lukewarm interest in the history of Spain in the 1930s but at the end of that lecture in particular, attitudes had radically changed. But for her grandmother's story Natascha might have been equally ambivalent at the beginning. She was ashamed that she did not take much interest in the search for information at the start of this venture but now she was really interested, she even felt a tremor of fear for what she might yet learn.

She drew herself back to thinking of Bartolomé again and how difficult it had been pushing him around the streets. Sadly, her hope that he might help with her enquiries started to wane because of his reluctance to provide her with the information she knew he must have. He had lived through that time, he had things to tell. But she had been revitalised with the revelations provided by the cleaner so she would persist and give him more time. Pushing him along the main street, into difficult places and up steep adjoining streets on his insistence seemed to Natascha to be a test of her strength rather than a place that he found interesting. The effort might yet have been worth it after all.

It was the side roads that classified Béjar a hilly town despite most of the main street following the level course of the valley. She had been told that in the past, Béjar was a well-to-do community with cloth-making factories strung alongside the river, like fat beads, making use of the fast-flowing water to drive the machinery. There was plenty of work for anyone who wanted a job beyond those working in the cloth industry. Don Tomás González Solar also provided employment, not that he ever paid his employees very much, but it was work and money in their pockets for the simple task of keeping the master's free-roaming cattle and horses in good order.

Things changed for the worse for his estate workers and their families when the government brought in a law allowing the working class access to parts of these great estates to cultivate for themselves. The aristocracy and other wealthy landowners viewed this action as a removal of their rights to extend estates by unchallenged acquisition. The benefits to the workers were short-lived as the rich believed that their rights of inheritance were beyond the law of the land. It was common knowledge that the Guardia Civil, the army and the church would support the wealthy rather than the undefended peasants. As a consequence, some of the poor were driven from their allocated smallholdings and where they showed any resistance were murdered. No authority, no lawyer, mayor or even priest, except the very brave, challenged the traditionally untouchable aristocratic masters.

Natascha referred to her notes to stimulate her memory on the reasons for civil disturbance but rationally took into account that the lecturer's comments were general and might have no bearing on what happened here. However, being here gave her an uncomfortable feeling of being included in a wicked and bloody past. Would she also be part of this distressing history as she uncomfortably delved into the past possibly uncovering facts that would reopen wounds, maybe placing her at risk? She laughed at the absurdity of such a thought. How could she possibly imagine this when it all happened so long ago?

Despite these unchallengeable actions by the wealthy and the powerful, the people of this district, for the great part, had enough to eat and survived cold winters with plenty to burn. Here there was little dissent amongst the majority although some felt aggrieved that the rich and powerful seemed to be beyond the law and some brave and maybe foolish people were not afraid to express these thoughts. They felt that their citizenship had been diminished by the pre-war actions of the Fascist generals. They were now lesser beings, and this may well have been the reason that they had lost the full protection of the law. The elected government was on their side but seemed unable to ensure the rights and safety of its citizens. The rich regarded their workers as a breed apart, lesser beings, not worthy of recognition. Democracy was deplored and many workers who had been permitted to vote were shadowed by estate men who ensured, by menace, that they voted in favour of the wealthy landowners.

Forget it, thought Natascha; it was all such a long time ago.

23

THE VENTA

Early Summer 2008

Natascha, once again, did her best to put her questions to Bartolomé in a manner that would not upset him. Over the weeks she had known him he had never once volunteered any information about that period in history in which she was most interested. It was so frustrating; she chuckled to herself knowing how she would have reacted to this sort of obduracy only a few years ago. Instead of the present patronising comment, mostly through her gritted teeth, something more vitriolic would have been delivered. His response to her request was yet another grunt and sigh indicating she had ventured into forbidden territory. 'Never mind, dear, you tell me when you are good and ready.'

Natascha held on to her smile, although she was bristling underneath, as he looked back over his shoulder up into her face. She saw the triumph behind the smile and in the naughty twinkle in his eyes. 'You are such a tease, Bartolomé; I think I might leave you here in the middle of the road as you're being such a rascal.'

His expression changed immediately. 'No, no, Natascha, please don't leave me, please don't leave me, I promise to help.'

Natascha was both shocked and shamed by his reaction to her counter teasing. 'Bartolomé, stop worrying, of course I won't leave you here, it was a joke. Don't get yourself so upset, I wouldn't do anything to harm you, you should know that. Come on, let's get on with our trip.' She felt disturbed as this was unexpected and completely irrational. *Why would he fear her in such a way? A series of questions coursed through her mind. Did he have a fear of traffic? Had someone in the past purposely put him in danger? He's so quiet about everything that happened in his past, maybe they were so awful he can't even bear the memories,* she continued to think to herself as she pushed him towards the car. Remembering her conversation with the retirement home cleaner she concluded there might be something in what she had said. *"He can't bring up the past whilst he is awake because he finds it too painful but there is not much he can do to keep it a secret when he is sleeping and that is why he screams out when he dreams."*

'Look, don't worry; we won't talk about those things that upset you. Instead we will have a look around this lovely country of yours. You can point out all the most interesting things and tell me about them; how about that for a plan?'

'OK, Natascha, good idea; and I can show you where we can get a really good cup of coffee and the best tostada for miles around.'

She settled him into the passenger seat of the car; he liked to travel up front with her so he could see everything about him and ensure she took the right roads. *'Right, where are we off to, then?'* She then looked across at him in his seat. *'Oh, make sure you have your strap on. If nothing else it will keep you firmly in your seat if we come across pitted and rutted road surfaces. You never know what last night's rain could have done.'*

'I'm locked in and ready to go.' He looked across smiling weakly at her. *'I'm sorry I got a bit panicky back there but it felt like I was to be abandoned again; it was really horrible just after Mum died.'*

'Don't worry, Bartolomé, I understand. I've been put in places I didn't want to be but I think I deserved it because I was a really naughty girl; that wasn't such a long time ago by the way. If it helps you to talk about it I'm all ears but I am not pressing you.'

'Thanks, there are one or two things I would like to tell you.'

Natascha couldn't believe her ears; was he finally going to open up to her?

They drove carefully through the underpass beneath the Ruta de Plata which carried traffic between Salamanca and Palencia. 'That road's only just been finished; to me it's more like a bridge than a road standing up there on its concrete legs.' Bartolomé chatted away to Natascha. 'Doesn't take that long to get to Salamanca or to those towns even further south.'

'Long enough on a bus though, Bartolomé; Salamanca is where I've come from, remember I told you?' cut in Natascha as Bartolomé continued to talk about the recent improvements to the road system.

He looked puzzled. 'You don't live there.'

'I'm only here in Spain for a short while; this is part of my education. It's supposed to improve my Spanish.'

'I know you're not Spanish, I can tell from your accent, but you are very good. I can understand you better than some of those people who come from down near Cadiz.'

Natascha could feel his eyes on her but because the road was becoming more demanding as it started to climb into the hills, she did not return his gaze.

'Did you hear what I said, Natascha?' Because there was no immediate response he continued sounding petulant. 'I said you were good.' He was hurt but continued. 'Well, maybe not that good; to me you sound a bit posh, bloody superior.'

My God, thought Natascha to herself, he is so sensitive. 'Oh, come on, Bartolomé, I can't help it, that was the way I was taught Spanish.' He folded his arms across his chest and shrugged his shoulders like a spoilt child. She continued to speak but cautiously, taking care not to allow their conversation to drift into those areas that caused most distress. 'I was brought up in France, you know; I went to school in France but I have English parents.'

'English,' he intoned. 'Really, people told me my mum could speak a bit of English, learnt it from her friend.' With that he sat up and looked across at her. 'Are you English then?'

Although disturbed by the knowledge that his mother had an English-speaking friend, Natascha knew that it was not the time to ask Bartolomé more questions. But she continued. 'I have to tell you I feel as if I'm French and I think that is because I have so many French friends. I speak only French at university and always French when I am with my friends. But at home we use English all the time, except when doing homework or watching television.'

'So, you're a clever girl,' said the less grumpy Bartolomé smiling towards her. 'If you speak English as well as you speak Spanish then you really are clever.'

Natascha laughed loudly at his compliment and felt she might have eased him back into a better mood. 'No, I'm not clever, Bartolomé, because I didn't work as hard as I should have at school; I was very lucky to get into university.'

'Well, I hardly went to school at all, I'm not certain why but I have a good idea; maybe I could tell you about that bit of my life and see what you think.'

Natascha made no immediate response knowing she needed to be sure that what she said next paved the way to allow him to tell her the whole story. 'Well, Bartolomé, for someone who hasn't been to school very much, you know a lot. I've seen you reading the newspaper every time I've come to visit you, and not one of the cheap, simple papers either but the one filled with politics and other quite boring stuff.' Natascha laughed at herself for drawing attention to her lack of interest in anything but the trivial.

'Oh, that paper, I find it quite difficult too but it is one of very few worth the effort.'

'What do you mean, worth the effort?' asked Natascha hoping he might start to give an insight into his interests.

'I think this is a long story; do you mind if I tell you about it when we stop for a coffee?'

'No problem, let's enjoy the scenery and you point out places of interest.'

The lower hills were a collection of different grazing areas. Rangy steers and young bulls in glistening black coats held court on the higher slopes with menace in their eyes and irresistible power in their broad shoulders but despite all their posturing they were butcher bound. Doe-eyed dairy cows advanced in line towards squat farm buildings settled below the gentler slopes brushing the top of the new grass with creamy udders while solitary cows tethered to large pegs grazed perfect circles just short of the vegetable plots. Natascha drew Bartolomé's attention to the neat rows of vegetables. 'Look, they're as pretty as any garden; look at the care they take, everything seems to be perfect.'

'They grow good vegetables up here. I should know, I stayed up here for a short while when I was a boy.' Bartolomé spoke back to her. 'It was one of the best places I ever stayed but men came looking for me and I had to move and hide away for a while.' His mood changed as he remembered some of the happy times. 'I used to give the farmer a bit of a hand in the garden, clearing out the weeds and doing a bit of tilling. I remember what he used to say to me time and time again: "Man can't live by milk alone." He loved his vegetable plot more than he loved his cows.'

On the higher, better drained land, there were small but beautifully tended vineyards with the vines standing in perfect lines like well-disciplined soldiers. Cherry trees interspersed with plum grew in small orchards within and about more rocky spots. The military precision was missing but it was clear that they were treasured, with the grass mown neatly beneath their branches.

Natascha was surprised by how much Bartolomé knew. 'Have you ever been a farmer, Bartolomé, or worked on a farm? I ask because you seem to know so much about it.'

'As a boy, as I've said already, I used to live on this side of the valley. I didn't have a choice. People kept moving me around telling me it was for my own good. As I grew up I got to know that the people who looked after me took a risk because apparently the bad men were looking for me. It was one of the reasons I didn't go to school much.'

'How could you be a risk, Bartolomé? You were only a very small child.'

'Well, I was, because I saw what happened and I knew the names of some of them, you know, the ones who killed my mum and her friends.'

Horrid facts were falling into place. She felt she couldn't drive anymore so she pulled up onto the grassy verge and stopped the car. She sat still for a moment then very gently turned her head towards Bartolomé. He was still; his chin on his chest as a single tear coursed slowly down a face tormented by memories. She looked at the old man, decrepit, too big for tears, an unappealing creature unloved and forgotten. Unexpectedly possessed by a sudden surge of sympathy for this emotionally ruined man-child, feelings normally completely foreign to her, she felt she had a greater understanding of the appalling life he must have led. She was overwhelmed by the need to comfort him. It was the moment in her life when her view of the world changed. She looked beyond the man and recognised the child orphaned by the bloodletting on the forest floor. Abandoned, hidden then hidden again with only one tormenting constant, the image of his mother's cruel death. Unaware of what she was doing she leant across to him seeing only a child's face aged by years of painful memories and took him in her arms. She pulled clear her handkerchief and wiped his old man's eyes and with her fingers brought order to unkempt hair. Very gently he pulled away to sit up straight. He looked back at her, as would a child, conveying appreciation of kindness shown. *'Sorry, when I talk about these things I get upset, I can't quite understand what is going on in my mind.'* He eventually found his own big handkerchief and blew his nose and wiped his chin. *'Do you know, I can still see them doing it?'* He said nothing more and Natascha waited patiently in hope for more; she would say nothing, not wishing to break the fragile spell; but nothing more was to be revealed so they moved on.

'Come on, old chap, let's go find ourselves a nice place to have a cup of coffee.' With that, she started the car and moved back onto the road.

They travelled on knowing soon they would come across a venta and be able to have their promised coffee, or as Bartolomé preferred, café cortado. He enjoyed this version of coffee best because it was always presented in a tall glass and had just the right balance between milk and coffee. Natascha said she was used to café au lait and hoped it would be as good as the French coffee. 'Believe me, Natascha, it will be better; it's something you can wrap your hands around on a cold day and just breathe in the delicious aroma before you drink it.'

'Sounds great, but we want a snack of some sort to go with it. What do you suggest?'

'Tostada, of course, there's nothing better.'

'What's that like? I know it must have something to do with toasted bread but is there something special about it?'

'Wait and see. Oh! And this is my treat by the way; I'll do the ordering so you sit quietly and wait.'

'Thanks, Bartolomé, I can't wait, let's hope a venta turns up soon.'

No sooner had she stopped talking than they found the ideal place. Just around the bend and settled into a cutting amongst great Chestnut trees stood a collection of old farm buildings, one of which clearly had been the farmhouse. Painted on the gable end in large but neat letters was "Venta". There was a collection of supplementary notices, the most noticeable advertising Cruz Campo beer.

'Sure you don't want a beer instead, Natascha?'

'Certainly not, I'm not that fond of beer except, maybe, in the summer when it is really hot. No, I've come for tostada and coffee as you have recommended.'

Natascha pulled the car off the road on to the vast gravel parking area. 'Wow, look at all these lorries, hope we'll find a place for us to sit down.'

'There will be plenty of room, don't you worry; and all these lorries are a good sign. It usually indicates good food is on the menu.'

Natascha pulled out the folding wheelchair, locked it into place and pushed it across to Bartolomé's door. 'It's ready, Bartolomé, can you get in?'

He settled into the chair and pushed down on the wheels to get himself moving. Natascha pushed from behind as they manoeuvred across the difficult gravelled surface but soon they reached the building and the door was opened for them. The scent of coffee was strong and there was more than a little smoke in the air. Natascha found a table against the window. Most of the men were congregated about the bar, some drinking coffee and eating tapas but many drank beer from the bottles. As it happened it was Natascha who made her way up to the bar to order food and drink following the strict instructions given by Bartolomé. It was difficult to find a place in which she could attract the barman's attention. She was a tall and slender young woman and it was not long before this was noticed.

'Come on, my lady, I'm quite happy to make room for you,' called out a short, stocky man with well-oiled hair, much to the amusement of others who now turned their attention towards her. Natascha felt uncomfortable but from past experience knew it to be unwise to show concern; after all, they were just behaving like others she had come across in France.

Bartolomé shouted at them from the window seat to let the young woman alone. 'She's looking after me, show some manners.'

'And what are you, old man, her sugar daddy?' With that, laughter filled the room.

Natascha turned to the man who was making fun of her saying quietly, 'Be kind, this is a special excursion for him and I want it to be a good day.'

He looked hard at her, noticing her accent. 'Are you one of those Russian girls you can get through the post?' he said leering at her.

'And are you so pathetic that you're not worth talking to?' she glowered. 'Can you not ask a sensible question or has your brain shrivelled to the size of a worm's? Now move aside and let me place our order,' she said with a sharpness only Natascha could provide.

The driver was taken aback by her response. He pushed himself up from slouching over the bar and standing upright looked about at his friends. Their expressions were enough to confirm his loss of face and he was determined to put this young madam in her place. He pushed his brawny arm about her waist, gripping firmly the soft swell of her hip, and squeezed. And to her left, the other put his hand on her upper back pressing his fingers roughly through the fabric of blouse taking hold of straps supporting her underwear. Natascha shrieked in rage and with both arms stretched across the bar she swept in both directions clearing everything within her reach to crash upon the floor. Not quite done she directed a venomous response to both men, turning her head between one assailant and the other, 'Take your filthy hands off me, you disgusting creatures; have you just crawled out of a cesspit? You smell as if you have spent your entire life in the shit.' All this was delivered in French but none of its meaning was lost on anyone in the bar. There was a shuffling of feet and nothing was spoken. She turned to the barman as he went to clear up the shattered crockery and spilt beer and coffee. 'Leave that and serve me my order,' she said imperiously. 'And what did you do to protect your customers?' He looked embarrassed and returned behind the bar.

'Madam, please accept your order free of charge.' His dark eyes were on her seeking forgiveness.

'No, that won't be necessary, it was not your fault. Sorry, I was too hard on you.' She turned from him and looked around. 'Except, you may wish to do something about those two animals; I see they are still here making themselves comfortable over there in the corner.' With that she picked up the coffees and took them to Bartolomé's table. The barman delivered the tostadas then walked over to the miscreants' table. She did not hear what he said but they soon left. Bartolomé watched them walk across the parking area with both men getting into the same vehicle.

'I've noted down the vehicle registration number.'

'Well done, Bartolomé. Now let's get back to the good time we promised ourselves,' she said cheerily. She felt anything but

cheerful, she was still shaking and when she looked up into Bartolomé's face she saw how pale he was. His voice also had a tremor and she believed it was more than that annoying little incident. The bar was not the noisy place they had arrived at; it was quieter now but people were starting to talk to each other again and hopefully about other things rather than that ugly little scene.

Quite out of the blue Bartolomé looked up at her and stumbled over a few words that did not make sense. He coughed and tried to clear his throat then suddenly said, 'Do you like the tostada? It's best when you put on salt before you pour on the olive oil. Oh, you know this is the best olive oil you can get in Spain, it comes from the groves around Cordoba but the Jaen olive oil is good and the bread is made locally just for tostada.' He spoke rapidly and seemingly to himself as if he was disguising his real thoughts by a flood of words. He then trailed off, sat quite still, his hands around the glass and peering into the top of the milky coffee. Natascha knew there was something else on his mind; something quite disturbing because he couldn't bring himself to look at her.

Natascha cleared her throat to gain his attention; she then tapped him gently upon the arm. It was enough to stir him out of the thoughts that were disturbing him. 'Come on, Bartolomé, what's the matter? I know it's not about the coffee; you're wrapping your arms about it as if it was some long-lost lover.'

He smiled back at her recognising her attempts to make him feel more comfortable. 'Yes, I do like the coffee but it's not that.' Natascha gave him a look that asked him to tell her more. 'It was what those men did to you; I couldn't help.'

'What! Don't worry about that too much; I think they had too much to drink and were just stupid. Anyway, I sorted them out.' Natascha relived the uncomfortable event in her mind once more and it made her feel very vulnerable. 'Actually, I was terrified; that's why I acted as a screaming bitch. Do you understand? I'm sorry if I have upset you.'

'No, Natascha, when it happened I was frozen and couldn't do anything, not even call out; what happened to you is what had happened to my mother.' He took a sip of his cooling coffee but held on to it, holding it beneath his chin. His body shook as a shudder passed through him enough to spill a little of the coffee on to the table.

Surprised, Natascha leant forwards and looked closely at him as tears formed in the corners of his eyes. 'Bartolomé, take it easy, don't let this upset you. Come on, I'm all right; don't worry.'

He put the coffee firmly down on the table spilling a little more. Natascha mopped up the spillage with a handful of the little paper napkins always available in ventas.

'I felt I was a child again over seventy years ago; what those men did to you is exactly how it started with Mum and the others.' Natascha raised her chin to speak to him again but thought twice about it for he was clearly angry now. 'No, do not speak, just listen to me; I can see it now, it was dark but everything was lit up by the lights of the lorry.'

Natascha waited a long time for him to continue but soon realised that he had lost himself in one of his long, silent sessions. A change of subject was usually the best way to break the spell. 'Bartolomé, I've had a super time today and it was a great idea to come to this lovely place. I don't mean the venta but the countryside about here is just wonderful.' He said nothing. 'You know, this is the first time I've tried coffee served at a venta and it was great, but I especially enjoyed the tostada.' Still he said nothing. 'Come on, Bartolomé, I must take you home now.'

He continued to sit still making no effort to leave. His demeanour had changed; he seemed to be empowered and he looked unashamedly into Natascha's face. This was not a time to speak and certainly not to ask questions, so she waited and then he told her. He left out no details, he'd even remembered some of the names, but it was the description of the horrific event and the emerging fact that it must have been her grandmother's godmother Joan who died with her that made her nauseous. She wanted to disbelieve all she was told but she knew it was the truth.

24

THE LORRY

Autumn 1938

The sun was low in the sky as he returned to the village, but it was still light enough to drive without headlights. It had been a very long day having set out early in the morning and he had needed the lights then; not only was it still dark when he set off but there were patches of mist to contend with all along the valley road. He had loaded the lorry the day before; that was difficult enough as he manoeuvred his vehicle as close as possible to the stack of acacia that his enterprising friend had cut from the forest earlier. Acacia was not native to this part of Spain but his friend knew that it could be found in a difficult place just above the river, unseen from the road. It had been necessary to pull the lorry off the road to be well hidden from prying eyes. The only way to achieve this was to reverse the awkward vehicle down the very narrow forest track that started not far, and still visible, from the village. His aching back helped him to remember that they still had to carry the heavy timber a long way to the lorry and then heave it up onto the high-level floor. Jorge knew it was worth the effort because it paid well; he'd made one or two runs down there before.

Acacia made great, long-lasting fencing posts and the area to which they were being delivered was notoriously damp down by the River Alagón close to Palencia. These were dangerous times and this little venture was even more dangerous as the acacia trees belonged to neither Jorge nor his friend.

There was little work about nowadays and Jorge knew he had no choice but to go out on his own; the local landowners no longer had any need for his lorry to cart around their goods since they had purloined the lorries of "Reds". They paid a heavy price for being poor and obstreperous. He had to be careful not to give anyone a reason to call him a "Red" particularly now that little shit Cortés had been promoted to running the show. He would never understand it, he was a useless sod who never did an honest day's work in his life; all he seemed to do was drink and beat his wife. *Well, you can't argue with them*, thought Jorge, *they hold all the power these days and a blue shirt is now the badge of honour.*

He was glad to get home and have a bit of money to pass on to his wife. Enough, he hoped, to have something decent to eat instead of making do. The lorry trundled up the hill in low gear avoiding the worst of the potholes that could so easily bring about a collapse of the suspension. He was already worried about the noise the gearbox was making; he'd made a mental note that first thing tomorrow he would change the gearbox oil. He had heavy-duty oil in the corner of the barn covered up with straw and other rubbish to keep it safe from the "new" authority. As he reached the top of the hill just before the track entered the village square he noticed one or two people engaged in conversation close to his house. It was the spot he parked the lorry most nights so he hoped they'd shift out of the way before he pulled into the space.

They moved as he turned right to take up his normal parking place. He then groaned as he noticed Cortés was part of the welcoming group. *What now?* he thought. *It's got to be trouble.* Normally he leapt down briskly from the driver's cab and couldn't wait to get inside his house out of the cold. On this occasion he took his time trying to rack his brains for the reason they wanted to see him; nothing came to mind. He scrambled down from the cab using the left-hand front wheel as a step. His back was aching so he took his time eventually turning to the group. 'How are you doing, chaps? You're out late, aren't you?' He managed a cheerful acknowledgement of the group although he didn't really feel it. He turned to Cortés smiling but feeling nothing but contempt for the man.

Trying to keep it friendly he acknowledged the contemptible little man, 'Hi, Al, nice welcoming committee you've got for me tonight; didn't know I was so important.'

Alfredo Cortés nodded his head and then spoke. 'Are you busy tonight because I've got a special job on?'

'Look, I'm knackered, it's been a long day. I've done more than enough hours and don't want to do any more. Also I've got a problem with my gearbox, so can't I do the job tomorrow?' Jorge knew that a "special" job was the last thing he wanted to do. It usually meant some poor sod was going to meet his maker.

Cortés sneered, 'I'm not really interested in how tired you are, Jorge, or whether you need to service this heap of crap you call a lorry or what you've been doing today.'

Jorge sensed he was on dangerous ground; Cortés was on to something about him. Maybe it was about the acacia; it was sure to be something that he wasn't going to like. Normally he was an obsequious little creep believing his oily words were seen as charm. *Couldn't be further from the truth,* Jorge thought to himself. 'Look, I'll see what I can do but you would be doing me a great favour if you let me go into my home to have something to eat.'

'Well, we're not quite ready ourselves but we wanted to be sure you'd be part of the plan after playing the unofficial timber merchant,' Cortés sneered.

Jorge was shocked; how had he found out what he had been up to? 'OK, thanks, you give me a call when you need the use of my lorry; I assume that's what you want.'

'Oh, we need you as well, Jorge, so you won't disappoint us, will you?' he said with heavy sarcasm. 'We've got a few people to call on before your precious lorry is needed.' Cortés looked about at his cronies who were all smiling enjoying the menacing tone of his demand. 'We've got business that will bring us a bit of fun, haven't we, boys?' He then turned back to Jorge who was making his way to the back of his house. 'Oh, by the way, Jorge,' he called towards the retreating back, 'should I let Don Pedro know you've done a bit of forest clearing for him? I'm sure he'll be delighted.' He moved off chuckling to himself as his friends patted him on the back.

There was no doubt he was in trouble and he knew he would have to go along with whatever Cortés asked him to do despite knowing it was bound to be nasty business. Jorge pushed against the door into his house. It was stiff and scraped across the stone floor catching a prominent flagstone and stopping abruptly. He cursed to himself as his face caught the edge of the door. *It'll probably bleed*, he thought, *but Christ help me, worse things are about to happen tonight*. His wife, Miranda, was standing still by the stove, just looking at him and in the poor light of the cottage he could see she was unnaturally pale. 'What is the matter? You look really upset,' he enquired but she didn't answer and nor did the children sitting on the floor close to the stove keeping warm.

'Did you hear that brute, Cortés, speaking to me outside? Is that what is upsetting you, Miranda?' He looked down at the boys; their eyes were wide and concerned. 'Hey, come along, lads, Daddy's home, there is nothing to worry about; come on, give us a cuddle,' he said as cheerfully as he could. The boys shuffled about on the floor but didn't rise so Jorge went over to them really concerned. This lack of enthusiasm was so unlike them.

Miranda served up the food on to an odd collection of different bowls and plates, from a big iron pot that had been moved to the side of the hotplate. Jorge had moved across to her and gently kissed her on the cheek. She stopped and looked into his eyes. 'He is such an evil man; do you know, he tried to push himself into our house; it was that loose flagstone that stopped the door from opening wide and letting that fat, ugly beast in.' Jorge was appalled. What would that monster have done if he had got into the house? Miranda continued, 'The things he said to me, Jorge, were awful and the boys heard every word. I just hope they didn't understand everything he said.'

'What did he say?' She turned away not wishing to look into the eyes of her overly protective husband; he would be enraged by what had been suggested and that the boys had been threatened as well. 'Come on, darling, tell me; I won't overact, I promise you.'

She continued spooning out the food then called to the boys. 'Come on, boys, come and get your food; be careful because it is really hot.' Jorge stood away to allow their sons to collect the food and take it to their place where they stood leaning on the table eating like it was the last scrap of food on Earth. Miranda smiled towards her sons as they set about making short work of the vegetable hotpot.

'This is great, Mama, really tasty. What is it?' called out

the younger of the two; their eldest, Pepe, was too busy eating; he wasn't going to waste any time on talking.

'Well, the secret ingredient is rabbit. Do you like it?' There was no response and she laughed with Jorge as they realised nothing else was going to get in the way of eating.

'Where did you get the rabbit, Miranda? You haven't been poaching, I hope?' He laughed trying to lighten the atmosphere. 'Never mind, I'm starving and I want my share before the boys start asking for more. Oh, and make sure you have enough for yourself, I don't want to see you go short just so you can spoil the boys again.'

Miranda passed the bowl of hotpot to Jorge but as he tried to move away she held on firmly to the bowl not letting him move away to the table. He held her with his eyes and waited for her to explain herself. 'What he said to me was, if I wanted to know what was going on tonight, to have a look outside and see what happens to the bitches, I'll know them when I see them. They'll be getting what they deserve. Enemies of the state, he said, and it could happen to me unless I was nice to him.'

'What? The insulting bastard.' Trying not to spill the food he pulled Miranda towards him and with voice full of emotion whispered, 'Dear God, not more poor souls; haven't we had enough of this killing? No one is innocent in this foul war and as the battle has been won this side of the line, why do they need to keep on killing our people?' Jorge took his food to the table then walked back to his wife who was now filling her plate. He stood behind her and gently put his arms around her. 'He can't do anything to you, darling, not while I'm around. Maybe I'll get a chance for him to have an accident; I've already told him there's something wrong with the lorry – it could be the brakes.' His laugh was hollow and Miranda didn't find it funny. 'But seriously, what can we do? We can run away, just throw everything we've got into the back of the lorry and take off.' She turned and looked at him; her face told him that it was a futile idea. 'I know, not a great idea. When the Falangists find us, the fact that we ran away will mean we are guilty. For what, God only knows, but it will be enough for them to kill us.'

'Surely not the boys; they wouldn't do that, would they?'

'No, you're right, they wouldn't do that. I have heard they put them in labour camps or schools according to their age; but I know many children have been executed as well as their parents, some as they ran away, others just because their dad was a councillor or union leader.' He took her plate of food from her hands and led her over to the table. 'Here, sit yourself down; you deserve this more than anybody.'

They ate in silence not wanting to continue the disturbing conversation with the boys within earshot. There was enough for them to worry about since the school had closed and no one knowing if there would be a replacement teacher or whether Rodrigo would come back. *No bloody hope of that*, thought Jorge. *He'll be dead by now*. They couldn't allow people like Rodrigo to be left unaccounted for; he was far too clever for the ignorant little bastards now in charge.

Miranda could see from his expression what was going on in his mind. She had heard what he was thinking many times before and she, like the majority of the people she knew, thought the same. This wasn't going to solve today's problems. Bad things were going to happen tonight by the sound of it so it was necessary to get the boys into bed and asleep as soon as possible.

The ritual of getting ready for bed had been completed and Jorge was telling the brothers a story told many times before but they loved it. Jorge thought it was a ridiculous story about an eagle that was too afraid to go hunting and had to eat cabbage to stay alive. Before long the boys were fast asleep their faces still and untroubled as they lay together on the straw mattresses upon the floor.

Miranda pulled out the second chair from under the table as Jorge picked himself up from the floor. He was stiff and moved awkwardly towards the table and sat down. Miranda had made some coffee for which her husband was grateful; he needed something to keep him awake as they both had much to think about. Turning to look towards the sleeping boys it was clear to them that their priorities lay with keeping the family together and out of danger. They knew they had to compromise some of their principles to ensure their safety but the welfare of their sons mattered more than anything else.

'You know Rodrigo's wife, Juana, yes?' She looked for his affirmation; he nodded his head. 'You know she's English but I don't think anyone would notice she wasn't Spanish,' said Miranda watching Jorge's face closely.

Jorge laughed, knowing Miranda, like the rest of the wives, always worried Juana might be, as the French put it, a "femme fatale". Everybody knew it wasn't true despite the hints dropped by Father Jaime. 'Of course I know who she is, you can't help noticing her, she's a great looking woman, but so are you. Just because Rodrigo's gone missing doesn't mean she's on the lookout for a replacement.'

'I know she's pretty, Jorge, and on top of that she's a really nice person; Juana is a good friend of mine. How many times has she come here and seen to the boys when they've been ill? When Rodrigo escaped a lot of people complained and she made a few enemies but that didn't stop her using her nursing skills to heal the children even of those who have treated her horribly.'

'Well, what's the problem with her? Surely everybody is glad that she has stayed around. She could have gone back to England. I don't know how she's done it but she is still here, God bless her.'

'Apparently the new party, the Falangists, you know, the Blue-shirts, have been spreading malicious rumours about her. And the priest isn't helping; he keeps dropping nasty little hints that she's a loose woman.'

'Have you ever watched the priest when he is giving Communion? He always spends more time with her than is necessary. When she takes the bread he always hangs on to her hand and you can see her trying to pull away; she colours up, you know, her neck goes pink.'

'Yes, I have noticed and so have many others but I've also noticed you and a few of your friends watching her as she walks up to the altar rail.' She laughed at Jorge's embarrassment. 'I would love to know what was going through your minds as she floats by up the aisle; bet you're not thinking about your prayers for the day, more like sins of the future.'

'Miranda, you're wicked, you've got a bad mind,' but he laughed along with her knowing she was right.

It was then they heard raised voices somewhere out in the square. The happiness generated from their light banter of just a few moments ago evaporated. They looked across the table at each other, the candles flickered but there was enough light for each to recognise the fear in the other's face. Jorge went to move but Miranda held firmly on to his hands. 'Wait, you may not be needed, everything might be solved by a war of words. I think I recognised Father Jaime's voice; he'll sort it out.'

'I doubt it, he thinks like the bishops do. They know Franco will protect the church and anyone who has disrespected the church will pay for their crimes; hardly a Christian outcome but it's going to happen.' He got up from the table and moved towards her. 'I'm going to be needed, Miranda; I promise not to antagonise any of that bunch of murderers; I've got three good reasons to keep out of trouble,' he said quietly as he glanced towards the sleeping boys. Miranda stopped him continuing by pressing her finger to his lips. 'There is little you can do without putting all of us in mortal danger. Be a shadow; drive if you have to but don't do anything else, don't touch anybody, don't say anything and come home safe.' She kissed him and helped him into his big jacket. He then went and stood by the door hoping never to hear the order from Cortés that would take him a few more steps closer to hell.

25

WHISPERS IN
THE DARK

Autumn 1938

Despite the difficult circumstances under which they met, Juana always looked forward to meeting with Pastora. The closeness of their attachment to each other had been built up in the early years when everything was simple and sunny; how different from today. Since the beginning of the war their once inconsequential little world had changed and tragically for the worse with little hope for the future. They were more like sisters than friends with an openness that tended towards disagreement over small issues but their love and loyalty to each other could not be questioned. In the immediacy of these destructive times, where cruel uncertainty and callous bloodletting ruled, they needed to be closer than ever, and so they were, but Pastora's extreme distress verging on madness was a task Juana felt was beyond her capabilities and certainly her patience at times. But she must persist, hoping and praying that her efforts would draw back her precious friend from corrosive insanity into the practicalities of the real world. There was

comfort in each other's company but at present little joy;
in fact no joy, she must admit, since the return to Spain of
Franco's Moors. With them came fear, poverty, persecution
and death and it had struck most cruelly at the heart of
Pastora's family when her loving and masterful Sebastián
was killed. In the past there seemed nothing that could not
be solved by either of these bright, attractive young women
with many in the village inspired by their energy.

Sebastián had been dead for many months now and,
distressingly to Juana, Pastora seemed to weep every time his
name was mentioned; it was obvious she struggled to keep
her tears under control but grief tore away constraint, often
leaving her inconsolable. Juana suffered too for Sebastián
was her friend and Rodrigo's too. In her heart she could
not see the value of such prolonged periods of weeping and
heart-rending sobs; it did not free you from the pain. It was
so exhausting; there must be a better way to come to terms
with her loss. Inwardly Juana chastised herself for apparent
lack of feeling; *how English*, she thought, *am I really that
cold?* She felt shamed and frequently left Pastora's company
having done little good and struggling with guilt.

The times Juana most dreaded were when they
decided to bring their children so they could play
together. Both Alicia and Pastora's son, Bartolomé, were
of a similar age and occupied themselves chasing about
under the overhanging vines outside the coffee shop.
Sebastián's pride and joy, Bartolomé, always looked about
the square in hope that Daddy would appear. Pastora's
grief-induced madness would often be triggered by her
son's simple question, "Where's Daddy?" *Well, it wouldn't
happen today*, thought Juana with relief. However, there
would be the drama of the square that would always exist
as long as they made it their meeting point. Pastora angrily
accused the square, as if it were a guilty participant in the

foul killing of her husband. A confused Juana found this extraordinary.

Pastora's recently adopted form of greeting was pleasant enough but disconcerting as she would unduly prolong their initial embrace seemingly to seek comfort from the closeness, enough to make Juana feel awkward. *Being English again*, she thought, unresponsive once more, she chastised herself. Upon release from her caresses Pastora would peer with disarming intensity into her eyes searching for help she seemed unable to give. All Juana could do was to inwardly pose unhelpful questions regarding the state of Pastora's mind, none of which she would dare to voice. *How mad is she? Does she teeter on the brink of sanity? Can I survive the soul searching? Can I make right the wrongs? Will God help me?*

The knowledge of the truth of Sebastián's undignified and horrible death, almost too painful to bear, moved those of rational mind and who loved him a little closer to a form of pragmatic acceptance. Juana had absorbed the appalling circumstances of his murder; slaughtered on the stones before the holy church and they affected her to this day; she involuntarily shuddered as if someone had walked heavily upon her grave. Smiling grimly, she hoped her entombment would be a good many years off into the future and chuckled at her bleak thoughts.

Since that murderous day Pastora had adopted some habits that were disturbing by their repetition. Time and again during unrelated conversation Pastora would inexplicably change the subject and painfully grip her friend's arm; she would then forcibly turn Juana's head towards a point within the square. 'Look, his blood still stains the earth,' she would whisper coarsely as anger closed up her throat. Other words were and continued to be difficult to catch as she mumbled tremulously over some mysterious incantation whilst scratching at the sand between the paving stones with the point of an elegant dancing shoe. It didn't seem to matter where they stood upon the square, for when the madness gripped her she would point back over her shoulder with an accusing finger. Unwaveringly it would home in, laser-like, on the blooded place and the grip she placed upon the hapless victim of her discourse would intensify as her mind transported to bedlam. 'There, you see, there congealed between the cobbles; look, it blackens the sand.' And with the grimmest smile continued, 'Smell it, smell it, sniff, Juana, sniff, can you not smell my husband's blood?'

Juana recognised the extremity of her friend's suffering; she had come across such cases in her early days as a nurse in England and not many of those who had suffered to such an extent regained a normal life. Let this not be the end of a purposeful life for her lovely friend, she prayed. She has much to live for; her son Bartolomé and for me, she sobbed inwardly. Juana cringed at the selfishness of her wishes, but it was true she needed Pastora as much as Pastora needed her.

'Do not step where he lies, let him rest,' she called out softly to the villagers who needed no prompting as they cautiously avoided the place of the fallen Sebastián.

Juana shook her head trying to remove the impact of these previous incidents; she must treat this next meeting as just another session to help Pastora get her life together and look more positively to the future. She had planned for this by asking her elderly neighbour if she would mind collecting Alicia from school and care for her whilst she was out on her hopefully brief visit. Pastora had already arranged to collect Bartolomé early so she could prepare for Juana's arrival at her home, happily not in the square this time. Juana knew she must not be too long as Pilar had explained she would care for Alicia in her home on this occasion and not as she normally did in Juana's home as it was necessary for her to prepare for her husband's saint's day celebration to be shared with his sister, a formidable relative.

Juana left the house later than arranged just as Pilar was taking charge of Alicia, leaving her daughter with a brief parting kiss and a cuddle, making her promise to be a good girl. She had taken no more than a few steps when she felt compelled to return and take her child into her arms again. She was unable to latch onto the intangible premonition but she certainly felt the coldness that infiltrated the very core of her body. 'I mustn't go back, it will only disturb Alicia,' she said to herself. 'I won't be long; I'll be home before you know it.' But she spoke to herself with uncertainty.

Daylight was starting to slip away, the distant sky an insipid turquoise now edged with pink. She tripped up the foot-worn track between the entangled branches of arching oaks and between the poor cottages of those who had fallen on hard times until she reached the open square. There were people in the plaza; unusual for this time of the day, she thought, when everywhere was still closed. It was family time when the men had come down from the higher slopes of the forested hills and wives were giving thought to the evening meal. Juana stepped back into the shadows. She did not know why but so many bad things had happened over the weeks and months it was sensible to be cautious when something unusual was taking place. They were talking but their voices were too low to make out what their business might be but it was disconcerting the way they huddled in their conversation, just like conspirators, she thought. Suddenly they all turned their heads to look down the road that led away from the village to the lower more major road by the river. It was a dark and dank place with overhanging trees and collections of river-worn boulders that had been swept down from greater heights centuries ago. Juana picked up the sound of an approaching car as it laboured up the deeply rutted road. *So that's what they're waiting for,* she thought to herself. *What can be so important about this vehicle?* And crucially who could be so important to warrant a welcoming committee? Juana knew she was going to be later than ever for Pastora but curiosity had got the better of her so she stayed in the shadows and waited. A short, stocky figure in an ankle-length black leather overcoat and a fedora used the open door of the car to heave himself up from the back seat. He stood briefly then removed his hat. Juana noisily drew in a breath and slapped her hands across her mouth; she stood stock still in fear someone might have heard her.

She pressed herself back into the shadows and crouched down to make herself as small as possible. This man terrified her. The villagers despised him. He was bad enough before the invasion, known then as a bully, particularly as a woman beater and suspected petty thief. But now he was leader of the dreaded Falangists, tasked by the rebel leaders with cleaning up after they had swept through and subdued the opposition. They worked under "El Caudillo's" instructions. No Republican sympathisers were to be left to ferment further trouble, they were to be cleansed and any who had been in contact with them were to be treated with suspicion and if in doubt of where their loyalties lay were to be cleansed too. Better safe than sorry.

She had hoped never to see this despicable little man ever again and was convinced his arrival was the prelude to something evil. Juana chose not to stride across the square like she would do normally but to edge her way around the open space keeping well into the shadows. It was difficult to keep hidden all the way around the square as side entrances between buildings had no cover at all. She remembered a tip Rodrigo had given her when playing "Hide and Seek" on the tree-covered hills above the village on glorious picnic days with friends in the wonderful time before their world had been turned upside down. Very slow movements were as good as hiding in the shadows he had said. Watch your opponent and move only when his eyes are not on you, freeze at all other times. She remembered telling him of a game they played in England called "Grandmother's Footsteps"; it's a bit like that, she declared. Rodrigo only partly agreed saying that Grandmother knew she was there in her game but it was important in his game that they didn't know you were there. She smiled inwardly thinking how silly it was playing this game trying to keep hidden from this pathetic group of self-important nobodies. But experiences from the recent past heightened her apprehension, demanding caution, so she took no chances. Having reached a point close to the assumed group of conspirators and in the last shadow before having to step out into the light she paused and could hear some of what was being discussed. Cortés was holding court, the aggressive movements of his arms emphasising the action to come. Apparently, he had been there some time earlier in the evening but had to go back for the tools. Juana was intrigued; what work could they possibly expect to do in the dark? Cortés never worked anyway, he was a miserable little scrounger, but he was their leader.

She was really late now and needed to meet up with Pastora soon as she would certainly be starting to become agitated. Juana went to move but paused when she caught the name "Francisca" being passed between them. She knew Francisca, the widow of the murdered *Guardia Civil* captain who died trying to rescue Sebastián. Juana stood still as the approaching night and listened, waiting to hear what else might be said.

'You two go,' said Cortés leaning out of the car window, pulling towards him the men standing nearest. 'Yes, you two, and make sure that widow bitch keeps her mouth shut; she still thinks she has the authority of her sanctimonious husband. Well, that bastard's dead and good riddance, I say. I can't stand that interfering old sow, I'll be glad to see the back of fucking Francisca.'

'I like that, boss, fat old sow; can't wait to hear her squeal as we grunt,' added another voice. They all laughed as they exchanged slaps across their backs.

'Get her back here soonest, and then we'll do the business with her before we bring in the other two.' Cortés paused then continued in a softer tone. 'Remember, boys, we save the tastier morsels for a treat at the end so keep your mitts off the pretty ones until I give the word.' He turned towards a tall man Juana recognised as one of Don Pedro's estate workers. She was surprised because she knew him to be a decent family man who was always polite. 'You, Mano, go knock up Jorge, but only when I give the word. Tell him we need him and his lorry now. Take no nonsense from him, remind him how pretty his wife is; that'll get his co-operation. And Mano, don't look so fucking reluctant or I'll let Don Pedro know you're not up to the job, you have a very pretty wife, too; take care, boy, you don't want to make me unhappy.' Mano scowled and walked away to wait. Cortés laughed slamming the car door on them all.

Juana was petrified. What could they possibly want with Francisca and who were the other two women they were talking about? Should she go home and bar the door in case they were talking about her, or should she try and get to Pastora's house and let her know what was going on? She knew she couldn't abandon her already distraught friend. *Alicia will be safe with Pilar*, she comforted herself.

She turned her head and watched as some of the other men moved towards the car to get in and join Cortés.

'Could be busy tonight, boss; you never know, we might be required to be energetic beyond the call of duty; know what I mean? So, might as well sit down whilst we can, in comfort, and conserve energy.' The laughter was loud, coarse and prolonged until Cortés called out for them to shut up as he turned to listen to a woman leaning into the car.

'What did you say? Couldn't hear you above this noisy lot?' Cortés's face was at the window looking towards the woman as she leant towards him.

Juana recognised her. A face from the past, once her friend from their meetings at the school gates. There was a disagreement; she couldn't remember what it was all about but she had avoided Juana ever since. The woman's voice was clear and sharp, Juana could remember it well, with every word clearly heard. But it was what she said that really shook her. 'I'm going home now, Alfredo; make sure the snooty bitch that's been pestering Father Jaime gets her comeuppance; you know, the one married to the runaway school teacher, him and his lefty politics?'

Cortés flicked his fingers at her. 'I don't fight your battles, lady; I've my own reasons for pulling that luscious little blonde in, and believe me, it's nothing to do with his or her politics.' A burst of laughter rang out from the car once again.

Juana cringed and felt she was unable to breathe. *She's talking about me; no, they're talking about me, all of them. My God, what have they got planned for tonight?*

She must move; she had to meet with Pastora but the news she brought would undoubtedly distress her further. Juana was now convinced she was to be the target for tonight's planned event and if this was the case the last member of the trio must be Pastora. Her friend had made herself the obvious target as she never missed an opportunity to harangue anyone from the Falangists or any who applauded Franco and his cronies. Even the priest had received the sharpness of her tongue on more than one occasion as it seemed to her that he was complicit in the murderous actions that had taken place on the square. Juana had always tried to calm her down when speaking to Father Jaime and usually ended up apologising for her outbursts. Time and time again Juana had explained to the priest how abandoned Pastora felt and that her anxiety was getting the better of her and could not he, her confessor, help her tormented soul. The priest was dismissive of Pastora's concerns and would turn his unwelcome attention on Juana. Even Pastora in her depressed state was conscious of how little interest he had in helping her overcome her problems as he seemed to concentrate all his attention on Juana. She recalled an earlier conversation she had with Pastora that established their mistrust of the priest.

'There he goes again,' she would say with an edge of bitterness to her voice. 'What is it about you, Juana, that turns our man of God into a love-sick boy?'

'I don't want to talk to him, Pastora; he gives me the creeps. He never stops looking at me, forcing me to check again and again that no buttons are undone and that I am modestly dressed.' Juana shivered as if touched by a cold hand. 'Sometimes I feel he's looking straight through my clothes and I am naked to his eyes.'

'You're right, I've watched the way he looks; I hate the way his features loosen, how his tongue constantly licks his upper lip. To me he is no longer a man of God; he's base, disgusting and one to watch; we need to keep our distance.'

'Who can we turn to, Pastora, if not him? He is our link to salvation, he is our priest and we must have faith.'

'Anybody but him; maybe the church has truly abandoned us. It seems as if even God has turned his back on us and we are no longer His children. Is that not why our brave men are never buried in consecrated ground, instead finding graves in ditches and crowded pits hidden away in forgotten places?'

At times like this her thoughts would turn to Rodrigo. As she turned to leave she prayed. 'God spare you, my love. Come home when the world has recovered her sanity.'

She stood up from the crouched position in the shadows wincing from the stiffness in her knees. With the first few faltering steps, keeping her hands close to her sides she moved cautiously into the light. She took short steps keeping her upper body rigid so as not to draw attention and covered the open ground. Without being noticed she slipped behind the most forward of the cottages on the plaza and approached Pastora's abode unseen. She tapped on the door and it opened instantly.

'Where have you been? I thought you had forgotten me.'

Juana put her fingers to Pastora's lips. 'Shh,' she whispered. 'Don't say a word, wait until we are inside.' Juana took the door from Pastora's hands and closed it cautiously, making sure it made no sound. 'We may have trouble from the "Blue-shirts", they've already gone to get Francisca from her hovel down the hill, luckily for us it might be some time before they're back.'

'What are you talking about, Juana? What has this to do with us? We've got enough trouble of our own than to worry about Captain José's widow.'

'I've just overheard that toad Cortés giving orders to his group of morons to bring Francisca back to the square before picking up the other two.' The full implication of Cortés's words was starting to sink in and fear emanated from within Juana's pale face.

Pastora noticed the change in her demeanour and she too started to feel fear crawl beneath the skin.

'My name was not used but I am sure they were talking about me.' Tears started to fill her eyes as she pulled a small piece of folded linen from her waistband and wiped her face. 'I'm so sorry, Pastora, I know I'm being a baby but none of us has protection any more. The Falangists can do what they like; they've been given free rein to do whatever it takes to remove any opposition to Franco's Spain however tenuous the reasons might be. I've seen it before and I heard what they said tonight; they've got double incentive to take us. We are women. Oh God, how I wish I was a thousand years old with the complexion of a toad; they wouldn't look at me then.'

'We've no men to stand up for us. Sebastián is dead and we don't know what's happened to Rodrigo. And don't forget Francisca; I may not like her much, bossy cow, but she is a woman without protection, too. Sorry, I shouldn't have said that, poor soul.'

'Surely the *Guardia Civil* will look after their own despite the lies that were told about José?'

'Francisca has been making such a fuss recently; she's complaining about the place she has to live in. I don't blame her, it is horrible and she's demanding the officers who shot her husband be put on trial. Nobody will do anything, they just laugh at her; it's been swept under the carpet and the two gunmen are being used to tidy up other similar irritations.' She paused for a moment, then continued. 'Francisca's husband did his best to apply the law honourably and look what happened to him. He was a decent man despite being a civil guard. Law? There is no law, it's all a charade.'

Juana was astonished by Pastora's rational thought. She had expected her to drift into the usual manic unrelated comments of the very recent past. The real threat of danger had shaken her and for the moment she was back to her normal strong self. *Thank God* she thought, *some good may yet come of this dangerous situation*. Juana stood looking at her friend wondering if this change for the better could last, trying at the same time to control her emerging sense of panic. They both needed their wits about them if they were to survive this threat. 'We have to escape now, not in five minutes but now. Only God knows when those thugs will be back.' Pastora seemed to be rooted to the floor. 'Now, Pastora, go and get Bartolomé dressed and yourself,' she said pointing at her flimsy nightclothes. 'Make sure you are really warm; we'll probably have to sleep out under the stars tonight. Quite an adventure, hey?' She smiled and a twinkle returned to Pastora's beautiful dark eyes. 'I'll meet you down beyond my cottage; remember, not my cottage, too dangerous, see you next to the old goat house. Stay in the shadows and don't cross the square. Cut through the forest at the back of the houses to reach me.'

Juana left and followed the route she had laid out for Pastora. It was darker and noisier than expected and she couldn't avoid the unseen fallen twigs that carpeted the forest floor. Time was of the essence, they had minutes to escape and she still had to retrieve Alicia from Pilar's protective arms.

26

FRANCISCA TAKEN

Autumn 1938

Francisca had been pulled half-dressed from her home. There had been no respectful approach; they kicked the door open, marched to the corner of the room and dragged her out of bed. She fell to the floor heavily and using their feet they encouraged her to stand. Francisca had been asleep and it was only when she had regained her composure by climbing to her feet did she come to realise what was happening. She started to scream and thrash around to break their grip on her arms; she was a big woman, strong, and the noise she made was deafening. A fist struck her firmly on the chin and she dropped to the floor unconscious. 'Christ, we're not going to have to carry her, are we?'

'No, you tosser, we'll wait until she wakes up. Go and see if you can find something to gag the old cow. We'll be in the shit if she wakes up the whole village as we drag her back to the boss.'

'I've found something we can use as a gag, a dirty old linen bandage, and here's a pot of cold water if we think she's been sleeping too long.' He laughed as he bent down to wrap up Francisca's mouth leaving just enough space for her to breathe through her nose.

'Come on now, long enough, wake the bitch up and let's get on our way.' He took the pot from his colleague and carefully dribbled it on her face. She stirred and groaned and pushed herself into a sitting position but didn't seem to be able to progress any further so he threw the rest of the water into her face. Francisca grunted behind the gag and struggled to her feet. The younger of the two men pulled a blanket from the bed and put it about her shoulders. 'You're getting soft in your old age, son; what's the matter with you?'

'We don't want her to die from the cold, do we mate? We've got better things for her to die from, haven't we?' They both laughed at the crude joke that did not register with Francisca as they held her by the arms and frogmarched her through the doorway. Up the stony path towards the square they forced her, with her head down upon her chest; she couldn't understand what was happening, all she could feel was numbness in her face and a constant ringing in her head as she was dragged up the track between the two young men.

Both pulled up short with Francisca stumbling between them as they noticed a movement amongst the trees just to their right. 'Did you see that?'

'I most certainly did; a woman, wasn't it? She just crossed the path and disappeared into the woods. And I know who it was, too!'

'Who was it then? I hope she isn't going to raise the alarm.'

'Don't worry, son, I think it's going to work in our favour; just wait 'til we get back to the boss, hey? He'll love it.'

Cortés heaved himself out of the car and walked towards the escorted woman staggering towards him, head still down on her chest, not quite conscious. That suited everybody as she was normally an obstreperous woman that no one could better. 'Boss, I think someone's been spying on us; we caught a glimpse of that pretty blonde bint flitting through the trees.'

Cortés thrust his head forwards eager to know more. 'What did you say, you? Someone's been spying on us? Who was that then?' he demanded taking hold of the young man's collar and thrusting his face menacingly close in his usual hostile manner determined to dominate this cocky young fellow.

'I can't be certain, but I think it was that young blonde nurse; you know, the one who had a look at your dick when you had the clap.'

Cortés boxed the young man's ears. 'I didn't have the clap, you twat, I had a rash in my groin and it was very painful. Comes from working hard on a red-hot day; I was all sweaty and it hurt more than you could bear, you pathetic little turd.'

'Someone said it was your dick but it was so small she couldn't find it so put the ointment elsewhere,' continued the risk-taker enjoying the chuckles coming from his colleagues. 'Anyway, how come you'd been working? That's not like you; if you had a rash it was probably from sitting on your arse.'

Cortés pulled a pistol from out of his waistband and pointed it at the young man; he'd had enough of the coarse humour at his expense. 'Shut your mouth, silly little boy,' he squeezed through gritted teeth. 'And be careful how you speak to me in future or I'll blow your fucking brains out.' He grabbed hold of Francisca and pushed her into the young man. 'Keep hold of her until we get back; if she gets away I will kill you and that's a certainty.' He turned to the rest of the gang. 'It's time we picked up the other women.'

Cortés knew there was no need for caution as Juana must have seen what they were up to, so they ran across the cobbles and down the path to the poorer part of the village.

But Cortés was wrong. Juana hadn't noticed the kidnappers taking Francisca up the other track; if she had she may well have planned her escape differently. With cautious haste she thought it would be better to run into her house to get a few essentials first and then pick up Alicia. After that she would make her way down the track to meet Pastora at the old goat house.

All her plans turned to dust as the men crashed through the unlocked door. The candle gave off enough light to illuminate their faces, smug and menacing.

27

ABANDONED BY GOD

Autumn 1938

'Have we a treat in store for you, lucky girl,' Cortés said grinning through tobacco-stained teeth. Juana felt helpless. Her first thoughts were for Alicia; what should she do? He must never take Alicia so best not to mention her. What of Pastora and Bartolomé? She must keep quiet about them, too.

She tried to buy time by engaging him in conversation. 'How can I help you, Alfredo?' she said keeping her voice as calm as possible then realising the stupidity of her question as she watched amusement settle onto Alfredo's face.

'I already have plans how you might help me, Blondie,' he grinned, as he spoke with emphasis. 'And the other boys, too,' he said indicating with his arms the rest of the men who had joined Cortés in the room. 'They will need help from you as well; very special help that only a woman of the world like you can provide,' he said with heavy sarcasm. 'It may be demanding work but pleasurable, certainly for the boys, and well within your capabilities I'm sure, enough to make Father Jaime jealous.'

Sickness welled up in Juana's stomach as she realised the implication of his words. She groaned as the muscles in her abdomen contracted in fear of what these men would do. Should she plead, should she fight or should she simply submit to their will? Anger and outrage built up an impossible pressure as adrenaline surged into the bloodstream and tightened the sinews; grabbing the iron pan from the cold stove and screaming in anger she struck at the men by the door. Cortés ducked but the man to his right caught the blow on the shoulder. It was a sickening sound dropping him to the floor wailing like an abandoned child. Juana was easily overwhelmed as the men slapped her with heavy hands and despair quickly returned. Undone, she sobbed loudly calling out Rodrigo's name repetitively as the moaning, injured man pulled himself up from the floor. With face contorted in anger he shaped to punch her but stopped, noticing that although she was struggling the others had a firm grip on her arms and legs. With sinister smile and vengeful intent he took hold of the front of her bodice and pulled slowly and relentlessly until the buttons came away. She pleaded with him to stop but he continued unremorsefully as all eyes, like beacons, appraised the revelation. Juana cringed with the sound of expelled breath and squeezed her eyes shut, cutting out the pain of lustful stares. She dropped her head forwards hoping her loosened hair would fall to cover her shame. It seemed pointless to struggle any more. Someone had closed in upon her; his breath was in her face as a calloused hand wrapped broad fingers about her exposed breast. Throwing back her head she called on Rodrigo to forgive her.

Cortés pushed firmly at the men holding the humiliated woman. 'Go on move, the others will be wondering what we've been up to. Don't want a riot on our hands just because they think you've had an early taster, do we?' They moved towards the door but left space for Cortés to step through onto the track.

'Juana, Juana, where are you, what is the matter?' Pastora called in a low and urgent voice, as she emerged from the darkness holding Bartolomé by the hand. 'We're already late.' Her enquiries came to an abrupt halt as she caught sight of Cortés as he was about to leave the building. Turning quickly to her son and pressing firmly in the small of his back she pushed him away. 'Run, darling, run, bad man is coming, hide.' Bartolomé scuttled away into the undergrowth. She turned back to the leering Cortés and venom flooded her veins. Without a thought to the consequences of her action she launched herself at him striking him in the face with her small canvas bag containing the essentials of her life. She followed through with a rapid kicking and scratching attack. 'You are the bastard who killed my husband. You will rot in hell but not before I rip your face from your filthy body.' Her hate-filled words were emphasised by each blow to Cortés's cowering body. The others pulled her away as he crouched pathetically on the ground. He struggled to his feet and stumbling forwards two steps towards Pastora slapped her hard about the face. As he steadied himself to launch a second strike she spat at him, 'Brave man who fights women, and only when they are held by others; such a brave man, come show your courage again, murderous scum.' As he stepped forwards with increasing anger Pastora shrugged against those who restrained her and swung a right-footed kick into his groin. He grunted and folded onto his knees then rolled slowly onto his side and curled up into a foetal position. He lay there moaning. One of his men started laughing quietly in the hope he would not be heard. The suppressed laughter was contagious and the others unable to contain themselves joined in.

One of them took control. 'Come, lets take the women back up to the square and leave Zorro to cradle his balls. I don't want to be around when the pompous little arsehole gets himself together.'

'Good advice,' confirmed another, 'and, for God's sake, no silly bugger laughing at him when he finds his voice speaking like a castrated duck.' Pastora saw this sudden lightening of the mood as an opportunity to escape but they held her too firmly.

'Let us go, free us; what have we done to deserve this? I beg you, let us go, we will tell no one what has happened.'

'We will leave the village so you will have nothing to fear from us. Please, for our children's sake, let us go,' pleaded Juana but knowing no such thing would happen.

'No way, you witch,' came a voice from the rear. 'I'm going to make sure you suffer more than any of the others I've done before. You've made a big mistake crossing me.' Cortés struggled with his words in a strangulated voice as he limped into the square behind them. His hands twitched as if he did not know quite what to do to relieve the pain apart from pulling down at the crotch of his trousers to bring relief to his assaulted testicles. 'I'm going to tear you bitches limb from limb,' he continued with a breaking voice. 'You will pay painfully for the insults you have inflicted on the honour of a Christian Spain.'

'Your bollocks honour Spain, do they Alfredo?' the cheeky youngster called out, risking Cortés's wrath but making the other men laugh.

'Shut your face, you little shit.' Cortés stepped in closer to the restrained women grimacing and gently rubbing his groin.

Pastora was further enraged by Cortés's closeness to her. She could not contain herself. 'You murdering bastard, you are neither a Christian nor an honourable man. Kill us if you have to but it will be murder, an unwarranted killing of innocent Spanish mothers. We're the ones who honour

Spain, not you, you scrounging low-life.' Pastora noticed
Francisca being held by two other men just to the side of
her and her heart went out to the proud, distraught old lady.
'And look there, we have a decent, honourable woman who
has dedicated her life to Spain, Francisca, widow of a just
man who also dedicated his life to the honour of Spain.'
Juana continued to sob quietly unable to raise the energy
that Pastora generated. 'And look here, wife-beater, look at
the nurse, Juana, who has brought comfort to the sick and
healed the wounded, even you with your sore arse, you foul
man.' Cortés tried to intervene. 'Don't you interrupt me,
maggot,' she screamed leaning forwards to the cowering
man. 'These are not my last words even though you plan to
take everything from me.' She caught something moving
out of the corner of her eye. It was the priest striding with
purpose across the cobbles. 'Ah, now look,' she called out
jeeringly, 'we have Father Jaime who comes to join us.
Come to save our souls, Father, or to satisfy the Devil who
has taken yours?'

Juana was shocked by the way Pastora spoke to the
priest. 'Pastora, that is enough, you must not speak to a man
of God like that.' She then addressed the priest directly
hoping for him to intervene. 'Father Jaime, what can you
do to save us; what have we done to deserve this?' He said
nothing but lifted a wooden crucifix in his hand as if trying
to ward off evil spirits. 'What is it you do, Father, holding
out the crucifix? Are we damned, are we black souls to
be excommunicated?' With her voice breaking in despair
she continued, 'What are we guilty of? What sins have we
committed?' He still said nothing but looked closely at
Juana as if he could see into her soul. She looked back and
was surprised to see his eyes fill with tears. 'Do you weep
for us, Father? Do you recognise our innocence and know
that a great injustice is about to take place?' He still did not

speak but wiped his hand across his brow and rubbed away the tears.

'Child, there is nothing I can do for you; we live in bad times and bad things are done to innocent people. But it is necessary for the greater good of God's children in a restored Christ loving Spain.'

'I am one of God's children,' said Pastora passionately. 'As are Francisca and Juana who never missed a mass, never missed a holy day, helped the poor and fed the hungry. We are God's children. Are you now saying God and His church must abandon us, even on the pain of our death? Why, to save a Spain raped by Franco's Moors?' The priest looked uncomfortable.

'That is so.'

Juana leaned towards him and appealed for his help. 'We will die, Father; will you bury us? Will you say prayers for our souls? Will you bury us, Father? Will you allow Francisca to lie in peace beside her loving husband?'

'That is not possible; I cannot go against the will of God; it has been declared you are no longer a child of God.'

'We are Christians; we have always been Christians, we were christened in the church, we were married in the church, we attended church every week unless we were ill. How can you let them kill us? We are innocent children of God.' Juana wept as she struggled with the words pleading with the priest to at least include them in the church at their death. 'Are we not free from sin? Are we not good people and good mothers? Would not Mary, mother of God, recognise our innocence and would you not be required to explain to her how you and your church conclude we are not innocent?'

Father Jaime dropped his head. He could not concentrate on that which God had commissioned him to do. He failed to look into her beautiful eyes as shame enveloped him. His lust for her was insurmountable; he was so close to her that he was barely able to control the stirrings within. It was physical pain suffered whenever she was near. He felt driven to possess her. His hands, his mouth like different creatures compelled to seek out the soft and most secret places. His curse dissolved his will. Lust lived beneath the cassock, his wickedness hidden within black cloth. This curse dissolved his will so he must cast her out like the Devil to save his soul. She must leave, she must be gone forever and she must burn. Only then could he release his body from the agony of his desire. Her death was the only way to restore his sanity and with the forgiveness of the Holy Father he would return to godlier ways.

'Well, Father, you have heard her. She is a good woman; a better woman than any I know. What is it, Father, what ails you?' Pastora pressed him with strident voice. 'You're supposed to be above all other men, Father, but I suspect you are no different from these salivating tomcats, this collection of disgusting degenerates.' Pastora turned and swept her hands about her to include all who stood in wait. 'Look how they lust for us, Father, and I can see it in your eyes too, Priest. You are consumed by the same base instincts; your godliness is overridden by carnality.'

Juana, still concerned for Pastora's soul, intervened. 'Father, forgive her, she fears death as much as I do but we are innocent of any crime against the state and we are God-fearing children. Why must we die?'

'Christ the Son of God died cruelly upon the cross to absolve us from our sins and He was without sin and God did not save Him. And you, woman, are mortal. Absolute obedience in accordance to the scriptures does not exempt you from sin, for you are a woman. The seeds of sin are within you; kindness, goodness, obedience to your masters is not enough. Christ was innocent, you are less innocent. In this lies the justification.'

28

JOURNEY WITH NO RETURN

Autumn 1938

Miranda sat down resting her head in her hands. Her elbows were on the table and she looked into the empty plates knowing her next job was to clear them away after their simple meal. She waited as Jorge stood facing the door; not a word was spoken between them. They picked up the sound of a woman weeping then the sound of a child, or was it the breaking voice of another terrified woman? Miranda shuddered as she imagined it could be Pepe, her eldest, and glanced to confirm he was still fast asleep by the fire. She felt ashamed at thinking only of herself but could not help it; she had promised to be strong for Jorge's sake but it was no good, she wept. Jorge turned slowly noticing dignity in her distress. 'I know, darling, this is awful but try to focus on our own predicament; we can't do anything to help these poor souls; there is no one on our side, all we can do is to ride out this storm and hope for the best. Where is God in all this? We are the weak, He should help us.'

'I think I know that voice,' she started and before she finished speaking someone beat loudly on the door. They were both startled and Miranda ran across the small room and threw her arms about Jorge.

'I must go. Take care, stay inside and bolt the door after me.'

'Come on, get yourself out here, Jorge, you're needed now; get a grip, start the engine and let's be on our way.' Cortés's lackey beat heavily on the door once again. 'Come on, Jorge, get a bloody move on.'

Jorge turned away from his wife and opened the door and stepped outside. He then pulled it firmly over the protruding flagstone to close it and called through the door. 'Don't forget to bolt the door firmly.' Forgetting Miranda's advice he continued incautiously, 'There's plenty of vermin out here.' Mano looked at him quizzically not sure to what he was referring.

They walked towards the lorry and Mano, knowing an insult was submerged beneath the words, said, 'What are you talking about? There are not many pests around at this time of the year.'

'Well, everything has been turned upside down for us ordinary folk, Mano, we don't know whether we're coming or going. I expect it's the same for all animals and especially vermin and there seems to be more of them about nowadays than we can cope with.' Mano shrugged his shoulders at his nonsense. 'They run around in little packs, Mano; safety in numbers they say; gives them more courage, you know?' Jorge heaved himself up into the lorry, turned and looked down at his escort. 'You OK?' He smiled down at the confused man. 'You happy in your work, Mano?' Jorge caught a look of concern in the man's eyes that could almost be taken for sympathy. *They're mostly shits*, he thought, *but this one could be different*.

Jorge backed the lorry the short distance from his parking place to within five metres of the assembled group. He could see the women kneeling before the priest in the reversing mirror but it was difficult to make out who had been taken by the Falange. Not wishing to draw attention to himself he climbed down quietly from the cab so he could get a better view of the proceedings. He couldn't make out who the older woman was because she seemed to have crumpled and was lying on the cobbles. The priest, in all his regalia, was easily recognised but Jorge could barely hear him; however, there was no doubt now who the other two women were, both good friends of Miranda. He was shocked. He stood frozen in his tracks with open mouth. He wanted to run away to go back to the house, pick up the boys and Miranda, put them in the lorry and drive away into the distance. The improbability of such action succeeding here and now was obvious and as he contemplated how he might do it in the future he noticed a small child at the edge of the square moving towards the group. Jorge sidled around the group keeping a necessary distance from them so as not to draw their attention as he moved towards the child. He knew the little boy. He was Pastora's only child, Bartolomé, and as he came closer he could hear him calling softly between the sobs for his mama. Jorge bent down and swept the child up in to his arms turning his back on the arresting party so he was unseen. *What now?* he thought. He turned back to the lorry but maybe he should sneak back to the house and leave Bartolomé in Miranda's care?

Francisca, as if startled, pushed herself up into a kneeling position pulling the gag away from her mouth and throwing her head back with arms outstretched howled her distress to the blackened sky, a sound to wake the dead. Again she called out even louder her late husband's name. It was prolonged and heart-wrenching, a sound that curdled the blood; within that one distressing call could be felt the anguish, the injustice, the irreplaceable loss and the cruelty to come.

Father Jaime stood up from the women and pressed his hands against his ears as he shuffled away towards the church.

Pastora, her face wet from weeping, called after the retreating priest in a voice broken by emotion. 'Release your ears, Priest; hear the sound of a better Spain purged of its sins by the blood of innocent women.' Pastora wept, her body shaking with painful sobs, unable to speak further.

Juana took up the futile cause and in desperation called out, 'Look at me, Father, look at what they have done to me.' She held the torn bodice of her dress with both hands. 'Look at what the saviours of Spain have done to me.' He turned back as she held the two pieces apart. 'Do I sin to show you the results of their abuse? Do I sin to let you know how much worse the abuse will be before they have finished with me?'

'Cover yourself, woman; know you that I am a man of God?'

'No, Father, you are a disciple of the Devil.' Juana sobbed heavily into her hands then raised her head to speak again. 'I have been a fool, Father, to wave aside your behaviour as innocent; all my friends have told me so. For God's sake redeem yourself, Priest; save us, I beseech you.'

Father Jaime just turned away without a word and made his way back to the dark shadows of the church. He could not wait to hide his shame and with the help of God heal his poisoned mind and wash away the guilt. What they said was true and he ached with the pain of it; the heaviness of his guilt consumed all rational thought. What had happened to all the worthy actions of his calling, to the comfort he should bring to those who suffered, to mercy, and forgiveness? But he could still feel the intensity of their gaze as they cried out first for justice and latterly for mercy. He knelt against the seat inside the confessional box with his arms enveloping his head and wept.

Jorge knew the proceedings would move forward now with the leaving of the priest, and Cortés would be barking orders to his band of thugs very soon. He wiped the tears and snot from Bartolomé's face and put him up in the cab of the lorry. 'Stay there, little man, Mama will be here soon and I'll be back to look after you; go to sleep if you can.' He returned to the back of the lorry just as Mano came looking for him. Jorge prayed that young Bartolomé would keep quiet; he didn't want him to be found and had no idea what would happen to the child once this ugly business was over. Mano was beside himself with grief and knew not what to do. He hated himself, his weakness knowing he could do nothing to help. The others, normally raucous men, were also quiet, but Mano knew this would not be for long. Jorge, of like mind, noticed the change too but had no sense of sympathy or understanding. 'I wish I had a gun,' he murmured to himself. 'I could so easily slaughter the lot of them.' But Miranda's advice repeated itself over and over again in his mind warning him against taking rash action.

Miranda might change her mind if she knew it was Pastora and Juana who were to be the victims. If he'd known what was going to happen he'd have made himself scarce tonight; he had no wish to be involved in anything like this. It was horrible especially as these young women were so close to Miranda; they were her dearest friends and they are my friends too. He choked upon the thought.

'Drop the back; we've got to get them on the lorry. God, I hope they don't make too much of a fuss.' Mano spoke in sombre tones to Jorge. 'I'm not happy with what's going on. Why women?'

Jorge wordlessly indicated his disapproval and then grabbing his arm stopped Mano walking any further. He pulled the tall man towards him and looked into his face. 'Well, do something about it.'

Alfredo Cortés moved in from behind the rear of the lorry and noticed the two men in conversation. 'Hey, you two, we've got work to do; no time to discuss the treat ahead or are you plotting your own little revolution?' His eyes narrowed. 'If either of you screw up this operation then it's your loved ones that'll pay the price; keep that in mind, gentlemen. Now, get the women on the fucking lorry.'

Mano held up the heavy tailboard while Jorge released the retaining catches and they then lowered it so that it hung vertically below the floor of the lorry. There were foot holes cut into the tailboard to make access possible. Mano climbed up and turned to assist Francisca who was struggling to lift her foot up to the first foothold. One held her from behind as another physically lifted her foot and placed it in the hole. Francisca couldn't reach Mano's hand. He called out to the others, 'I need help here; this woman is no lightweight. Come on, give her a push.'

Juana and Pastora watched as they loaded Francisca, cattle-like as if for market, all her dignity stripped as her clothes were disturbed and rode up over her hips. She sobbed as the men treated her to a barrage of insulting comments. Mano pulled her up and seated her in the forward corner behind the cab of the lorry. One of the younger men had climbed up far enough to lift his head above the level of the floor to continue with his stream of caustic remarks. Mano trod firmly on his fingers. 'So sorry, I didn't see them there,' he said with barely disguised sarcasm. 'Oh, and keep your filthy tongue to yourself in future or you'll have to deal with me.'

'Oy, what's going on?' demanded Cortés.

'He stamped on my fingers, boss. I don't think he's one of us; he's trouble.'

'This job would be easier to do if we didn't have scumbags like that little shit involved, boss,' retorted Mano. 'Just let us get the job done properly and do it with a bit of dignity.'

'But we came here for a bit of fun before putting our world right. I'm committed, boss, just like you; a little slap and tickle isn't going to do any harm, is it?'

'The slap and tickle comes later; just get them on the lorry and no more fuss. Oh, and watch it, Mano, right?' Cortés patted the pistol pushed into the waistband of his trousers and looked hard into Mano's face. The implications of this action were not lost on Mano. He knew what a brute Cortés was and didn't want to test him. 'Come on, pretty ones, we haven't got all night.' The young women had made a silent pact. Their virtue and dignity were sacrosanct; they would do whatever was possible to preserve them. Pastora shrugged off the men's hands and stepped unassisted towards the lorry. She was a slender young woman and although she had lost her shoes somewhere along the route on being dragged to the square, still walked like the dancer she was. Her head held high she approached the lorry and brushing away the hands of the men who stood by, climbed with ease and walked to where Mano directed. Juana did the same pushing away the hands and climbed with less ease than her friend. The nearest of the men moved swiftly forward and thrust his hands beneath her skirt; she screamed her disgust at the violation and with that Mano stepped forward swiftly kicking at the men's heads. One, caught by a hefty blow behind the ear, fell heavily to the ground whilst the others attempted to climb onto the lorry to attack Mano. Cortés stepped in shouting at them to stand back. 'We've just been through all this, you idiot,' he said poking his toe at the man lying on the ground. 'Just didn't listen, did you? Get up and join the others by the car. You're travelling with me to a very special place.' The man stood and moved menacingly towards Mano still standing at the back of the lorry. Cortés pulled the gun from the waistband of his trousers and pressed the muzzle into his cheek. 'Do as you're told, you dolt; go to the car.' Cortés then addressed Mano. 'I don't think you have made yourself a friend. In fact, I think you are very much on your own, Mano, so watch your back, you've plenty of enemies.' Others climbed up into the lorry to join Mano as prisoner escorts looking sourly at him as they passed and settled into their seats.

Jorge waited to receive instructions from Alfredo Cortés. The car moved to overtake the lorry and lead the way to the destination no one but Cortés seemed to know but Jorge had pulled up his lorry too close to the entrance of the exit road. Cortés made several attempts to squeeze by the area strewn with rocks and made impassable by deep water-cut gullies. He got out of the car and shouted up at Jorge driving the lorry. He replied, 'I can't reverse because I don't have enough grip in the sand behind me; I've tried already.'

'Well, go ahead then,' said Cortés. 'But when we get to the junction I'll overtake and lead the way. Remember, when you get to the bottom keep well to the right so I can get past without breaking the fucking suspension; there are six of us in the car and all big buggers.'

Jorge drove off steadily; he knew how bad the surface of the road was since the last downpour but with care they should get there without a mishap. Under normal conditions the drive to the junction took about nine or ten minutes but this time it would be closer to fifteen. As instructed he kept well over to the right when he reached the bottom. The right wheel travelled in the deep water-cut gully and took the lorry to the right almost like it was on rails. He stopped to allow the car to overtake and then tried to follow as the car turned to the left. It was impossible; he couldn't get the wheels to turn left as a result of the deepness of the right-hand gully. They had no choice but to continue to the major road to Béjar then try and turn. Cortés was banging on the side of the lorry again. 'What the hell are you doing?'

'I had no choice. I pulled over to let you by but the front wheels were stuck in the gully and I couldn't turn back, so here I am.'

'OK, we've no choice either. It's getting late so we have to do the business here.' Cortés thought for a moment or two then came back. 'Look, drive up the road a few metres then reverse down the hill and stop close to the car but make sure your lights illuminate that pile of rocks there.'

The sick feeling had ridden up almost to his throat making him swallow and it dawned upon him that what he had feared would happen was only minutes away. With a sinking feeling Jorge did what he was asked, parking as close to the car as possible. He switched off the lights hoping Cortés would overlook this part of his instructions. He sat still in the cab and rested his hand on the sleeping Bartolomé. The child, warm under his jacket, slept innocently while the violation of his mother was being planned.

29

THE END

Autumn 1938

Pastora and Juana held Francisca between them as they watched in fear men animated in their discussion by the car. They did not know what was going on; the air was filled with jubilant shouts countered by angry outbursts, all horribly disconcerting. Eventually, with decisions made, they moved as children, excited and energised, back towards the lorry. Mano sat apprehensively still as the group gathered about the rear of the lorry. The other guards leaning forwards in their seats were agitated, wanting to know what was to happen next. Francisca continued to mumble to herself unaware of what was being planned, but Juana and Pastora, realising the men's foul intentions, started to weep. Mano tried to console them but they swept away his attempt of comforting arms; he was crushed knowing he was partly responsible for what had happened. Guilt tortured his innards; it was becoming difficult to breathe.

The tailgate dropped with an ear-splitting crash that drove night-perching birds from the overhanging branches and shook Francisca from her disengaged state. The real world tumbled in on her; in terror she screamed towards the stars but her wailing reached none who could help. With returning strength she flung her guards about like puppets as they dragged her to the end of the lorry where they unceremoniously threw her to the ground. She fell heavily amongst the stones. Appalled at what the men had just done, Juana and Pastora slipped out of Mano's hold and raced to the older woman's aid. They dropped lightly to the ground and gently lifted Francisca to her feet. Blood ran from a wound on her head and she limped painfully as they tried to get her to walk. Cortés stopped them, standing immovably in their way.

'Where do you think you're going?' he commanded as he leant forwards into their faces. 'Not far, that's for certain.' He pointed towards the ditch that ran at the edge of the road. 'Take the old biddy over there by the cutting; that bit like a wall at the side of the track.' The women moved only a few paces then stopped by the deep drainage trench that ran at the foot of the steep bank bordering the edge of the road. 'Come on, turn around, let's have a look at you, show us your best bits.' Cortés laughed coarsely.

When they turned he was closer, standing a few paces from them with his hands behind his back. Francisca had started her unintelligible mumbling once again whilst the other two held her close, as much for their comfort as support for her. 'Lights,' Cortés called out to Jorge, who, without thought, responded. The lorry headlights illuminated the area about them making them wince. They felt even more vulnerable and stood even closer to each other. Cortés drew himself up to his full height, as might Napoleon when addressing his troops, and started to recite the words written on a document held in his left hand. 'I am empowered by the Christian state of our Glorious Spain to ensure the loyalty and purity of our citizens by eradicating any who by their race or ideology are a corrupting force.'

Without a pause he continued, 'You three by association are as guilty as your husbands who were declared enemies of the state. They have been eliminated and the people of a God-fearing Spain are safer for it.'

This was the news that Juana feared she would receive one day. 'Not Rodrigo, not my lovely Rodrigo,' she said stumbling over words. 'You have killed him?'

'Not me, my love, he died at the end of a Moroccan bayonet or two, or three or even more I'm told.' He laughed again. 'I understand they held him up on the points, like skewered meat and as he died, he danced.' The horrible news was received in silence. 'He was very light-footed I hear, Pastora would approve.' Still not a sound and with the lack of response, Cortés's mood changed. 'And like all enemies of the state he'll never be found; he's been stuck in some hole in the swamp, by the road where it crosses the river.'

Juana dropped to her knees, letting go of Francisca and buried her head in her hands. Pastora moved to be beside her but Cortés leant forwards and took hold of her by the hair. 'Stay where you are Gypsy bitch and stand up.' He roughly hauled Pastora to her feet. 'Get together as you were, all of you, I haven't finished yet.' Juana struggled to stand upright as grief overwhelmed all other feelings. The women stood together once more, trembling, their frailty visible to the men who shuffled forwards menacingly. 'Prisoners, look at me, come on, you whores of the Republic.' Their chins lay upon their chests. 'Come, you slags, look at me. I command you look at me.' Slowly the women lifted their heads realising Cortés had moved towards them and was even closer. He could almost touch them. Pastora and Juana still held Francisca steady but could feel her strength draining like water seeping into sand.

Cortés drew his right hand from behind his back and pointed the pistol at Francisca. Without a word and as the women stood frozen, he pulled the trigger. Francisca was thrown backwards by the power of the shot and slipped from the supporting arms of the others. In horror they looked down on the crumpled form that was proud Francisca; her eyes and mouth still open in surprise. Juana knelt quickly beside her in the hope it was all a mistake but as blood started to seep through the thick fabric of her dress she knew there was nothing she could do. Pastora rearranged the murdered woman's disturbed clothing and Juana gently closed her eyes. She prayed for her soul; Pastora joined in with the well-known words believed by the church to bring relief to the bereaved. This was too much for Cortés and he turned towards the men. 'Go, get them; they're yours for the taking.' The men moved tentatively but determination to head the queue seized the many; they squabbled like loose-tongued drunks shoving and pushing to gain advantage. The women prayed. Crystal voices reached high into the branches of the overhanging trees but seemingly not beyond as doubt permeated their minds. Is their Saviour deaf or does He weep unable to comprehend the actions of His church?

They were carried by eager hands towards the boulders, the sacrificial rocks, and held painfully by tortured limbs as others jostled peevishly to be the first. The assault scratched only at the surface of their dignity and, in truth, could not sully their innocence. These were noble women, but the indelible stain of others' foul actions would shame and persecute them through their soon to be extinguished lives. And the victors, in palaces of stolen gold, will demand liars to reconstruct history, laying blame for the monstrosities of this filthy war on those who are nameless and blameless and buried in some distant ditch. Juana could do nothing but pray as her joints were pulled awkwardly backwards to the point of dislocation and the pressure on her body was forcing her spine and shoulder blades onto the teeth of the unforgiving rock.

She knew they were upon her. Could feel them at her flesh. There were teeth upon her neck and coarse bristles on her breast but the pain of dislocation masks the greatest shame of all so she blessed the Holy Mary for an answer to her call.

'Hail Mary Mother of Grace, Hail Mary Mother of Grace, Hail Mary, sweet Mother of Grace.' Pastora picked up the plaintive call finding strength in the chant. *Is there comfort in knowing we suffer equally? Is there truth in trouble shared is trouble halved? God knows.*

Pain, unavoidable pain, and the sense of wrongdoing wrings out all hope as despair, like leeched blood, traces hot lines through the burning guilt. How plaintive is the whispered call of those who gave us life, fed us and left nothing for themselves, kept us safe and answered for our failings, and still at the point of death will try to save us from ourselves.

How will we be judged? Is this sordid crime my crime? Did I unwittingly bring fervour to their lust; unknowingly did I wake temptation in the dormant beast that sleeps so lightly in the recesses of dark minds? Am I not the crime? Pastora wept and strained her pretty head to seek one lasting glimpse of her perfect friend. *Juana, touch me, kiss me as the light fades; pain is nothing but distant thunder beyond the shadowing hills. I am now lifted to pause amongst the highest soft-limbed branches; leaves caress the air and from here I see, I'm gone.*

Jorge had remained in the lorry's cab, rigid as if in death unable to breathe. Gripped by the horrors of the unfolded events he could not pull his eyes away from that which followed. Safe in the false thought that the child Bartolomé still slept, he leant forwards onto the dashboard and peered through the misted windscreen. Mano had not dismounted from the back of the lorry; being tall he looked out over the cab as he leant upon its roof. He knew the women were to be executed but the killing of Francisca had taken him by surprise. He was horrified. Unknown to Jorge it was the very same shot that woke Bartolomé. Mano kept watching but Jorge turned away to rest his mind from the appalling images, unaware that Bartolomé now perched upon the seat, peered through the quarter-light.

Unable to draw his eyes away the child, of so few years, watched as cruel images seared his mind, such images to question his sanity in the years to come.

Jorge opened his eyes; he had failed the child. 'Bartolomé, no, don't look, hide your eyes, for God's sake, hide your eyes,' Jorge hissed in shame as Bartolomé witnessed the savage scene he had tried to protect him from, that which would torment him for the rest of his life. 'God grace him with forgetfulness.' Jorge tried to assuage his guilt knowing it would be unlikely as the horrific events were now indelibly etched on his own toughened mind. He would bear these scars for the rest of his days as would the child Bartolomé.

And what of Miranda? How could he tell Miranda? He held Bartolomé close to his body with his face away from the window. *They must not know he is here, or they will take him, too.* Jorge wrapped Bartolomé tightly in his jacket, enough to restrain his arms and placed him in the footwell. In despair, Jorge willed the child asleep. Does not sleep salve the horrors of the day? With imperceptible shaking of the head he tearfully denied the hope. He gently rocked Bartolomé with his foot, and allowed himself to continue looking through the screen awaiting what next these monsters would do.

30

MANO'S REMORSE

Autumn 1938

The brutality of the rape was over and the men were standing or sitting, some adjusting clothing but none in conversation; they were at a loss as eyes sought unrelated sights upon the ground or gazed blankly into the accusing shadows of dense foliage. Pastora had been turned and now lay on her front with her toes barely touching the broken earth. She was finished. She sprawled like carelessly left washing drying in the heat of the night. Her bright red dress lay about her with remnants trailing like pennants over the slenderness of her dancer's legs. The colour of the dress and black silken strands of hair held by moisture about her bared shoulders were the only indications of who this might have been. The stillness belied the drama. She was nought but something forgotten from the day before. To them, who could not look another in the face, this had been Pastora savaged, brutalised and broken. Here she lay, the lifeless remains of a once beautiful dancer; the crimes of which she was guilty, her beauty, an infectious personality and the joy her dancing brought to others.

Mano sobbed at the sight. Guilt twisted every organ in his body choking each function making it difficult to breathe. He was a coward, a spineless, shameful failure who could not find the courage to go to her; nor could he save the kindly Juana who selflessly tended the sick. His self-loathing brought bile into his throat; snot, tears and vomit were coughed upon the roof of the cab as he struggled for his breath. On weakened legs he lowered himself to the floor and wished to die and it was that thought that gave him purpose. It gave him strength, a steely purpose to reclaim some honour and with it came a stiffening of the sinews as adrenaline increased the pace of his heart. He pushed up from the floor with his hands gripping the coiled rope that lay amongst the year-long debris.

Both he and Jorge, unaware of each other, caught the movement of Cortés as he lifted himself from the embrace he'd forced upon Juana. The light smile upon his coarsened features shrivelled into the meanness that best reflected his mind. He struggled with his clothing and rebuckled his thick leather belt then took the long-handled shovel from another standing by. He looked over his shoulder towards Juana and smiled again. She was still arched painfully over the rock as she struggled to raise her head. Her fingers clawed at the cruel surface trying to gain purchase; but she failed. Her collapsing body slipped towards the ground. With knees splayed, she wrestled with the effort to straighten her legs and regain some control. She persisted, groaning as she struggled to be in an upright position by pressing back onto the rock with her hands. Cortés took his opportunity and jabbed her sharply in the midriff with the handle of the steel-bladed shovel. Gasping, she lifted her head and at that moment Cortés swung the blade striking her on the head. The sickening sound told all who stood by that life had been driven from her. Bleak silence gripped the appalled observers as the last breath was exhaled; a long regretful sigh that deflated form as head, shoulders, arms and torso folded slowly upon collapsing legs settling uncomfortably at the foot of the rock. And she was still.

Cortés turned to his men, thrusting his hips forwards like a triumphal matador and using his left arm, indicated his slaughtered victim. Mano strode past him brushing him aside making him stagger into the men nearby. The tall man's attention was solely on Juana. He dropped to his knees beside her whispering a prayer. With no thought to those who stood around he lifted her gently away from the foot of the rock and laid her respectfully upon a clear space. He pulled down what was left of the skirt of her dress covering her below the knees. The bodice had been torn into strips and that which had been shredded hung by threads about her waist. Mano felt uncomfortable with intimacy of his duty but pulled together just enough of the fabric to cover her breasts. With fingers as light as feathers he closed her lifeless eyes and picking up the rope he stood. With heart breaking he lowered his eyes in shame hoping that he had done enough for her to forgive him. But it was not enough for him to avenge her so turning swiftly on his heel he moved rapidly in on Cortés and stood uncomfortably close to him.

'Well, heroes of our glorious revitalised Christian Spain, have we celebrated enough?' he bawled with straining voice. 'How will your achievements of tonight be viewed in the future? Will you tell your grandchildren how you saved Spain from such enemies of the state as these?' Mano swept his hands around taking in the bloodied evidence of their night's work. No one would look at him; even Cortés had turned his head away. 'Look to your leader; an honourable man, visionary and not without courage; did he not slaughter the enemy singlehandedly. One against three: Francisca, fifty years old with a tongue as sharp as a razor; he took her down with one shot. Bravo! And Pastora, a terrifying dancer who may snap her castanets too close for comfort. And what of Juana? Did you know she put a stinging cream on our fearless leader's sores? Let him be an example to us all. Our *Cid*, *El Cid* of the rejuvenated Spain. Did you not witness his courage standing up against her? Did you see he crushed her skull with his shovel? She won't threaten anyone with her healing any more.'

Cortés could take no more; with a roar of exasperation he pulled his pistol from his waistband and pushed it into Mano's face.

'Do your damnedest, foul little man, pot-sized demon. Pull the trigger and do me a favour.'

'I'm not going to kill you now, treacherous bastard, we're going to take you back and make you suffer first.' Cortés turned to his men and spat out, 'Bind him, use wire like we do on Republican scum; treat this traitor as he deserves.'

Not one of the men stepped forwards, some even turned their backs on him. 'Come, I order you, take charge of the prisoner. I want him bound now!' he shouted. 'Thrown into the back of the lorry, now, I say; throw the bastard in the back of the lorry.' He screamed but no one moved. 'And when we get back to the interview room I want him covered in blood; not a tooth left in his mouth, you hear? And cut his bollocks off; if they're still in place when he gets there, I'll have yours instead.'

Still no one moved, and Cortés knew he would get no help. What had happened tonight lay heavily on the consciences of the many who made up the cleansing group; bastards as they were, shame laced their latter thoughts. Cortés now knew he would have to resort to the simple action; kill him here and now. Mano recognised the change in his opponent's expression and knew what would happen next. He didn't give him a chance. He backhanded the little bully catching him in the face. Cortés hung on to the pistol and was bringing it back up to fire just as Mano returned his right arm in a brutal hook to the head. Sadly, for Mano, it caught Cortés over his ear sending him to the ground still conscious but fortunately the pistol slipped from his grip to disappear into the shadows. Still no one moved; Mano looked to them for some response. There was none.

'I'm done with this, we've dishonoured all that is good.' He spoke in lowered tones. 'I am not guiltless; it is my shame. I am undone.' Mano lifted his head and looked hard at his one-time friends imploring them with his eyes to speak in assurance that what he felt was true for them too. 'What have we done in the name of God and Spain? Where is God in what we do? He's not here; it is the Devil who masquerades as Him. We live a lie.'

The men had moved together as if to seek safety in numbers, but none spoke, no one would look another in the eyes. Mano shook his head slowly acknowledging that their confusion rendered them mute. He had said all he could say, he could form no other words and with a backward glance at the destroyed Juana he put one hand across his mouth and wept, struggling with his final words, 'I weep not just for what we have done but for our souls. We allowed a monster into our midst, the Devil's disciple, who will continue to feed on us and our children; God help us.'

Holding the coiled rope in his left hand he walked between the assembled men, some of whom touched him gently on the back. Across the road he walked, down the steep wooded slope towards the oaks deep in the forest. So deep in the darkest place that he may never be found.

Cortés had regained his feet and found the pistol two strides away. Brushing himself down and struggling to regain his authority he demanded the men carry their victims to the deep drainage ditch where Francisca lay tidily in isolation.

'What, now, boss? I thought we were going to dig holes in the forest for them.'

'We're out of time; the drainage ditch will have to do. It's deep enough, just make them fit the space.' Cortés stood at the edge of the ditch and instructed the men about their gruesome business. They put Francisca into the ditch first then lowered Pastora so that she was head to head with the older woman. When they carried Juana forward one of the men pointed out that the ditch was shallower towards the Béjar road so there wouldn't be enough depth to completely cover the blonde one. 'Well, turn her round, legs to legs and push her up the ditch. Let her straddle the others,' said Cortés. 'There's enough room if you double the legs up in that part of the ditch.'

One or two of the men treated the women's remains with as much respect as was possible. They crossed arms across their chests and rearranged clothing to create as much modesty as possible. Hair was pulled into place about their broken heads and fragments of torn material from the dresses were placed across their faces before the soil and stones were shovelled in to cover their brutalised remains. All but a few were silently respectful and others hid their tears of shame. Cortés snatched the shovel from the hands of the one responsible for filling in and walked over the grave patting down the areas of loose soil. 'Is that really necessary, boss? That's a grave, you know. Show them some respect.'

'Get stuffed; they were slags and got what they deserved. Trouble with you, baby boy, is that you don't know nothing about women. Keep them in their place, I say. That's either the kitchen or the bedroom.' He then laughed raucously at his own ages-old insult. He stopped surprised when he realised no one else was laughing. 'Right, get back in the vehicles, we're going home.' He walked across to Jorge who had not moved from the driving cab throughout the whole disgusting rape. 'Wake up, you idle bastard, we're going, so get a grip.' He turned back to him with the usual cruel grin upon his face. 'You shouldn't find it so difficult for this old crate of yours to make it back up the hill, now that you're not carrying so many passengers.' He laughed again and for the second time he laughed alone.

31

JORGE GOES HOME

Autumn 1938

The distraction of keeping young Bartolomé safe and away from the prying eyes of this band of thugs did little to save Jorge from the most brutal of sights. His hatred of these wicked men built up in him like over-pressurised steam to the point that he might throw caution to the wind and set about them with the steel starting handle he now held in his right hand. Bartolomé, stirring in his sleep, reminded Jorge that his adrenaline-charged energy would better serve the victims of this foul crime by being used for more humanitarian purposes. Pastora's child needed him. Logic saved him from irrational action that would undoubtedly have ended in his own death. He shuddered at the thought knowing Miranda, the boys and now Bartolomé would have become victims also. He watched them bury the women and was appalled at the disrespectful manner Cortés finished off the work. It was not necessary for the disgusting little man, blue-shirted saviour of Spain, to have stamped heavy feet upon their broken bodies nor for him to have beaten the soil with his murderous shovel to complete the job. The men had stood back, heads bowed, believing the job to have been done well enough but Cortés seemed to relish his dancing on their grave and the grin on his face made Jorge's skin crawl. One of his men took Cortés by the arm speaking sharply to him as he tried to pull him away. Cortés responded by throwing off the man's hand and taking a swipe at his legs with the sharp-bladed shovel.

Jorge felt bitter contentment as he recognised the first stirrings of disharmony within the group. Mano stomping off into the forest did not surprise him, for he was a good man; how he got tangled up with this lot he did not know. Probably his joining the Falange was a direct order from his arrogant boss, Don Pedro. *A callous bastard*, thought Jorge, *the swine would rather have empty cottages than give shelter to the penniless.* This was a man who saw destitution as a crime and charity as a sign of weakness; despite all this he was known and respected as a good man. The church applauded him; surely godliness and wealth were just what the church needed. This last thought drew a wry smile from Jorge. In his view Christ Himself would find recovery of this church almost beyond His reach. The God of his people, loved by all, who protected simple folk, would never condone the actions of those who claimed to be His representatives. Not those who strutted on marble floors in silk and silver thread, nor they who congregated amongst the pews intoning mysterious sounds that halted the breath and reached beyond the Moorish arches laced in Inca gold.

With each thought he felt himself stepping further away from that which had been so important in his life. What use was Father Jaime in trying to save those tortured, wretched women? You would have thought the priest would have tried harder to save them, especially with his rumoured favouring of Juana. Maybe he saw her as too much of a temptation and would be glad to see her gone. Difficult to believe he could be so callous. Who would trust him again? 'I'm going to say my prayers in the forest in future,' he mumbled to himself, 'and we'll make our own little church under the trees.' These thoughts comforted him as he imagined Miranda on his arm with his boys and trusted friends all seeking untarnished peace in nature's simple temple. A fragment of his anxiety gave way to hope.

His reverie was broken when Cortés slapped his hand on the driver's-side window. No, he wasn't asleep contrary to Cortés's coarse remarks and sadly he was right; it would be easier on the lorry as it climbed the hill back to village with fewer people on board. This was not his major concern. It was what he was going to say to Miranda that troubled him. He must maintain a semblance of neutrality for safety's sake; can't have Cortés seeing him as any form of threat. One of the men tried to open the passenger door to get in but Jorge had fortunately locked it to stop Bartolomé from opening the door and revealing his presence. 'Sorry, mate, the door's broken and I can't open it; and anyway, look at the state of your boots, I can't have you bringing all that mud in here. Get in the back with the others. It's only a short journey.' Jorge gave him what he hoped would be seen as a friendly smile. There was no argument as the man climbed up into the back of the lorry with the others. Cortés hooted as he drove his car back up the Béjar road and disappeared. *So, I've only got the local boys*, thought Jorge, *and I'll be glad to get rid of them*. He had no idea what time it was as he guided the lorry over the pitted surface of the village road nor did he know how long the men had been about their monstrous business. It seemed like hours with every horrible event being drawn out sadistically. It could have all been over in a matter of minutes if Cortés had kept control of his men but that vile man relished cruelty. His wife, cousin to Jorge, was a poor little creature reduced to nothing but a shadow of her former self. She was never a great beauty but she was kind and attentive and a great chatterbox but look at her now; a bitter, old-before-her-time bag of bones who seemed to forever carry evidence of his heavy hands.

Within fifteen minutes or so he pulled the lorry to a halt in the square close to his house. He climbed out of the cab and helped the men down. They didn't speak nor did they acknowledge him but Jorge was determined to get some response from them. He knew these men didn't live in and about the main body of the church or the houses that clustered about the square. 'Got far to go, boys?' he said with false levity.

'What's it to you?' said one as he stepped menacingly close to Jorge. 'Why would you want to know where we live? You a fucking spy then?'

'Don't be daft, boys, I'm only interested, wondering if you've got far to go. I could make you a coffee if you have a bit of a journey ahead; just being friendly.'

'Look, don't bother being friendly; we noticed you did bugger all down there. I suppose you think you're better than us, just because you didn't get your hands dirty.' The other men had stepped away from the lorry and entered a ramshackle old building, a lean-to against the church wall and returned with the bicycles. 'Thanks, Bart,' said the tall, obstreperous man ignoring Jorge, for the moment, as he took charge of one of the bicycles being wheeled towards him; he then turned back to Jorge and addressed him with barely concealed anger. 'Now look, Mr "Driver" waste of space, I'll be happy never to see you again but if I do, it'll be to beat the shit out of you and especially if I hear you spreading lies about what really happened tonight.' He poked his finger into Jorge's chest. 'And to satisfy your curiosity we're going to cycle down the northern track to our cosy little homes and our lovely little wives. I suggest you get yourself back to yours; enjoy it while it lasts. We know where she lives.'

Jorge was inflamed by the implication and stepped up close to the man taking him by the collar and causing him to stumble over his bicycle as he hauled him towards him.

'Easy tiger,' the man smiled wickedly. 'We may be shagged out but there are three of us here and we'd be happy to give you a battering now if you like; comes as second nature to us. If you've a problem with that have a word with the dead, they'll confirm it.' He pushed Jorge's hand away and mounted the bicycle. They rode across the square laughing with each other and Jorge watched in disgust until they disappeared noisily into the forest.

Climbing back into the lorry he reversed it into the spot beside the cottage then picked up the sleeping Bartolomé from the cab floor, holding him tightly as much for his comfort as for Bartolomé's. He felt the events of the evening getting the better of him; he left the lorry, making sure he closed the door without a sound. As he approached the door of his small cottage it opened and Miranda stood waiting with a candle in her hand. She looked at the child and understood what had happened. She moaned softly. 'No, not Pastora, oh God, please not Pastora. What have you done, Jorge? What have you done?'

Jorge, shocked by her implication, looked back into her candle lit eyes imploring her to understand. 'Not me, my darling, how could you believe it could be me?' He stepped inside the house and looked for a place to put the child. Miranda indicated their own bed and Jorge with great tenderness placed the sleeping child in the security of the centre.

'Oh, my poor Pastora, is she dead? What has happened? Did you see what happened? Where is she now and why have you got Bartolomé?'

'Miranda, she's dead.' All the pent-up emotions started to erupt; he could no longer hold them in check. He was not a man to tolerate the sight of other men weeping but the horrors of the night had eroded his resistance; he just stood with his hands covering his face and sobbed. He felt her arms about him bringing warmth and comfort but it did not take away the pain or his increasing sense of shame.

'Was she the only one? I heard Francisca's voice earlier; has she been taken, too?'

'If bad news such as this could be any worse what I have to tell you is more painful than just the loss of Pastora.' Jorge stopped unable to carry on until he regained his composure. Miranda put her hand gently under his chin and lifted his head so she could look into his face. 'They took Juana as well; both your lovely friends are dead and so is Francisca.'

'Where are they? What have they done with my lovely sisters?' she whispered with a voice breaking within the weight of such horrible news. She was barely audible.

'They are buried in the forest; they are all together. Small comfort but they are all together.'

Unnoticed by Jorge because of the failing candlelight his wife also wept as she had done long before Jorge came to the door. She had picked up the sharp exchanges between her husband and the men outside and already knew the danger in which they lived. 'We are living through horrible times, Jorge; we must be careful to do nothing that might aggravate those who hold over us the power of life and death. We must move to somewhere away from all this wickedness or make ourselves invisible somehow.'

'Miranda, I have seen things tonight that would make God himself curse and I ache for vengeance on these most evil of men; men I know who've changed for the worse because of this filthy war.' Jorge paused again to assemble his senses. 'When I think clearly, I know it is not just me that will suffer if I take on the Falange, for I will most certainly lose against that force and it will be my beautiful wife and my lovely boys who will pay the price.'

'Stay safely with us, Jorge, use the head and ignore the heart. We need you.'

'Come, we must sleep; we'll be no use to man nor beast unless we rest,' he mumbled. 'There's much to discuss tomorrow and we need to recover our energy.' Within minutes he was asleep, but he turned, twisted and groaned in subconscious torment. Miranda anxiously looked on as she changed Bartolomé, the surprise addition to her family, into the outgrown, clean, dry clothes of her youngest son. The child slept soundly but Miranda could only lie open-eyed and think of all that had been lost, the fear that worse was yet to come and that God and His church had abandoned those who needed Him most. They had no place to go and no one to turn to. Sleep slipped even further away as she recalled the threatening words spoken to her husband less than an hour ago. It was they who raped and slaughtered her friends and, without doubt, would do the same to others. Once they had tasted blood, how much easier it would be for them the second time.

Jorge had slept through what had been left of the night and woke as the sun rose enfeebled by the mist that hung above the forest floor to stain the morning red. The firmament beyond lay still, vast and pale with shadowed mountains dark against the subdued light while flocks of birds insensitively squabbled in branches of the tallest trees. The freshness of a new day and the hope it so often brought was missing. The horror of the previous night's bloodletting gnawed at the mood of all as neighbours moved cautiously to peer through opening doors.

Did the priest call all his parishioners to Angelus? Or did the bell toll for those who lay cold in the cloying earth of the still dark forest? 'We must dress, Jorge,' said soft-voiced Miranda, 'and be ready for any eventuality; be prepared, those murderers might yet return to confirm we will never trouble them again.'

'They won't be here this early but we must let all decent people know what happened although I expect it's already common knowledge.'

'Tell them the whole truth Jorge, leave no detail out. Crush their chance to distort the truth and save us who suffer most, from their lies and insidious rumours.'

'I will not fail the painful truth, precious Miranda. Anguish, like acid, courses in my veins and raw-fleshed images from last night possess all thoughts. I can do nothing but tell the truth. It has strengthened my will, given me courage and I will tell it to those who can bear to listen.'

Miranda looked back at Jorge with anxious eyes. Something else disturbed her. 'If Juana is dead, where is Alicia?'

32

BURIAL GROUND

Summer 2008

Although Santo Domingo was no great distance as the crow flies from Bartolomé's care home it was quite a long way by the tortuous road that cut through the mountainside and then followed the river as it meandered through the high valley. Nevertheless it was awe-inspiring and Natascha spent most of the journey gracing each view with approving sounds. The day was perfect for a journey into the hills; all the early morning haze had gone and powdery clouds peppered a vast blue sky. She was taken by surprise by the sharpness of some of the switchback bends having to use the full width of the road to negotiate them; each time she prayed nothing would be coming towards them from the other direction. As they climbed into the more densely forested areas driving was made even more difficult as they were forced to take the corners blind. Natascha could not see through the foliage that grew up so close to them from the edge of the road. This is like driving through a tunnel, she thought. It was a leap of faith, but she took them slowly giving her as much chance as possible to stop if necessary.

'You don't half drive slow, Natascha; do you think we'll ever get there?' Bartolomé teased her.

'Take care, Bartolomé, if you don't behave yourself I might leave you on the mountainside.'

This time he knew she was joking and just smiled to himself.
'It's not far to go now anyway and I'm starting to feel just a bit
nervous.' He fidgeted in his seat and glanced over to her for
reassurance. Natascha could feel his agitation growing and she
knew it was nothing to do with her driving, but more likely their
destination. His voice changed and Natascha knew what must
be going through his mind. 'I don't know why we're joking and
laughing because this is a terrible place. It is full of bad memories.'
He seemed to have shrunk into the car seat and was uncomfortable
with being seen from the outside. 'It's not just me, other people have
said the same. I'm not even sure what I remember, everything comes
back all broken up. It's jumbled, all out of order, I know. What
some of the really old people told me helps me remember.' She leant
across to reassure him and tapped him on the knee. He was silent
for a while and Natascha knew from experience it was better to wait
and say nothing. He was talking to himself as his thoughts flowed
over the memories and images in his mind. Then he looked up at
her. 'What happened to you in the venta, Natascha, that also helped
my memory to work.'

Natascha knew she had to treat him as gently as possible and
looking towards him said, 'Look, I'm here with you; we've been
through other frightening episodes together and survived. Don't
you remember how nice you were to me after what happened in
the venta? You were great then and it's time now for you to be
great again.' Natascha surprised herself by being able to ignore his
elderliness and treat him like a distressed child. It was only recently
that it had dawned on her that Bartolomé was as much a victim
of that horrible war as any who had died in it. She recalled the
conversation she had had with the cleaner in the home talking
about the nightmares Bartolomé suffered, his nervousness at being
left in vulnerable places and other more minor incidents. Yes, there
was quite a lot of child in Bartolomé and she was convinced the
emotional damage he suffered must have happened that night his
mother was kidnapped, raped and then murdered. It was not quite

the way Bartolomé put it to Natascha in the venta but she knew exactly what he'd seen. Natascha noisily drew in a breath then held it. This evoked a quick and questioning glance from Bartolomé. On breathing out, an involuntary shudder coursed through her body; was this place still haunted by a great wickedness?

'Natascha, stop here, please; I don't want to go any further for a moment or two.'

'It's difficult to park here, Bartolomé, but if I just pull up on to the grass verge there should be enough space for any other cars to pass.' She slowed the car to a stop and then changed her mind. 'Look, I'm going to use the other side of the road; I'll get out on the grass because it will be easier for you to get out on the paved area, OK?'

Natascha swung the car across the road to the opposite side; then looking carefully through the windscreen made sure her selected parking spot was clear of hidden drainage ditches or large stones, of which there were certainly plenty around. She drove the car up into the long grass and bumped along the verge to park. Neither of them moved nor did they say a word. Natascha waited as Bartolomé prepared himself to walk once again to the place where his mother had died. He had been here only a few times in his life. The last time was with a stranger, some official, and his secretary or so he thought she was his secretary; she was a woman, anyway, and very kind and did all the writing.

'The last time I was here I was brought by an important man and a very kind lady. They wanted to know what had happened on that night and he kept asking whether I was sure this was the spot.' Bartolomé looked annoyed still wondering if the man had been accusing him of being stupid. 'Of course it is the spot, I told them, getting a bit cross. Everybody I've spoken to has told me it is the spot, even the old man who came down and covered them over properly told me it was the spot and I knew him. He's died now, you know?' Natascha waited for him to continue knowing he still had more to say. 'Anyway, as I said, I got a bit upset and the lady

took me back to the car whilst the man took out a map and wrote something on it. He also took a few photographs; you should have seen the size of the camera; it had a big wooden tripod.'

'When you're ready, Bartolomé, do you think you could take me up there?' Natasha said very gently and waited a while before adding, 'Do you want me to help you get out of the car? Or we could wait a bit longer if you like; we're not in a hurry, are we?' It was clear to Natascha that his irritability was starting to come to the surface again and she feared he would have another tantrum and demand to go home. She pre-empted him by saying, 'Look, would you like to go home?' He didn't reply but instead opened the door and swung both of his feet onto the road surface. Natascha left the car and moved quickly around to get the wheelchair unfolded and in place.

'No, I don't want to use that, I'm going to walk using my stick and lean on your arm. Is that all right with you, Natascha?' She pushed the wheelchair up on the verge where it was hidden by the car.

Natascha left it there because she was certain he would need it before the walk was done. 'Of course, dear sir, it will be my pleasure to walk with you.' They set off up the road towards a collection of big rocks. 'Wow! Look at the size of those boulders, Bartolomé. They're enormous and so smooth.'

'They're not smooth; they're like a cobbler's rasp,' he said crossly. 'That's where it happened.'

Natascha stopped in her tracks, shocked and slightly overbalancing Bartolomé who was hanging onto her arm for support. She stood as if frozen not wishing to move a step closer; it was well over fifty years ago that this appalling act had happened but you could almost feel it in the air here and now. To Natascha it seemed like only yesterday. This was the site of the brutal attack; could there still be evidence? Why did so little grow here? It was spooky. Would the women's blood still stain the ground? Of course not, but this was a dark place full of menace that perpetuated the mood of that dreadful night over half a century ago.

'Don't be frightened, Natascha, there are no ghosts here,' said Bartolomé trying to make light of what had happened.

She looked at him as if he had been disrespectful. 'Bartolomé, how can you be so casual about this place? This is where your mother died.' Natascha paused as she noticed the pain in his eyes. 'Sorry, Bartolomé, you were only trying to be brave.' She put her arms around him and held him steady. They both wanted a short time for contemplation. 'Come on, show me the ditch where they were buried; that's what we came for, isn't it? That's the place we should say a little prayer.'

They walked past the boulders across the difficult, unsurfaced road that switched back on itself and wound its way up to Santo Domingo and then into the adjacent lay-by. It was just like a widening of the road with the part closest to the cutting having been used recently to store piles of road-repairing gravel. It was not a place that cars or other vehicles could pull into easily or should use to park as it was on the hairpin bend that took the traveller down into the river valley. Larger vehicles than cars including the infrequent bus needed to use the space to navigate the sharp bend.

They stopped walking close to the cutting wall. 'There's no ditch here, Bartolomé, just the remnants of gravel and mud.'

'Well, you've got to know what happened. The drainage ditch used to run at the base of this high bank, the cutting done by road workers years and years ago. Anyway, there used to be a deep drainage ditch that took most of the rainfall around the back of the road and dropped it over there,' said Bartolomé pointing across the road. 'Go and have a look; you can still see the old channel to this day.'

Natascha walked around the outside of the bend noticing that some recent work had reinforced the lower side of the road with concrete buttresses. Looking down the steep wooded hillside she noticed across to her left a deeply cut channel. There was no water but the stones and rocks were covered in beautiful rounded mounds of moss. It was really a very pretty sight. 'Yes, I see it; it's a lovely spot, Bartolomé, *a fitting natural memorial to those who...'* She let her voice fall away as there was nothing that could compensate for the loss of his mother. She made her way back to Bartolomé who was using the steep bank for support.

'I can't come here very often for obvious reasons but I'm glad you've seen the place.'

'What I don't understand is why the ditch has been filled in; what happens to the rainwater now?'

'Natascha, I told you what happened; isn't it obvious why the ditch is filled in?' He started to become anxious giving way to his belligerent behaviour of the past and it alarmed Natascha. She knew she had to calm him down quickly. He beat his stick upon the ground in rhythm with his words. 'I've told you before, they put them in the ditch here,' he pointed, 'and then they covered them up.'

Natascha realised her stupidity. 'Yes, you did, Bartolomé, I'm just being a dunderhead. Of course I remember.' He stopped using the stick to bludgeon the ground and allowed Natascha to take his arm. 'I think we need to let you sit down, you've been on your feet quite a long time now. Please, tell me again what you saw. We'll talk as I help you back to your chair.'

Bartolomé used his stick again but to point out to Natascha the fine gravel scattered along the pull-in area. 'They used this spot to unload piles of gravel for the winter; it gets very cold up here and icy on the roads, so if someone gets their vehicle stuck on that bend there,' he said pointing with his stick at the sharp bend to the right, 'they get out their shovel and scatter it under the wheels. There used to be a shovel left here to do the job but thieving hands kept taking it; so you've got to have your own shovel now.'

'Do you mean to say that the authorities used this place where the ladies were first buried as a dump for gravel?'

'They're still there.'

'What?' called out Natascha in astonishment. 'Are you telling me those poor souls are still buried here?'

'Yes, they are, nobody is allowed to move them. People have tried but the council don't want them moved and anyway the churches don't want them reburied in their graveyards as they're sinners.'

'Do you mean to say that your mother and my grandmother's godmother are still lying in that ditch?' She looked hard into his eyes and the coldness and anger there affirmed that this was so. Natascha helped him into the chair. 'There, is that better? Do you want a blanket? You're not cold, are you?' She stood up from the chair waiting for some sort of answer but his head had dropped to his chest. 'Bartolomé, I'm just going back over there for one last look and then we'll go home.'

'Don't be long,' he mumbled. 'I am tired and this place always upsets me.'

'I'm not surprised; I promise I won't be long.' With that she turned away to cross back to the graves.

'A car's coming, I can hear it,' called out Bartolomé.

'Don't worry, I'll keep out of its way as it takes the bend,' called back Natascha. The car was labouring on the uphill climb and she knew it would be a little while before it took the bend by the graves but she needed to hurry for Bartolomé's sake. She crouched down in the place where the ditch used to be and looked closely at the ground. It was deeply scored where a machine had picked up loose gravel and had scraped away some of the topsoil in the process. Out of curiosity she picked at something beneath the disturbed surface yellowed with age, and she pushed it unseen into the side of her trainer.

'Hey, you! What do you think you are doing?'

Natascha turned to face the smartly dressed young man who approached her in an aggressive manner. 'I'm here to pay my respects to a person who was buried here many years ago,' replied Natascha annoyed by his attitude. 'What business is it of yours, anyway? Why don't you clear off and leave me alone?' she snapped at him then turned back to what she was doing and tried to imagine him not being there. He grabbed her roughly by the arm.

'Who are you? What are you doing in this place?' He now held her by both arms and shook her. 'Answer me, damn it, answer me.' Natascha responded by bringing up her knee into his groin and pulled away from his hold. She ran towards the car, but it was pointless as she couldn't leave Bartolomé behind so instead she turned towards her infuriated assailant and waited with her back to the car for protection. By this time two other men equally formally dressed had got out of their car and stood leaning against it as their friend limped towards Natascha. He was red in the face and obviously hurt but he still made an attempt to get hold of her again. She slapped him hard enough to make him step back away from her; she heard the others laughing and calling out ribald comments as he turned away from her and held his assaulted face.

'Can you get yourself into the car, Bartolomé, whilst I keep this animal at bay?'

'I'll try but what about the wheelchair?'

'Forget the wheelchair, Bartolomé, get in. I'm really frightened of this man.' The assailant turned and walked up to her but kept a safe distance not quite knowing what she might do next. Natascha then turned her full attention to the man. 'I'm doing no harm. Why do you want to attack me? This place is where my grandmother's godmother died; all I want to do is pay my respects.' He said nothing in reply but kept on looking at her closely. Natascha felt his eyes crawl over her body and she knew that he had other intentions; fear seeped in replacing the strength she felt quickly slipping away.

'So, you are related to one of the treacherous bitches that were executed here all those years ago; my grandfather did for them, you know?' Although a handsome young man his features twisted and Natascha felt she was looking into a cruel face from the past. Would the young women who died here have witnessed such latent savagery? Of this there was no doubt, but it was a baying mob that took them, Natascha recalled. He continued with undeserved pride. 'Our grandfathers rescued Spain from a bad lot, the commies, the Jews, Freemasons, homosexuals and other dross. I suppose you're *one of them, too,' he said with menace. 'Pity we can't see you off in the same way.' He turned towards his companions leaning against the car. 'Hey, you two, come and have a close look at what I've found, very tasty and all alone; well, almost, that old cripple can't get in the way but maybe we can tempt him to join in just to keep him quiet?'*

'You touch me again and you will regret it,' said Natascha unconvincingly as she reached back for Bartolomé's stick. She felt some comfort as Bartolomé had manoeuvred his chair towards her and pressed the stick into her hand.

'Leave her alone, Alfredo, you drunken lecher; show some responsibility, get in the car,' called out one of his friends as they both walked towards Natascha.

'I need to search her. We officers have a duty to make sure the wrong people aren't causing trouble in our country.' With that he lunged towards her grabbing hold of the front of her clothing pulling her into a clinch. 'My God, she's tasty, come and get your fill, you losers.'

Natascha couldn't get a full swing of the stick to strike him as he was up too close so she screwed the brass handle of the stick, from behind, into his lower back with all the force she could muster.

'Christ, you bitch,' he screamed but still held her firmly up against him. His breath was hot and rancid as he pressed his mouth into her face seeking out her lips; his knee pressed between her legs and she was starting to feel she was losing the battle. She struggled to do further damage to his back with the stick but to no avail as his companions pulled back her arms and held them by her sides. This is the end, she thought, I can't hold off three men. As hope seeped away she felt resigned to her fate; all she wanted to do now was to survive the attack.

'Stand back, Alfredo, let her go; give the girl space or you'll have me to contend with,' shouted the taller of the two men angrily. Alfredo looked in astonishment at his colleague. It was not what he expected; surely they would like to take advantage of this rare

opportunity? Her left arm was let go and in a flash the tall man swung behind Alfredo pulling back his head as he wrapped his arm about his throat.

'Get your hands off me, I'm your senior officer; stand back and let me do my duty.' His whole attitude had changed from rapist to arrogant official. 'You two, hold her while I search; she could have illegal substances secreted about her.'

'Right, Alfredo… sir, I mean, but you be careful you stay within the regulation guidelines and don't let those fingers of yours go wandering where they're not supposed to go. I'll be watching and I won't tolerate any deviation. Understand this, we're not going to cover for you if you go too far.'

'I'll be the judge of that,' said Alfredo with venom, 'and I won't forget your attitude. Just do your duty and hold the bitch still.' He pushed his fingers through her hair then down onto her arms that were being held horizontally by the others. The man pushed his fingers into the short sleeves of her blouse onto her bare shoulders and into the armpits then down towards her breasts. Natascha was beginning to feel nauseous and couldn't stop the tears coming. 'Let me go, please, let me go, I haven't done anything wrong. Please let me go, you've got it all wrong.'

'She's right, boss, we haven't any reason to do this. Me and Miguel are really unhappy about this.' The second of the two men remonstrated with his senior officer. 'Take your hands off her, boss, and let's go home.'

Alfredo looked into their faces and smiled lasciviously. 'You're just jealous, I've got the best part of the job, as you can see rank has its advantages.' He laughed and then continued running his hands down over her hips and onto her thighs and as he pushed his hands between her legs she wailed. It was a heartbreaking sound.

Both men shouted their disapproval at the molester. 'You disgusting bastard, let her go.' It was at that moment that the stone thrown by Bartolomé struck Alfredo high upon the head. He lurched backwards holding the wound as blood eased between his fingers.

Both his men jumped forwards and held him firmly as he reached inside his jacket for his gun. 'We're going home whether you like it or not,' said Miguel forcibly as they frog-marched him to the car.

Natascha was sobbing into her hands as she leant back onto the bonnet of the car for support. Bartolomé could do nothing but stroke her shoulder from the awkward position he was in leaning across the car. 'Come on, let's leave, let's leave now, we must get away from them.'

Miguel had come back to the car and stood close to the weeping young woman. He put out his hand and touched her. She lifted her head in panic and tried to pull away. 'No, no, please no, let me go, please,' she pleaded.

Miguel was shocked at her state of distress. 'Don't be afraid, I'm not here to harm you, all I want to do is to find out if you are capable of driving back home.'

'I don't know, I feel terrible, he is such a horrible man and he has power; he could blame me for all this. What's going to happen to me?' Natascha looked up at him as if she had remembered something really important. 'Do you know I'm not Spanish?' A shadow of concern passed within Miguel's eyes. 'I'm British and French.'

'Please forgive us, Señorita; my colleague has done you wrong. I am determined to report this incident to my superiors, you have nothing to fear.' She said nothing but continued to look intently towards Miguel as if searching for reassurance. 'You have every right to complain, Señorita; is that what you want to do?'

'No, I don't want any more trouble; you've done what you can to help me and I am grateful.' She lifted her head as if struck by yet another problem to be solved. 'I need to protect Bartolomé; he has many problems to contend with. So let's keep quiet about this.' Natascha went to help Bartolomé into the car but turned back to the officer. 'Why is that beast like he is? Haven't your people suffered enough without raking up the horrors of the past?'

'There are too many men like Alfredo in the Guardia Civil. They still hanker after the power they had in the past; but we will

*solve our problems in time. Adios, Señora, may God bless you.'
He started to turn to go but wanted to say something more. 'The
Spanish people are a loving people; our families and our friends
mean everything to us. I feel so ashamed that we have done something
that goes against our nature and puts us in the worst possible light.
Forgive us, Señorita.'*

*'I love the Spanish people too because they have shown me,
a foreigner, great kindness, especially as a student at Salamanca
University.'*

*He acknowledged what she said with a nod of his head and a
small, admiring smile. 'You are a clever young woman; may I wish
you success and happiness in the future. Once more, please forgive
us.' With that he turned and went back to his car. He waited until
Natascha had driven off to find her way back to Béjar. He looked
over his shoulder at Alfredo with his mouth hanging open as he slept
a drunk's sleep. He looked in disgust towards Miguel, pulled on the
steering wheel, turned the car and went in the opposite direction.*

33

FAREWELL BÉJAR

Summer 2008

'I'm leaving today, Bartolomé,' she said leaning on the doorframe and feeling uncomfortable with the lack of interest he was showing her. 'I only want to say goodbye and thank you for your friendship whilst I've been here.' She paused and waited for a response. She tried again. 'I really do mean what I say, Bartolomé.' He said nothing but continued to lean forwards in his chair resting his chin in his hands. He peered unfocussed through the small window out across the buildings that surrounded the care home towards the sturdy trees that lined the river. The nurse continued to work in the corridor behind her separating the newly laundered bedding into different piles before storing it in the linen cupboard. Natascha looked towards the nurse expressing her frustration in a glance wondering whether her friendship with Bartolomé and the interesting times they had together had all been for nothing. She sighed heavily in exasperation.

'Don't worry too much, Natascha, we all suffer from his moods; you know how he is.' The nurse came and stood by her looking through the doorway. He had reverted to his old, uncommunicative and sullen self but Natascha now knew he had good reason to feel this way. She couldn't blame him.

'Bartolomé, I'm going to miss you but I have to go; you know I was only allowed to be here for a limited period of time. It's not my fault if you think it's too short.' She waited for some response but there was none. 'Come on, Bartolomé, let's part as friends; I will write to you and I would hope you will write to me.'

He turned swiftly in his chair and spoke angrily to her. 'The Guardia Civil called to see me after you left yesterday; Senior Nurse Patricia told me.'

'What did they want to see you for, Bartolomé? You've done nothing wrong; I know that.'

'Well, Patricia said they couldn't see me unless they had the proper authority and when she asked what it was about he didn't answer but asked another question.' He turned away from her and continued to stare out of the window.

'What was the other question, Bartolomé?' Natascha sensed the second question was the source of his extraordinary behaviour. 'Come on, tell me what it was; we don't have secrets do we?'

He looked back at her, holding her gaze. She waited in surprise; it was unusual for him to look so brazenly into her face. Normally his eyes would slip away demonstrating his incurable shyness. 'I think they asked about you.'

'What! How do you know it was about me?' Natascha said anxiously feeling tendrils of fear creeping through her skin as she remembered the horrible man body-searching her in the forest close to Santo Domingo.

'He said they wanted to speak to a foreign woman about something important and they knew she was a friend of mine.' Bartolomé recognised Natascha's fear and tried to smile to put her at ease but it transformed into a fearful grimace making Natascha feel even worse.

The nurse turned to Natascha. 'I know. Patricia told us it when she got back to the staffroom. She sent the cocky young devil off with a flea in his ear, told him you had already left for Salamanca and wouldn't be back.'

Natascha tried to ask another question but Bartolomé told her to wait, there was more. 'Patricia likes you, Natascha; she said you've done me a lot of good so she told the guard to inform the Salamanca office that he was looking for you.'

'What? That's not going to help me? Why did she do that?'

The nurse, who had returned from the linen cupboard, spoke up adding more to the conversation. 'Patricia has known this civil guard since he was a boy and wasn't afraid of him. He was a bully as a child and continues to be a bully now. He used to intimidate the weak and vulnerable and it's rumoured his grandfather did some pretty horrible things during and after the war. It's a case of grandson like grandfather. Anyway, Patricia knew what she did would scare the coward off.'

'That's still a risk to take. So, what happened?'

'I heard a lot of this conversation, Natascha, as they were speaking outside my door; just where you two are standing now but he didn't know it was my room. Patricia didn't tell him. He said it was a private matter and he expected to get special treatment from the foreign bitch; those were his words, Natascha, not mine. He then went and said answer the question or else he would make big trouble for the fat man.' Bartolomé stopped and looked appealingly at her. 'I'm not fat, am I, Natascha?'

Natascha, ignoring Bartolomé's concern, was appalled. Whatever could he have meant? Although it was obvious what he wanted from her. She could handle that side of the problem she told herself but she now felt worried for Bartolomé. 'Will he be safe after I've gone? I'd hate to think they would make trouble for him because of me.'

'He's not at all interested in a lame old man, Natascha, only a beautiful young woman who might do him a few favours.'

'Well, he'll be very disappointed if he thinks I'll be obliging such a nasty little man.' She then laughed unconvincingly. 'Do you think he will contact the Salamanca office?'

'Not a chance for it would simply confirm what a sexual predator he is. There have already been a lot of complaints about

him and, even though he has influence, it could lose him his job.' The nurse closed the cupboard door and using one of the keys hanging from a chain at her waist locked it. *'I must go now and leave you two together to say your goodbyes. And you, Bartolomé, be polite to Natascha and thank her, she's been wonderful to you.'* She stopped and turned back to him. *'Oh wait, Bartolomé, why don't you tell Natascha about the old lady who comes here nosing about; you know, the one who says she used to live in a village up in the mountains like you did decades ago. She was a strange old woman.'* Patricia screwed up her face. *'A bit weird, I'd say.'*

Natascha was not sure she wanted to know about some old stranger so didn't prompt Bartolomé to tell her anything else. *'Can I come in, Bartolomé? I can't say goodbye from a distance.'* He nodded his head and she entered. She had always waited for an invitation to enter; he was quite old-fashioned in that way. In a few strides she was standing beside him as he continued to look out of the small window. *'Have you drifted off again, Bartolomé?'*

'No, I was just thinking about that old lady who visited me many times through the years I've been here. I don't know why the nurse mentioned her.'

'Well, never mind, let's just say our farewells and exchange addresses.'

'You know my address already; you worked here, remember.'

'It was just a turn of phrase, Bartolomé, but you don't know my address in France, do you? I need to give you that, right?'

'You know, it was funny, that old lady said she was called Maria-Luisa; it was a name given to her by the nuns but I think she had another name before that one. It's normal to do that when you live so long with nuns. Nuns could do no wrong as far as she was concerned.'

'Very interesting I'm sure, Bartolomé, but I've got to be on my way very soon.'

Bartolomé ignored her and continued. *'When she first came here she was still working in a school not far from where you're going; Salamanca. She was younger then of course, and I have to say quite pretty. Anyway, you could tell she was from up north because she had blue eyes and very fair hair but rolled up tight under her hat. What was strange was she always carried an old notebook. It was the same book year in, year out, just like one of those you got in school to write your spellings. It had a faded brown cover but the inside of the cover was bright red. I think it was just old. Very strange, I must say, and there was a name written in coloured crayons on the brown cover that certainly wasn't Maria-Luisa. I don't think it was her book, I think it was somebody else's.'*

Natascha didn't want to prolong the dialogue so she simply listened patiently until it had run its course but she was struck by the oddity between the name given and the name on the book. She couldn't help herself; she had to say something. 'What was the name on the book, Bartolomé?'

'Every time she came she took the same book out of her bag and opened up the pages; she never put it down and I never really saw what was written in the book but it certainly wasn't used as a vocabulary book because there were drawings; child's drawings; you know, really silly, baby ones; stick people and scribbles.'

'Is that all? Nothing else?'

'Oh, yes, there was, when she opened the book to find a clean page, towards the back, there were more mature drawings, really good ones and some looked like maps of places surrounded by trees and roads and rivers but I couldn't make sense of it.'

'Did she ever speak to you or did she just stand there with the book in her hand?' Natascha was starting to become anxious; was this a waste of her precious last moments before the bus left for Salamanca or something really important? She didn't know why but felt the stirrings of concern grow within her.

'I wasn't the only one she spoke to; I gather she asked the same questions of everybody. Don't get annoyed with me, Natascha; I know we've only got a little time before you go. Give me your address. I know you've written it down.'

Natascha felt bad about letting her concern show and urged Bartolomé to continue. 'Come on then, what was the name written on the outside of that strange old lady's book?'

He looked up, relaxed and smiling; he wanted always to be her friend and he had every intention to write to her in France. 'Well, there were two names with the first letter of each larger than the rest and illustrated with bright colours, you know, the way kids do, a bit of a mess really. The first name started with an 'A' with the second letter being a "b" or something like it; maybe even an "l", I don't know. The second name started with a "J" and full of "u's" and "n's" and small letters like that. I wasn't really interested.'

Natascha was shocked. She couldn't believe it; could this be true or was her imagination working overtime?

'Did she say she knew you at any time in your life, Bartolomé?'

'No, she couldn't remember me and I couldn't remember her but she thought we'd been babies together. You know, babies' memories are not very good.'

'But your memory as a child was very good, Bartolomé, you were an amazingly brave little boy.'

'Let's not go into that again, Natascha. Let's just say goodbye.'

'How old do you think she was, Bartolomé?' Natascha asked tentatively.

'Oh, my age, I think. Don't be late, you've got a bus to catch.'

Natascha spoke quietly to herself, 'Alicia, could this possibly be Juana's daughter Alicia?'

Bartolomé looked at her, then turned away.

34

AMENDING

2010

Natascha did not sit down at the kitchen table but leant instead against the sink absorbing the warmth of the early morning sunlight as it poured through the window. Her father and brother had already left the house to meet up with a local man selling flagstones. She could never understand why Dad had to work on Sundays. Surely the flagstones would still be there on Monday. 'No, they won't, Natascha, they're difficult to find nowadays, everybody's after them and I must get there first,' he growled at her then softened. 'I really won't be long.' She sipped at the coffee he had left for her and nibbled at the toast.

Her mum, also, had been a bit grumpy; but that was yesterday when she picked her up from the station. 'If you'd come on the same train as your brother you could have saved me a journey.'

'I had things to do, Mum, things I couldn't have done during the week; they work me hard you know, running around researching for the senior journalists and at the same time I'm trying to write an article which I'm sure they'll reject just like all the other ones. It's a bit depressing but I'll get there in the end, don't worry.'

The day before, a friend had run her out to a brocante on the outskirts of Toulouse. She informed Natascha that she would rather share dinner with a dog than explore the rubbish in that dump so she sat waiting in the car listening to the radio. As Natascha traipsed between enormous pieces of brown furniture and chipped enamel pots and bowls she came across a large, heavy, wooden crate full of all sorts of junk including bone-handled cutlery tied up with string, chipped plates and porcelain candle-holders and other unattractive items. The crate was marked "All items only 1 euro" and rummaging around she came upon exactly what she was looking for. It was a wooden crucifix set into a metal spike. It was very dusty and covered in some tacky gunk but altogether seemed to be in reasonable condition and would probably clean up very well. Looking up she caught the eye of the scruffy-looking assistant who was in the process of removing then examining something unsavoury from her ear. Doing her best to disguise her unkind internal appraisal of the woman, Natascha smiled insincerely and asked if she could buy it. The woman came over to her, constantly sniffing, and asked for five euros. 'But it says one euro on the box?' said Natascha.

'Five euros or you can't have it.' Sniff. 'Take it or leave it.'

Natascha tried to negotiate the price down but her opponent was adamant and she had to pay five. As she left Natascha suggested nastily to the woman that she might spend the money on soap. But the skirmish was a home win as her opponent produced an evil black-toothed grin that sent Natascha scuttling for the door. The battle was over but the price still annoyed her, even now. However, it was a better crucifix than she had imagined it to be when in the shop. The wooden cross was carved in oak with simple decoration on all sides. The holder and spike were in bronze and it too had a pattern cast into it. All in all, she was very pleased. She had not shown anybody the crucifix nor the box in which she had placed the relic. The box, lined with purple faux-velvet, had once held a Saudi silver necklace that Mamie and Papie had given her many years ago. This was now hanging on the corner of her dressing-table mirror at her place in Toulouse. Papie had explained that the necklace was part of a bride's dowry, which would be sold when she became widowed or abandoned. For many wives abandonment occurred as they became older as they were replaced by younger women and effectively cast out. *Is there nothing that is happy in this world?* Natascha thought to herself. Dreams disturbed her; she still suffered, even during the daytime, from the distressing events that had occurred in Spain. Dark spirits of someone else's past still haunted and intruded upon her life at times of joy, appearing unexpectedly like Banquo's ghost.

She swilled out her coffee cup and left it on the drainer. Opening the heavy oak door and stooping below the low lintel she stepped into bright sunlight and walked up the stone pathway towards the gate. As she passed the lime tree she noticed Mamie sitting upright and unmoving in the shade. Her book lay open on the table with her spectacles resting across the pages. Natascha stood still and looked in concern towards her. *Was she well?* she thought. Her grandmother slowly lifted her head and looked sadly into her eyes. 'Was it bad then?'

'It was horrible, Mamie; no, worse than horrible; I have told you what I can in all decency.' Her grandmother willed her to go on. 'It's all too late to put things right but I am going to do something that might bring some justice or peace of mind to her.' Natascha's voice broke and she rubbed at her eyes. 'It's all so pathetic, Mamie, but I must do something. It might be just about me and not about her at all, but I must do it.' Natascha took a small faded photograph from her canvas bag and passed it across to her grandmother. 'Do you want to look again?'

'No... yes...' She was hesitant. 'Yes, I'll have another look but you hold it for me then take it with you when you leave.' The old lady kissed her index finger then placed it on the pale, fading face of a beautiful young woman. Her eyes were smiling seemingly amused by the bright young woman who was clinging onto her arm and laughing uproariously; she too was very beautiful with shining black hair that fell almost to her waist. She slid her finger across the photograph where it came to rest on a dark-haired serious-looking *young man who was standing behind the women; close to him was a man taller than the others but clearly a friend. Natascha had been given the photograph by a man called Bartolomé a couple of years before and Mamie had confirmed what she had already deduced. Looking at the faces just made it all so much sadder; all four had been killed within a year of the photograph being taken.*

Mamie looked up at her. 'There was a child wasn't there?'

'Yes,' she paused, 'Alicia,' admitted Natascha tearfully, 'and I'm doing my best to find out more about her.'

Her grandmother nodded and gave her a comforting smile. 'Off you go, my darling, and say a prayer on my behalf; remember how important Joan was to me and how much I loved her.'

Natascha said nothing; she put the photograph back in the bag and continued on her journey. She wandered up towards the village and walked through it. There was nobody about, it was so peaceful. She glanced down towards the church and noticed the clocks were still slow then walked on up past the blacksmith; the entrance to which was, as usual, cluttered with harrows, seed drills and ploughs all awaiting his attention. She caught a glimpse of him in the arcing light as he tried to weld some life back into a terminally ill machine. She chuckled to herself, 'He works on Sundays as well, not just Dad.'

The cemetery was just beyond the kennels housing hunting dogs. This breed was used to hunt wild boar or hares on foot and their owners were lean and hardened men of France. The dogs howled as Natascha walked on by; all walkers received the same mournful, deafening sounds. There was no way to avoid it.

Within a few strides and hidden from the dogs by the cemetery wall the sounds diminished and she reached her destination. She pushed against the unmoving iron gates and squeezed through the narrow gap. She didn't want to be disturbed so she unsuccessfully attempted to close the gate behind her; she failed to move the rusting hinges one millimetre and with a sigh of exasperation she turned and wandered unseen up the path between centuries-old graves.

The more recent ones were towards the top of the slope, many of which were adorned with fresh flowers held in tipsy containers. Natascha noticed in the corner a prepared grave with neatly banked soil awaiting its return to place. She nodded to herself knowing for whom it was prepared; Laetitia, as delicate as a flower and one who seemed to have lived forever. So easily it ends for those whose life was blessed. But this was not the way for all good folk, of which she was so painfully aware.

She hadn't asked for advice nor had she sought permission for what she was about to do. Her faith in the church had been dented by what she had learned in Spain. She knew it was a different country but it was the same church that had been unable, if not unwilling, to help the oppressed; it was the same church that sided with the oppressors giving little comfort to their victims.

Where the gate swung into the cemetery, close to the ancient stone column that supported it, was a small patch of ground. It was triangular in shape and untended. Natascha noticed with relief it was an area not infested with the usual nettles, docks or other brutish sort of weeds. This will do nicely, she thought, and set about her task with a strong sense of purpose. She needed a hole just big enough to accommodate the box and plant the corms. It took no time with Mama's new trowel but she was careful to keep the grass in one piece. She took the box from the bag, and lifting the little clip, opened it. The fragment of bone was stained by age and the minerals found in soils from a distant mountain; it was wrapped in a child's embroidered handkerchief. Natascha rewrapped it making sure the dainty embroidered rose was uppermost. She caught the faintest smell of sweet perfume as she clipped the box together and then lowered it into the ground; she placed at each end a small number of cyclamen corms. These will bloom early in the year and are different from everything else here, thought Natascha. She then closed her eyes and whispered to herself the prayers that had been in her head for years. She tumbled the soil over the box and returned the grass to its place and stood holding the small wooden crucifix in her right hand. *Did she feel better, and could she smile a little more easily now? Maybe, but the memory could never be erased. I will learn to live with it, she intoned, and I don't think I ever want to forget.*

'Well done, Natascha, that was beautiful; Mamie and I are so proud of you.'

Natascha had not heard a sound; she must have been so engrossed in her task; but was comforted by her mother and grandmother being there at this time. She wept softly and her mother held her head onto her shoulder. Wiping her eyes she went to her grandmother. 'Who would ever have thought that we would find ourselves here today?'

'I thought there was little hope of anything being discovered but I was driven to ask you to do the impossible.'

Natascha lifted the cross into view and holding it with both hands offered it to her grandmother. 'Will you help me put this in the right place, Mamie?'

Smiling sadly, she took the cross from her granddaughter's hands and stepped forwards. Taking the crucifix to the rear of the resting place she paused briefly then pressed the bronze spike into the soft earth.

They left, walking to the cemetery gates and pressing through the narrow gap they pulled ineffectually on the gates to close them. Her mother stopped and turned to look closely at her tearful daughter. 'If this is the final chapter, Natascha, will you please tell me once more how it all started?'

'You know, Mama, I've told you before but maybe not well enough,' *said Natascha shrugging her shoulders.* 'What you must understand is, I wasn't that interested to start with, but as I picked up accounts of what happened such a long time ago from all sorts of people, I became upset, or more truthfully, really angry. I could not believe the appearance of normality shown by these people; they should be psychological cripples as a result of what had happened to their families. They recounted their versions of abuse, sometimes under more than a little pressure from me, I must admit. These gross acts of violation and, in my view, criminality by those who seized *power must be one of the greatest cases of injustice ever... They got away with it; these days they'd be jailed for life.'*

She turned and continued to walk towards the car. 'Go on, Natascha, where did the story start?'

'With what Mamie told me; it all started with a wedding in a beautiful city in Spain, Burgos. It was there that Mamie's godmother married a handsome Spanish schoolteacher. And, I'm not sure when, maybe a couple of years after the marriage, certainly after Alicia was born, they moved to a mountain village near the town of Béjar. It was there that Rodrigo, the husband, became the village schoolmaster. Is that enough for the moment, Mama? Let's go home. I'm exhausted and I'm sure you two must be as well.'

They left together in her mother's car and travelled the short distance home to tea and chocolate cake.

ACKNOWLEDGEMENTS

I am grateful to all at Matador who not only thought my work worthy of their attention but also provided advice and services second to none.

Closer to home my thanks go to brother Stan, daughter Sally and especially to daughter Kate who cajoled, guided and used her invaluable experience to squeeze the best from my limited resources.

This story is based upon an awful event catalogued in Giles Tremlett's book 'Ghosts Of Spain'. The unequalled scholarship of Giles Tremlett, along with both Paul Preston, 'The Spanish Holocaust' and Antony Beevor, 'The Battle For Spain' continues to be, to me, inspirational. The story is fiction but I have done my best to build it on the authority of the incredible research by the three gentlemen mentioned above.